The

Niki Mackay studied Performing Arts at the BRIT School. She holds a BA (Hons) in English Literature and Drama, won a full scholarship for her MA in Journalism. Under Niki Mackay, she is the author of *I, Witness* and *The Lies We Tell*, as well as the gangland thrillers *Loaded* and *Taken*. Under NJ Mackay she has published two standalone psychological thrillers, *Found Her* and *The Girls Inside*.

Also by NJ Mackay

A DI Sebastian Locke Mystery

THE
SWEET
HEART
KILLER

NJ MACKAY

hera

First published in the United Kingdom in 2024 by

Hera Books
Unit 9 (Canelo), 5th Floor
Cargo Works, 1-2 Hatfields
London SE1 9PG
United Kingdom

Copyright © NJ Mackay 2024

The moral right of NJ Mackay to be identified as the creator of this work has been asserted in accordance with the Copyright, Designs and Patents Act, 1988.

All rights reserved. No part of this publication may be reproduced or transmitted in any form or by any means, electronic or mechanical, including photocopy, recording, or any information storage and retrieval system, without permission in writing from the publisher.

A CIP catalogue record for this book is available from the British Library.

Print ISBN 978 1 80436 489 5
Ebook ISBN 978 1 80436 488 8

This book is a work of fiction. Names, characters, businesses, organizations, places and events are either the product of the author's imagination or are used fictitiously. Any resemblance to actual persons, living or dead, events or locales is entirely coincidental.

Look for more great books at www.herabooks.com

Printed and bound in Great Britain by Clays Ltd, Elcograf S.p.A.

For Graham S – Thanks for the Friday coffees

PROLOGUE

I watch her making her way around the shop. Her hair is so bright it is like fire. A true redhead – the real deal. It is the sort of shade which henna tries, and desperately fails, to recreate. No box dye could give you this; even a really good hairdresser would struggle. It hangs like a velvet curtain about to be lifted for a show down to her waist, which is offensively small. She has pale shoulders and on them are smatterings of freckles. Little brown sunspots that might look awkward with other colouring but on her look exactly right. She pauses for ages in the vegetable section, picking up courgettes and broccoli, feeling everything as she goes.

She's stopped now, the girl with the flaming hair. Younger than me by at least five years, I estimate. I don't estimate at all actually. I know because I've looked at her Facebook and Instagram profiles along with her Twitter feed, and rarely used TikTok account. Scant though the public information is, her birthday fundraiser posts are out there for all to see.

Hannah Smith. An ordinary name, though she is anything but. She is like an exotic peacock in a field full of brown hens. It is as if she's been pulled into glorious Technicolor whilst the rest of us languish in crappy black and white.

I swallow thickly, tasting my own envy, bitter like acid. I hitch my shopping basket farther up my arm. The metal digs into my skin. It is warm outside. Only early April but unseasonably hot already, the pressure of a heatwave making the air so still and so heavy that it looks like it's shimmering out there.

In here, amongst the fridges and the fresh produce aisles, it's fine. Too cool even. My skin, slightly darker than hers with no freckles at all, is goosebumped.

Tills now. Shit, my basket is empty. I hurriedly grab a few of the nearest things and almost lose the spot behind her to a tall, thin, grumpy-looking man in an ill-fitting suit. He frowns like he's about to have a go and I look up at him and murmur, 'Sorry.' His face softens and he shrugs, gesturing for me to go first.

No one's fooled by that crap though. Chivalry isn't dead, it never existed. He's letting me go first because he is a man who is older than me and I am attractive to him. I nod my thanks, my eyes drifting fast to his wedding ring and away.

Of course.

She smells of sweet perfume. Something young and inexpensive but not awful. It might be that Ariana Grande one. It's popular with her age group. One of the eau de toilettes under £20 that doesn't make an adult gag. Something happens to smell as we age, I think. Once, at fourteen, I had considered The Body Shop's white musk to be the epitome of sophistication. Now I know that really only a good Chanel leaves the kind of glorious waft that makes people think of beautiful things. She puts her goods onto the belt with the grace of a ballerina, the red locks swish-swishing as she goes. I hate her so much I am finding it hard to breathe. A strand of her hair gets caught in her watch strap. She fiddles for a moment, flicking it from her finger, then it is released. It lands at the end of her shopping, just over the plastic separator and onto my side. She is oblivious to it. Eyes now on the clerk at the till. Her voice, deeper than I thought it would be, making polite conversation. 'It really is hot, yes, nothing to do but sit around sweating.' And the classic English catch-all, 'Shouldn't complain, it'll rain again soon enough.'

And it will, of course, and we'll gripe about that too.

I put my stupid items behind her things, three bottles of… I look at the label, strawberry-flavoured water. Sounds utterly vile, plus Angela will be annoyed because I was meant to be buying something for dinner. My fingers linger on the black conveyor belt where, for just a minute, our combined shops sit. Hers colourful and abundant, vegetables, fruit, wine, I wonder if she'll drink it with him. Mine: three pathetic bottles of something surely only teenagers would drink. I pinch the hair that she's dropped, pressing it up and sliding it into the zip-up bit of my handbag.

CHAPTER ONE

SEB

A low sun hangs in the air. It is only April but it is an unseasonably warm and bright day already and it has only just begun. The bluebells are early this year; they stretch out underfoot as DI Sebastian Locke makes his way up the hill, carefully treading between the bright blanket of fragrant blooms and protruding, gnarled roots. He passes stacks of sticks lent upright like wigwams. Bivouacs. He's built his fair share in these woods, as has, he imagines, every parent in the area. It's been a while since he and Tilly did that, though, he thinks with a pang of nostalgia.

There are no children playing here today.

Today, despite the idyllic bounty of nature, something evil lurks. Instead of ramblers, dogs and shrieking children, there are officers in uniforms with serious faces standing guard to deter any onlookers. Here, deep in the woodland of Thames Park, it feels like a cavern of sorts. It will change as the weeks progress and turn to months, the bluebells switching for scorched, sun-baked earth and then dry crunchy leaves, browns, yellows and reds. But for now, it is springy moss, the heady scent of a glorious summer to come and a crime scene too.

'Bugger.'

He turns, stretching out a hand for Lucy who has lost her footing. She winces. 'Thanks.'

'Not one for hiking?'

She shrugs. 'I like nature through a window, not like this when it's trying to attack me.'

He suppresses a smile. 'Nearly there.'

She mumbles something incoherent and, he suspects, fairly obscene.

'Come on Lucy, you're on murder now.'

She sighs. 'It's too hot for this.' It's too hot for much. An early heatwave making everyone twitchy.

'We're almost at the top,' he tells her. For a man who prefers to work alone, he was more surprised than anyone to find he liked having Lucy as his unofficial partner.

'Alright guv.' Finn is half running, half skidding down the hill. Seb tries not to laugh. 'Bloody hills,' Finn murmurs. Seb nods agreement, though he is steady, sure-footed and fit. Finn says, 'You've not even broken a sweat.' Looking at Lucy. 'Unlike you.'

She swats at him.

'Alright you two. Enough.' He gives them a stern frown.

Mumbles of 'Sorry guv' as they finally reach the top. Finn huffs more than Seb feels is necessary and says, 'Over there,' pointing to Dr Martina Mathewson, who looks up from where she's crouched, masked up, hair under netting.

She waves a gloved hand from what is clearly the reason they are all here.

They head over and Seb asks her, 'ID?'

'Hannah Smith, according to her driving licence. Harry tried her home, no answer. Called her work, boss says she's not shown up, which is unusual.'

'Right. Family?'

'Up North. She's at university here, final year.'

'Lives alone?'

'One flatmate, Katie Hardwick.'

'Right then.'

Martina stands, giving instruction to the scene of crime officers and pulling up her mask. Seb looks at the body, laid out amongst the flowers. Her hair is a ginger so bright it clashes with the blooms. She could be sleeping were it not for the horrifying bruising around her neck and the pool of blood peeking out beneath the vibrant purple carpet. The smells mingle: copper and rich spring blossoms. A nauseating combination of life and death. He notes that her hands are on her chest clasping a small bouquet of bluebells.

'After she was killed,' Martina tells him.

'Excuse me?'

'She was positioned like that, after her death. Fingers snapped due to rigour.'

'Right,' he says, forcing himself not to grimace. Martina has a higher tolerance for killer's contusions than he does. 'She was posed, then?'

'Yep.'

He lets his eyes go to the fingers and can see that they are dangling like teeth coming loose from the gum. Her nails are short and neat, painted a pale pearly pink and chipped at the edges.

'Time of death?'

'Hard to say exactly.'

'Roughly,' he says, resisting rolling his eyes.

'Early hours.'

'She might have been making her way home from somewhere?'

'Most likely. It's a cut-through.'

'I'd have taken the lit roads,' Lucy says.

Martina nods. 'Me too.'

'Maybe she wasn't alone, then?' Seb says.

Martina nods. 'That would be my guess.'

'Mine too,' says Lucy. 'No women I know would take this route alone.'

'It's unlikely,' Seb agrees, 'but she might have.'

'I suppose,' Lucy says, though he can see she's unconvinced. 'Postmortem?' he asks Martina.

'Next twenty-four hours.'

'Thank you.'

CHAPTER TWO

STEVIE

The alarm pulls me from sleep. I am immediately aware that my head hurts and that I am freezing cold. I sit up, wincing as my eyes open and my bedroom comes into focus. The window is wide open, cool early morning air washes in along with the faint glimmer of the sun rising. My curtains are drawn, but still the faint light makes my eyes hurt. I blink, and it feels like I'm closing my eyelids over grit and sandpaper. I am on top of my bed covers and force myself onto my hands and knees, which is when I realise I am in a vest and knickers. No wonder I'm freezing. I let my head lurch down, my legs are goose-pimpled, the small hairs on my thighs raised in response to the chill. I shunt off the bed, standing up, and my stomach lurches. I throw a hand out to catch my dresser and steady myself. I am hungover. I try to think about the day before.

A failed supermarket shop in a store I wouldn't normally visit but have been to twice now because it's where she goes. I'd got back to the flat aware that I was going to annoy Angela, who had been quite specific about what we needed. The lifts were still broken and the stairs had been hard work. I'd paused at the front door. I could hear the radio from inside and Angela singing badly. It made me smile, until I remembered my lack of shopping and pushed the door open with a too-bright grin.

She had looked up. 'Did you get dinner?'

'I thought I'd treat us to a takeaway.' The words slid from me quickly because I did not want a confrontation, nor any probing into why I might have been distracted. I also couldn't really afford a takeaway and was doing mental gymnastics trying to think which card I might be able to use which wouldn't get refused.

She frowned. 'But we needed other things too.' She looked at the pitiful bag in my hand, adding, 'I wrote a list.'

'I know and I'll go tomorrow. It was so busy in there.'

'Right,' she said, still frowning.

'Sorry, I had a long day at work.' That was a lie; Easter holidays were within reach and we were all slowing down. I'd left the school as soon as the bell rang, shoving piles of books to be marked into my bag. Then, I'd stood outside the office Hannah works in, waiting, waiting. Checking her social media whilst I did.

Angela's phone rang and I knew by the way her face lit up that it was Mark. She sort of waved it at me, the phone, by way of explanation, and headed into her bedroom to take the call.

I put the three strawberry waters in the fridge. I remember thinking they might be nice with ice and vodka. I went out onto the balcony; I can see far across London from there. It was one of the reasons I knew as soon as I walked in that I wanted the place. I looked out over one lower block. Behind it is a road that is lushly green. In the springtime the trees offer up an array of blossoms like beautiful jewels presented as gifts.

From my balcony, I can see into his garden. I had wondered if I'd see flame-haired Hannah there too, perhaps carrying the wine I'd seen her pay for. I knew for a fact that his wife, Zoe, was away.

I opened the door slightly and leant my head in to listen. I could hear the faint burr of Angela's laughter from behind her closed bedroom door.

I shut the door, sure she was distracted, at least for now, and opened the plastic box at the edge of our tiny balcony and took out my binoculars. Garden empty. Lights off inside, wide bifold doors closed.

'Stevie?' Angela's voice made me jump. I slid the binoculars into my lap, turning to her with my fake wide smile.

'Pizza?' I said; it's her favourite.

'I think I'm going to go to Mark's actually.'

'Oh. Okay.'

Once she was gone I poured the first of many drinks.

Vodka and strawberry water, it turns out, are as grim a combo as you'd expect. Once the strawberry water ran out I moved to vodka and lemonade, and then eventually just vodka.

Wobbly and leaning on the edge of the balcony, breath heavy, eyes pushed to my binoculars. He'd come back late and not alone. In that respect, fidelity, James hasn't changed at all. I'd watched them both go into the house, sat on the balcony, keeping vigil, knocking back sharp drink after sharp drink.

Had I gone out? I try and think: yes, I had. I'd gone to the Amersham Arms. I remember talking to a man with dark hair who smelt of lemon cologne and then? I look for my clothes; I'd been wearing a loose black dress over the underwear I was still in. The dress is slightly damp to touch, mud caked at its hem. My black vest and knickers also feel slightly crunchy and when I pull my hand away there is a red tinge to it. Had I cut myself? I head into the kitchen, noting Angela's open door and her absence. At least I'll be saved the safety lecture from her then, though I've noticed of late she puts far less effort into it.

I throw the dress into the washing machine, adding my underwear.

I force myself into the shower, turning the water up to hot, and feel immediate relief as it pummels my sore, frozen skin. I close my eyes. When I open them, I see small scratches up and down my arms. I run my fingers over them, fresh still, not yet scabbed. Had I fallen down? I remember feeling wobbly on my feet, laughing, at what, I can't recall, something someone said... who? It feels just beyond my reach, but I think I fell into a hedge? Spiked twigs catching at the skin on my arms. The man who smelt like lemons. We'd left the pub, walked home threading our way through Thames Park. He'd kissed me. I'd felt sick. Had I told him to stop? His face frowning. Him pushing me back, the feel of the damp wood-land floor beneath my bare skin. My arms flailing, twigs scratching. Then... nothing. Him standing, doing up his belt, reaching a hand to me.

That's happened more than once. Anonymous night-time encounters, slippery memories that don't quite tell the full story.

I rub shampoo through my hair as my muscles start to slowly loosen. I force myself to keep my breaths long and even.

Dressed, hair dried, I apply make-up ignoring the slight tremor in my hand. In the kitchen, I manage a cup of coffee, washing down two ibuprofen with its dregs.

I get to school just on time and walk into my classroom greeting the children as they file in, waving small sticky-fingered hands at me. 'Hello Miss Gordon,' they chant and I welcome each one by name whilst nausea swills around with the coffee in my stomach.

I make it to lunchtime without puking up, which I take as a win. In the staffroom, Bethan has brought in an enormous box of donuts, which are now being grabbed and picked up with lots of 'I shouldn'ts'. I get one, slumping down in one of the overfilled chairs, the stuffing on the arm bursting out in an orange foamed lump. Bethan looks at me and sighs, 'God you're so lucky, Stevie, you can eat anything and still stay so slim.'

I force myself to smile and say, 'I'm at the gym a lot though.' I'm not, I'm there once a week. The sugar hits me straight away and the slightly dizzy feeling I've had all morning subsides a bit. I try and think of when I last ate. I'd drunk a lot last night, vodka mainly. I hadn't had dinner and we didn't get a takeout because Angela went over to stupid Mark's house. Yesterday was Monday. I'd had a latte at Starbucks, where Hannah had met a friend after work and I'd pretended to scroll through my phone whilst watching her. Just before the supermarket trip. I'd had a Twix at lunchtime from the vending machine here. Sunday, Angela had made a curry.

'I must join,' Bethan says. She won't though, despite her moaning she won't find the time. Between school, her husband and her children, she doesn't have much to spare.

'Definitely, we could do classes together,' I say, though I can't think of anything worse. She heads off and I am left by myself trying to piece together last night and finding the blank spots too blank to do so. Eventually the bell rings, yanking me from my thoughts and I stand up take a deep breath and switch myself into teacher mode.

CHAPTER THREE

SEB

Katie Hardwick looks so young, Seb thinks. She is twenty-one but baby-faced with wide sad eyes which are currently red-ringed.

'Do you know what happened?' she asks Seb now, as if him giving her details could somehow eradicate the awfulness of this.

'That's what we're trying to work out,' he says as kindly as he can, not giving her much of an answer. She nods as though he has and he's relieved when she doesn't push it. Some things, he thinks, are best left unknown.

'Do you know where she was last night?'

'No. I was at work, we have clients in other time zones and I had meetings. Anyway, she sent me a message saying she'd be late and not to wait up.' Her face crumples in on itself again. 'God,' she says. 'Sorry.' As though being shaken up by your flatmate's murder was an overreaction on her part.

'Don't be,' Lucy says, giving the girl one of her warm smiles. 'Shall I pop the kettle on?'

'That would be nice actually. Everything's on the side, milk in the fridge.'

'I'll get you tea, coffee?'

'Tea please. Can I have sugar?'

'Of course.' Lucy gives her the warm reassuring smile again and it does the trick despite the fact, Seb thinks, that she isn't much older than the girl sitting on the sofa.

'Was Hannah out a lot?'

'She has been lately.'

'Oh?'

Katie sighs. 'She's been… seeing someone.'

'You don't sound happy about it?'

'I, well… she's kept it all on the down-low, you know?'

'Oh?'

'It wasn't an ideal situation.' She runs a hand across her face. 'I'm sorry to say we had a few words about it. As a result, we agreed not to discuss details. I don't even know his name. Oh god, I should have pushed her, shouldn't I, for information?'

'If she didn't want to tell you, what could you do?' Seb says, though obviously it would be much easier if she had a name. 'Do you have any idea why she didn't tell you?' he asks as gently as he can, because he suspects he already knows the answer.

'I think he was married.' Katie gives him a faint smile. 'Actually, I know he was.'

'Ah,' he says. 'Complicated.'

'Yes.'

'You two were close?'

'Yes, very. We've lived together since we started at uni. I finished a year ago, Hannah's doing a fourth year with a work placement. Or she was.'

'Normally she confides in you?'

'Normally yes, we'd… this has been a bit of a sore spot. My, uh, my dad had an affair and I guess I have opinions on this sort of thing.'

'That's understandable,' Seb tells her.

15

Lucy comes back in, putting a steaming mug in front of Katie. 'Here you go.'

'Thank you.'

'We really were good friends,' she says, her tear-streaked face looking from Seb to Lucy. 'This… man was honestly the only thing we really argued about.'

'I understand,' Seb murmurs.

'And even then, we didn't really argue. Just agreed not to talk about it.'

Seb nods and asks a few more questions but Katie didn't know where Hannah had been, who the mystery man was or anything much. The most important thing they learn is that Hannah's behaviour had changed along with the affair.

'In what way?' Seb asks.

Katie shrugged. 'I hate to say it, but she was happy, I guess.'

–

'We need to know who that man is,' Jackie's voice booms from the loudspeaker in the car.

'Yes,' Seb agrees, 'and we should have a better idea by the end of the day. Finn is at the station with her phone, I'm sure he'll get into it soon.' Finn was their team's unofficial technical analyst. Seb was pushing for him to get more dedicated training in this area and so far Jackie had signed off on a few courses and Finn had access to the analyst working out of Hendon when he had questions. Despite having a fierce exterior, Seb had found Jackie a good boss who was normally willing to invest in people.

'And her laptop?'

'That's at work, Harry will pick it up while he speaks to her colleagues. He's due to be doing that about now.'

'Her parents?'

'That's our next stop,' Seb says, dreading it. 'We're meeting them at the morgue.'

'Poor fuckers,' Jackie says. And neither he nor Lucy sitting alongside him disagrees.

They get there in twenty minutes; the local police had already been out, informed the parents and brought them in. Katie had made the official ID at the station with the Smiths' permission; they needed to move fast and Jackie had wanted the murder reported in the press as soon as possible to encourage witnesses to come forward. No one had yet, but it was early days.

'Ready?' Seb asks Lucy, who nods, thin-lipped. It's a stupid question, no one in their right minds would ever be ready for this conversation. Though, Seb thinks, at least for once he isn't breaking the bad news.

They meet an officer at the front entrance. 'How are they?' Seb asks him.

The young man shakes his head. 'How you'd expect.'

'Thanks for helping out.'

'Of course,' he says. 'Though if it's alright with you, I wouldn't mind going. They're booked into a hotel here for a few days.'

'That's fine,' Seb says. 'And drop me an email, I'll message your super and say how brilliant you've been.'

'Really?'

'Yes.' Seb says. It's little things like this that can make a difference; he had seen plenty of higher-ups not turning round and reaching a hand back to offer support for younger officers. He'd seen plenty of higher-ups steal credit for work they hadn't done. He would not be that guy, no matter what.

'Thanks so much,' the young man says, standing up straighter. 'I'd love to do what you do, one day.'

'Stay in touch, let me know if I can help.'

They shake hands and he's gone.

Seb and Lucy get through reception and see a couple sitting, pale-faced and spaced out. 'Mr and Mrs Smith?' He looks at them thinking of their daughter, laid out amongst the flowers, blood thick and congealing beneath her by the time Seb and his team arrived.

The man looks up. 'Adam, please. You're from here, Thamespark?'

'Yes, sir,' Seb says, getting out his ID, but Adam Smith waves it away.

'This is Carolyn, my wife.' Adam Smith gestures at the small woman beside him. She is bent forward, shoulders curled in, her hands gripping a small raggedy thread of a tissue. 'Carolyn love.'

She looks up dazed. Adam slides an arm across his wife's shoulders. 'These are the police from Thamespark.' Hannah had her father's colouring but looked more like her mother. Seb can see a whisper of how she may have matured had she not had that chance stolen away from her.

Carolyn Smith's gaze meets Seb's, eyes teary but intense and alert too. 'Why would someone do this?' she asks him.

'That's what we're trying to find out, Mrs Smith,' Seb says. She shakes her head. 'I know this is awful.' He doesn't know how it feels of course, but he can imagine.

Carolyn breaks down in soft silent tears, head slumping forward.

'We told the others we don't know all the ins and outs of Hannah's life here,' Adam says.

'Of course,' Seb says. 'You knew her flatmate?'

'Katie?'

Seb nods.

'Yes, lovely girl. They've roomed together since the start of university. She's been to visit us with Hannah a few times. They liked to be there for gigs, the festivals, that sort of thing.'

'Hannah loves music,' Carolyn says, her head back down, eyes on the floor in front of her.

'So, she went to a lot of concerts?' Seb asks.

Carolyn doesn't respond. Adam, tells him, 'Yes, always has. She thought about studying it at university, music, but did business and marketing instead.'

'And she worked in marketing for a local energy company?'

Adam nods. 'That's right. Well, it's an internship in conjunction with her university. Very junior, of course, not brilliantly paid. We help her with rent.'

'Did you know her friends from work?'

Adam shakes his head. 'Not really, no.'

'Boyfriends?'

He frowns. 'You mean Tim?'

'Was she currently seeing him?'

'Oh, no. They broke up, oh…' He rubs his chin, frowning.

'Almost two years ago,' Carolyn says, her head rising, meeting Seb's eyes again. 'A nice lad. He adored her.'

'You liked him?' Seb asks her.

Carolyn nods. 'I did, yes.'

'Why did they break up?'

Carolyn sighs. 'Too young for it, I think. Like I said, he adored her and, I think, would happily have settled down with her.'

'She didn't feel the same?'

Carolyn shrugs. 'Said she was fond of him but wasn't ready for all that.'

'Which is fair enough at that age,' Adam pipes in.

Seb nods agreement. 'Yes.' Then, 'Do you have his contact details?'

Lucy makes a note of them. Seb waits one beat, two.

'You don't think she was seeing anyone at the moment then?'

'No,' Adam says.

'She's quite open about these things,' Carolyn adds. 'She'd have told us if she was.'

'You speak often?'

'Most days,' she says, the pain evident in her voice.

Seb nods and concludes the interview.

Out of earshot Lucy says, 'Is there any way this investigation pans out and they don't find out she was seeing a married man?'

Seb sighs. 'Probably not, no.'

'Jesus,' Lucy murmurs.

'But they needn't find out today.'

CHAPTER FOUR

SEB

They'd paused for lunch; Seb had grabbed a sandwich and called home to check on Val his once mother-in-law, and Jackie had messaged him saying he needed to get back to the station now. He arrives at the same time as Lucy. She's carrying a Starbucks iced drink in a see-through plastic cup. They are something his daughter Tilly has recently become partial to. From what he can gather, they are ninety per cent sugar and wildly overpriced. Lucy throws him a frown. 'Don't judge, it's too hot for coffee and I need the caffeine.'

'Never too hot for coffee, Lucy.'

They make their way up to Jackie's office. Seb knocks and Jackie yells, 'In.'

Martina is there, already seated, in a long black dress, her sharp bob immaculate as always.

'Hello Seb.'

'Hello Martina, autopsy done already?'

'Almost.'

Jackie frowns at Lucy's drink. 'Is that a milkshake?'

'No, it's a frappe.' Lucy's face flushes red and Seb suppresses a smile.

'Dear god,' Jackie murmurs, still frowning. 'Sit.' She waves a hand holding out a stack of papers and passing them to Seb. 'Martina did the autopsy on this woman and thought it may be of interest.'

Seb flicks through and comes across a picture of a very young woman. Dead, eyes closed, a blanket pulled up to her chin, which, Seb thinks, is another type of staging. Beneath her is damp green grass, the picture so close up he can see dew on some of the blades.

'Where?' Seb asks.

'Leigh Valley.'

'I don't remember this case?' Seb says.

'Leigh Valley took it. It made the papers, as I recall, but locally at least the DaSilva case took over around here.' Seb, of course, remembers that one. The one he'd made his name on, a cold case that had been unsolved for fifteen years until he re-opened it.

'That's not the real reason no one heard about it,' Martina says.

'Oh?' Seb asks.

Jackie sighs. 'She was a stripper.'

'Ah.' Seb feels a spike of indignation, his mind flashing quickly to police reports he'd read on his ex-wife, Charlie: long lists outlining various charges, solicitation being the one that always got him straight in the heart. It also meant that this case wouldn't have held the same public interest. In the eyes of most, her life would matter less.

'Okay,' Seb says, pleased his voice sounds even and steady, 'so what does she have to do with Hannah?'

'Roughly the same age, not far from here, but the real overlap is the same cause of death: stabbed in the first instance, in the stomach same as Hannah, strangled while the blood ran out of the wounds.'

'Jesus,' Lucy says.

'Right,' Martina agrees. 'A gruesome way to go and a tiring way to kill.'

'Tiring?' Jackie says.

'Stabbing someone takes a lot of force but strangling someone takes even more.' Martina pauses, Lucy picks up her drink and sips through the straw. It makes a silly sound and Jackie throws her a look.

'Sorry,' she mutters.

'It's not the most efficient way to get the job done,' Martina says. 'And it's unusually specific.'

'Anyone caught?' Seb asks, his mind whirring.

'No one.'

'Suspects?'

'A boyfriend, one of the university lecturers who sent her poems.'

Seb screws his nose up. 'What?'

Jackie nods. 'Yeah, she made a complaint about him, said he was stalking her.'

'Right.' Seb searches through the file. 'His name is Colin Aftermore. He's still at the university.'

'A strong suspect?'

'Not strong enough, obviously,' Jackie says, as though he is a bit stupid. 'You'll need to go over, talk to the officers involved and talk to him.'

'Any other linked deaths?' he asks Jackie and Martina, looking from one to the other.

'Not that we know of,' Martina says. 'And it just happens that I did her autopsy. As I started with Hannah Smith, I was reminded of her.'

'Right.' Seb turns over the information.

'Look over everything,' Jackie says. 'Make a plan. This is your case, Seb, but I'll oversee things. Briefing first thing tomorrow, please.'

'Yeah, okay. Will you be talking to the press?'

'Yes, but I won't be mentioning this or, for now, our mystery man either.'

CHAPTER FIVE

STEVIE

The children are unreasonably noisy all afternoon, or perhaps they are responding to my exhaustion by ramping up their energy. Either way, by the time I leave, I'm exhausted. I do stop and do a quick shop, grabbing the things on Angela's list and shoving them into my oversized bag for life. I get the bus back to the flat and find Angela and Mark in the living room. They are curled up together on the sofa, limbs intertwined.

'Hey,' I say. 'I went shopping.'

'Oh, so did we,' Angela says. We, as if Mark lives here and I have two flatmates. 'We're going out soon anyway.'

'Okay, cool,' I say.

I go to my bedroom, close the door and lie down. I pick up my phone and open my secondary Instagram account, one with a fake picture. Then I click onto James Cowley's page. I watch his stories. Reunited with Zoe, his wife. It's a picture-perfect scene of them taking selfies on the doorstep. Little does she know he had company this week whilst she was away working.

My phone rings and I jump, almost dropping the damn thing. It's my mum. I watch it ring ring ring, think about just leaving it…

'Hello.'

'So you are alive then.' The words shunt into my head like needles. The myriad of various pains that she causes me.

'Yes,' I agree. Because I am in fact alive, despite her best efforts. 'How are you?'

'I don't know, Stevie,' she says, and sounds bewildered. I force my eyes closed, feeling a headache clamouring behind them, a sharp wave of pain in my stomach as though I am ten years old again and she's mixed poison with my porridge. 'Have you seen the doctors?' I ask the silliest of silly questions.

'Yes. I have pills.' The usual solution, as if they can drug her into obedience. I suppose they have, in a way.

'Right,' I say. I was thirteen when the police came, taking my mum away in handcuffs, me bewildered, sick as usual, standing at the door sobbing because we'd never been apart. It was a doctor who'd finally caught up with her, who'd seen me in his office one too many times, reviewed my notes and realised that something wasn't right. She could have gone to prison. Perhaps she should have done; instead, she was deemed unwell and sent to a psych ward. I went into care and wondered many times if I'd have actually been better off staying with her. We'd never know.

A silence stretches out across the phone line.

'How's work?' she asks eventually.

'Okay actually. I've got a lot of marking.' I try and think of something else to say, anything, but as is often the case between us, I am at a loss.

'Well then,' she says. 'You had better get on with your marking.'

'Yes.'

'Do visit when you can.'

'I will.' I don't point out that I am there at least once a week, sometimes more. When she's gone, I go back to scrolling. Eventually, Angela and Mark leave and I head into the kitchen.

I make a sandwich and sit on the sofa, turning on the news, and almost drop the plate as I see the headline in lurid red letters across the bottom of the screen: '*Body in bluebell woods identified as twenty-one-year-old Hannah Smith*'. I watch the ticker tape. A crime scene has been set up and DSI Jackie Ferris has confirmed this is a murder investigation.

Any appetite I had dissipates quickly. Now I am turning the volume up and scrolling through my phone for more information. Hannah's Facebook page is awash with horrified outpourings of grief. The local online papers are all running a near-identical story. DSI Jackie Ferris is saying in a solemn but stern voice that there is no further information right now, but more will be released in due time. She is appealing for any witnesses to come forward as a matter of urgency.

One of the articles says the time of death is thought to be the early hours of this morning. Her body was found in Thames Park.

I think of the long, red hair that is likely stuck with static to the bottom of my oversized handbag. The feel of familiar woodland beneath my back, the man who is senses rather than a recognisable person, the smell of lemons, surprisingly soft hands running up my thighs.

I curl my arms around myself, folding my legs and pulling them in. My hands meet the tiny scratches that run the length of my arm. A bush, its small spiked twiggy branches nipping at me? The twigs as I lay on my back for a stranger? Not the first time. I always hope it's the last.

Dark, cool night air, contrasted with the pleasant spring day that was more like summer. Me waking up, here, in my bed, shivering, my clothes damp to touch.

I head into the bathroom and throw up the tiny amount of bread and cheese I'd managed and lie down, my cheek pressed against the cool tiles of the floor.

CHAPTER SIX

SEB

Seb feels nothing but miserable as he drives home. The faces of Hannah Smith's parents will stay with him for days: stricken and lost. They'd spent the afternoon trawling through her social media accounts. Hannah had been clever, driven and likeable. She played netball every Thursday evening and volunteered at a local school, giving free music lessons to children whose parents couldn't afford to pay. She had a bright future ahead of her and he is determined to find out who stole it. Nothing can bring the Smiths justice, of course. You were not meant to outlive a child; it's just not the way it should be. But, he'd get the killer, he'd see that person behind bars.

He parks up on the drive, taking a few seconds just to decompress. He tries his hardest not to let his job follow him into his house, tries his hardest to shield Tilly from the darkness waiting in the world like a small hunched demon with long fingers, poised to grab her. As he settles, he sees Faye's pink mini across the road and finds a smile creeping across his face despite his terrible day.

He knew she'd been coming for dinner but with everything else it had slipped his mind. He looks at the clock on his dashboard. Seven. They will probably already have eaten.

He opens the door and finds the cat sitting on the bottom step staring at him. Her perpetual hunger and need for almost continuous affection are not really in keeping with all the feline tropes.

'Hello Mimi,' he murmurs.

'Hey Dad,' Tilly says, Kai a step behind her. She reaches around him for her coat.

'Where are you going?'

'To Kai's,' she says.

'Oh. Right.'

'Hello Mr Locke,' the boy says.

'Well, don't be too late.'

Tilly rolls her eyes. 'Kai's mum has said she'll drive me back.'

'Still.' He frowns at her; she has recently developed what Faye tells him is known as sass.

'Yeah okay, not too late, got it.'

He opens the door to the kitchen. At the table is Val, his once mother-in-law, and Faye his new… girlfriend he supposes. His stomach flip-flops but his face remains calm. 'Hey you two.'

'Ah, Seb, there you are. Faye waited to eat with you. I'm off to bridge.'

'Oh yeah, it's Tuesday.'

''Tis,' she agrees and says to Faye, 'You can set your clock by my routines.'

'It's true.' Seb smiles at the small woman, who gives him a kiss on the cheek as she goes. 'You saw the young 'un?'

'Yes, off to Kai's. I said not too late.'

'His mum's dropping her back,' Val says.

'Still.' Seb feels like he's having deja vu.

Seb plates up food for him and Faye. She opens a bottle of wine, handing him a glass. As he sits down at the table, he realises he's starving.

'Have you not eaten today?' Faye asks, watching him eat.

He grins. 'The last of the Tesco sandwiches.'

'Bet they were shit.'

'Yeah. Though few things compare to Val's meals.'

'That is true.' Faye bites into the tender hunter's chicken. 'You lucked out with her.'

'Yeah,' he says and he had. Charlie had broken his heart – worse still, she'd made Tilly's life more difficult than it should have been – but his mother-in-law had remained a constant, calming presence. Without another adult at home, there was no way he could have managed his job. Certainly, there would have been no way for him to have worked his way up the ranks as fast as he had done.

'How was your day?' he asks Faye, feeling happy, the same way he does whenever he gets home to find her here, something that is happening more often than not right now.

She sighs, 'It's been a tough one.'

'Daniel?' A young man whose care Faye is overseeing, she's a psychologist who splits her time between prisons and her own clients. At the moment, she is focused on Daniel, who is in Feltham Young Offenders. He had been convicted of manslaughter after stabbing his stepdad. Faye was quite sure the boy had been protecting his mother, but the mother was adamant that her new man had been a saint and had, effectively, left Daniel to hang. He, unsurprisingly, had severe depression.

31

'Yes.'

'He's not getting better?'

She gives Seb a quick smile. 'He's not in the right environment to get better.'

'No,' Seb agrees. The whole prison system needed reform, a topic he and Faye have discussed often. 'But he's got you to help him and he won't be in there forever.'

'No, I know.'

'Sucks though.'

'Yep. And you're working the case that's all over the news?'

'Hannah Smith.' He clears the last of his food in two bites, his stomach giving a welcome moan after. Faye refills their glasses.

'Sofa?' She points.

'Yes.'

'She was found in the park?' Faye asks as they settle down, turning to face him, knees bent. The tips of her socked toes touch his thigh, which makes his mind wander for a moment.

He feels his face blush slightly and rearranges himself. 'Yeah, the weirdest part of it was she was kind of arranged and quite specifically.'

'Oh?'

'If you ignored the blood, of which there was plenty, she could have been sleeping and her hands were clasped over her chest holding a small bouquet of bluebells.'

'Posing,' Faye murmurs.

'What's that?'

'A profiling term.'

'Like staging?'

'Not exactly. Unless – does the way she was posed send a message to you or any other officers?'

'I don't know, not really. It was just... odd.'

'So, there's a difference. I mean, according to psychology, which is the most inexact of all the sciences.'

He grins. 'Obviously.' Another conversation they have had often enough: the pitfalls of her job, and his really, being that a lot of it comes down to feeling your way through.

'So if a killer is "staging" the victims it's normally for the benefit of investigating officers and might be done to confuse or attempt to mislead you.'

He frowns, pulls up the picture of Hannah Smith in his mind. 'I don't think that was his intent.'

'In which case this is more likely to be posing, which feeds into some fantasy held by the killer.'

'That sounds more likely.'

Faye tilts her head to one side. Her long hair swishes around her waist. 'If the killer is at that stage, I'd also suspect this may not be his first time.'

'Funny you should say that.'

'Oh?'

'Martina found another murder, same method. The killer stabbed the victim then strangled them.'

'That's overkill.'

'Yeah, and really sadistic. Both women would have been in agony and known what was coming.'

'How was the other victim left?'

'Not posed exactly, but she was covered with a blanket.'

'Guilt?'

'Maybe, yeah.' Seb sips his wine. 'Or maybe nothing to do with Hannah Smith at all.'

'Quite a coincidence though.'

'Yes, it is.'

He leans forward, putting the glass on the table at the same time Faye leans forward to do the same. Their hands brush. She grins at him. 'Never mind the case right now, you need to relax.'

CHAPTER SEVEN

STEVIE

Angela is there when I get in. Early for her, because I left straight after school, lugging exercise books to look over at home. My brain fizzes with the news about Hannah Smith, my memory serving up the dark-haired man who smelt like lemons and the feel of woodland beneath my bare arse. I'd been in the woods. I'm sure of it. Had I been going to James's? Perhaps. I don't drink often, or try not to, but when I do, the results are wildly unpredictable. I'd been hoping to get in to an empty flat and now Angela is talking. 'Sorry, I missed that,' I say.

'I uh, wondered if we could talk?'

'Oh,' I say. 'Sure.' I put my heavy bag down in the hall and follow her into the kitchen and living area. I sit at the little table, my head full of dark, intrusive thoughts, my heart sinking as Angela delivers the news I knew was coming and which will spell financial trouble for me. I smile and nod along to the conversation, which meanders for longer than we need around her and Mark's wonderful relationship. She's telling me in a very long-winded way that she's moving out and I am forcing myself to try and at least look pleased for her.

'The thing is, Stevie, it makes sense.' And it does, for her, and for Mark.

'What about him moving in here?' I ask, worry making my voice sound sad and pathetic. I hate Mark. He hates me, too. I can think of few things worse than living with him but abject poverty is one.

'We want our own place.'

'Right,' I say.

'Will you be okay?' she asks, duty stretching the words from her.

I force the smile again. 'Yes, of course. I'm a big girl.' I feel like a tiny, terrified child.

'You'll get someone else soon, I'm sure.'

'Yeah, you're right,' I tell her, a headache starting up behind my eyes just at the thought of having to go through that process again. I *would* find someone, but I'd have to sift through all the weirdos first. Ideally, I'd live on my own. Angela hasn't been too bad, though her worried, turning to exasperated, judging looks have worn thin of late. I won't miss the '*Do you need another drink? Should you be going out on a school night again? Have you been on the balcony all night?*' Implying I had a problem when clearly I don't as I can go days without drinking. Weeks even if I have to.

I was put here straight from care and it was supposed to be temporary, but I'd managed to get my key worker to argue for me staying, despite having an extra bedroom I didn't need. I liked my flat; had done from the moment I'd opened the door.

By then, my mum's older brother Tom had got in contact with me just after I was released as a ward of the state. He helped me wade through the paperwork and jump through various hoops until I was able to by the flat for a reasonable sum I think he felt bad for not being around when I was growing up. He'd been working in

America for years. By the time he came home and we connected I'd been taken from Mum and put through five years in care. He has since been a rock and even helped me out with university fees, but I didn't want to bring any more problems to him. The issue now is that I have racked up an insane amount of debt on various credit cards, so even my very affordable mortgage feels like a stretch, but I have a wardrobe filled with designer clothing.

'I'm happy for you,' I tell Angela, not meaning it because I am sadder for me, to be honest. I find myself wishing, not for the first time, that we could switch. Not just our lives now and today, but the lives we have already lived.

Maybe then, I'd still be with James. If I'd had normal parents who loved me like Angela's did. She moans about them all the time, of course, like so many people do. I've met them a few times; they turned up here the day she moved in. Her mum had made her dinners that filled my freezer. Just looking at them made my stomach rumble and called back thoughts of my own mother's dinners, which could so often be lethal.

'Thanks,' Angela says.

'When are you going?'

'I'll be off this weekend.' A few days then. 'Obviously I'll pay the last month's rent though.'

'Thanks, that's helpful.'

Her face softens and she reaches across the table, sort of patting my hand. It makes me feel young and stupid. The way I often feel around this woman, who is my age but so much more together than me. 'Let me make dinner for us tonight, yeah?'

'Sure,' I say, my stomach groaning at the thought of food. I *am* hungry.

Fifteen minutes later, I take the bowl of stir-fry with a 'This smells great.'

We sit side by side on the sofa and Angela turns the telly on. BBC One comes to life with the six o'clock news and there she is again: Hannah Smith, fierce red hair, super white bright teeth. A great photo, one where she is full of life. In direct contrast to the awful words being spoken about her now. I hear them slip in and out of my ears like worms wriggling.

'Stevie… Stevie.'

'Sorry, what?'

'Are you okay?'

'Yes. Fine.'

'You dropped your fork.'

'What? Oh. Yeah. Thanks.'

'You're also white as a sheet.'

'Yeah, no, actually. I don't feel great. Sorry,' I say.

'Are you ill?'

'Maybe. Probably kid germs.'

She shifts slightly away from me.

'I, um, don't think I can manage dinner. I'm so sorry.' I push the bowl onto the coffee table. Noting the slight quake in my hands as I do so.

'Don't worry about it,' she says. 'Get some rest?'

'Yeah. I think I'll lie down.' I add, 'Thanks though, for dinner.'

'Sure.'

—

I lie on my bed, my breath coming out in short, sharp bursts. The image of Hannah Smith, bright, beautiful, healthy. *Alive.*

Found in the middle of Thames Park, the news had said, repeating yesterday's information. She'd been found in the woodland that occupies acres of the space surrounding the playground, tennis courts and skate ramps. Murdered. An ongoing inquiry. Anyone with any information at all, no matter how irrelevant, is being asked to come forward. That's me, isn't it? *I* have information. I know Hannah's movements almost as well as I know my own. I know where she'd been, when and with who. Did I know she'd been in the park last night? I force myself to slow down my breathing and try and think.

When James moved in to a small house within view of my flat, I'd been flummoxed to start with. The fact he'd come back to Thamespark at all had surprised me; he'd been so adamant that he was moving on to bigger, better things. I still spent a lot of time replaying our last conversation.

'I've got itchy feet,' he'd told me. 'I need to just… go get on a plane, see what's out there in the rest of the world, you know?'

I'd nodded whilst my heart shattered into a million pieces, falling from my chest to my stomach, lacerating my insides, the start of yet another ulcer where the lining of my intestines sent fire up my throat. 'I could come with you,' I'd said, trying to make it sound casual, reminding myself to be fun, light, breezy. 'We could see the world together.'

He sighed. 'I want to go alone.'

I agreed as though the words hadn't battered me from the inside out.

'I'll wait for you then, for when you get back home.'

'No.'

'So, we're breaking up?' I was that stupid, that deaf to reality.

'It's been great though, hasn't it? We've had fun yeah?'

I nodded. We *had* had fun. I had felt normal. We had 'gone out' back in school. It had lasted long enough to unbridle me of my virginity. I'd been in foster care by then, lost, lonely, missing my mum despite everything. He was one of the handsomest boys at school, an athlete, outgoing, popular and in the year above. I'd been amazed when he started chatting to me. We both walked home the same way after school. It had been short and, for me, sweet. Then he had just stopped calling me. I bumped into him after he came back from university and we picked up where we left off, in some ways, but this time I managed to be his girlfriend, to keep the door mostly shut on my murky past. James knew me then as a student teacher in my first placement and working towards qualified teacher status. I was a keen reader, someone who liked plays and gigs and the cinema. I'd cooked elaborate meals for him every single time he came over, depleted my body of all unappealing hair and made sure I was in fresh, seductive lingerie. I'd answered his drunken calls close to midnight, opening the door to my flat, my legs and my heart to him. We had had fun, sure, but I'd fallen head over heels in love too. I'd allowed myself for the first time ever to think of a future where there might be an 'us' instead of the awful past where for so long there had only been 'me'.

Off he'd gone, again. Here I'd stayed, single and broken hearted, and that's when I started keeping tabs on him I suppose. When he came back to town I knew because I still checked all of his social media at least once a day. I knew, for example, that he'd met Zoe whilst he was travelling but also that he still liked a lot of photos that his university sweetheart posted. I'd found out where he was working, followed him from there to his house. Realised I could actually see that little house from my balcony. It had felt like a sign.

I scroll through news stories about Hannah Smith. They all say pretty much the same thing, which is not much at all.

I jump when there is a knock at my door.

'Come in.' I slide the phone face-down onto my covers.

'How are you feeling?' Angela's pretty face is scrunched up in concern.

'I'll live,' I manage, with a sort of forced chuckle.

'You still look pale.'

'Yeah, I need to sleep it off probably.'

'Okay. Shout if you need anything.'

'Thanks.'

After she's gone, I grapple around in my bedside drawer, pulling out a flat half-bottle of vodka. I take a large mouthful, wincing slightly as the liquid burns my throat, reminding me of the remnants of yesterday's hangover. I drink enough that the room mellows around the edges and I drift off thinking, at least once she's gone I'll be able to drink in my own living room again.

CHAPTER EIGHT

SEB

Seb feels the scattering of butterflies in his stomach that he always gets before he goes into the briefing room. He's fairly at ease around Harry, Finn and Lucy. They work together most days. They are all young, which is good. Seb had run-ins with some of the old boy network. Luckily for him there are less than a handful still working in Thames-park, which, though officially part of the Met, operates slightly differently to the inner-city stations. He keeps his team small and select and generally has happy relationships with his colleagues. Martina is here and Jackie has given him Ken for office manager as Seb had requested. He's an old boy, Seb supposes, but he's one of the good guys and Seb is pleased to have his wisdom. Ken nods at him now. *No need to be scared*, he tells himself. Jackie is at the back of the room, arms folded standing by the door.

Still, he takes his place at the front of the room and clears his throat before speaking, in order to buy himself a few seconds to push down his shoulders and ground his feet. It is a technique Faye taught him for centring himself. Initially, he'd laughed it off as mumbo-jumbo, until he'd tried it a few times and found that it worked. A psychological trick he is pleased to utilise and more proof, which he didn't need, that Faye is awesome.

'Right. Morning everyone, thanks for being here. As you know, we have had a murder in Thames Park. A single victim, Hannah Smith, found early in the morning yesterday, Tuesday 5th April. Cause of death was strangulation, but she was stabbed repeatedly first. A merciless and gruesome crime.'

He waits then, leaves silence for one beat, two, three. He lets everyone get their heads into the heinous nature of what they are dealing with. Behind him is a cork board where evidence will collect. There is also a screen linked to his laptop and on it is an image of Hannah Smith in the woods. Her skin pale and slightly mottled in her summer dress, her red hair spread out, twisting amongst the bright blue flowers.

'Martina estimates time of death to be between one a.m. and three a.m.?' He looks at her and she nods agreement. 'The pattern of blood leads us to believe that she was rolled over and posed after death.'

Ken looks up, eyebrows raised, pen poised.

'As you all know, most murders are heat-of-the-moment affairs committed within the home or on the streets.' Murmurs of agreement. A horrible statistic, but most people are killed by a relation or spouse. Most murders, Seb had found, are easily solved because of this. The majority of cases he has covered were men who hurt women who loved them. Sick but true.

'We have ruled out Hannah's parents who were at home in Harrogate. They had a takeout delivered at ten, confirmed with the driver, he answered the door, she went to get a tip. They wouldn't have made it down in time, she has no siblings, and her flatmate Katie Hardwick, who she was probably closest to, has an iron-clad alibi. She was working when Hannah was killed, overnighter in her office for meetings in different time zones. Came home in the morning, assumed Hannah was in bed.'

'A reasonable assumption,' Lucy says.

'Yes.'

'We need to sift through all correspondence on social media, email, etc. and see if we can put a face to the name. Tedious, potentially long but absolutely vital work, which has been started by Finn.' Seb waves at him to stand up. Finn rises, awkward and gangly. He has a sort of little boy face Seb thinks, which is turning red now. 'Any technical questions, he's your man, right Finn?'

'Yes, well I'll try.'

Seb nods that he can sit down, then asks, 'Any questions so far?'

Harry's hand goes up.

'Yes?'

'Why do you think she was posed?'

'I don't know exactly and we're not profilers.' A few eye-rolls at that: TV cops are abundant these days, but mostly in the UK profilers aren't used. 'I uh, did run it past a psychologist I know and she suggested that it was feeding into some fantasy the killer had. The other option would be to send us a message.'

'Us the police?' Harry asks.

'Right. But that doesn't seem to be the case here.'

'No,' Harry agrees. 'I suppose a note saying whodunit would be too much to wish for,' he quips and receives a few chuckles back.

'Whatever the reason, the chances are it will be good old-fashioned police work that will catch our killer, so that's what we'll be doing.' More murmurs of agreement.

'We do have another murder that occurred almost two years ago and which we think may be linked.' Seb clicks

44

a button and the screen changes. 'Sam Carmichael.' He says as they all take in the image, a young woman, olive brown skin, dark hair short and fanned around her face, a frozen expression which almost looks like surprise. Green grass beneath her body, dew sparkling on the single blades, blanket pulled up to her chin as if she'd been put to bed and tucked in. 'Almost two years ago, in Leigh Valley.'

'What's the link?' Harry asks.

'They were killed in the same way.'

Harry frowns. 'Don't remember the case.'

'She was a stripper. According to notes, she'd worked that night and though no one saw her leave a few of her colleagues said she took private jobs,' Seb says. 'No one was charged and I think local police probably thought it was a job gone wrong.'

'Not the same demographic as our vic then.'

'No, but the same unusual mode of killing. Stabbed extensively and strangled. She was covered after her death.'

'It's like she's been put to bed?' Harry asks.

'Yes, so another posed victim.'

'What a sicko,' Harry says. Jackie throws him a frown he doesn't see. Seb suppresses a smile. There are reasons Harry does a lot of the in-station work: he wasn't the most carefully spoken member of Seb's small team.

'Another thing that might link them is a college lecturer called Colin Aftermore. He was a regular at Sam's club and though he doesn't appear to teach any of Hannah's classes he is still at the uni. Lucy and I need to go visit Hannah's parents and ask about the affair. Harry can you start compiling a list of people Hannah was in regular contact with?'

'Yeah, course.'

'In tandem with Finn please, who'll be trawling through whatever we can get access to.'

Jackie stands. 'Also, go through everyone Hannah had contact with at the university, at work, at any nightclubs. Cross-reference everything and anyone that ties these two women together.'

Harry and Finn nod.

'Try and do it discreetly, we don't want the press knowing about a link until we are more sure,' Jackie says.

'We'll need to warn people, though,' Seb says. 'If there is a link.'

'Not today,' Jackie snaps. 'Also look at any assaults, historical or not. Sexual assault in either of these cases?' A quick subject change directed at Martina.

'Hannah had had sex recently, protection was used and there are no obvious signs but we can't rule it out,' Martina says.

'So no DNA?'

'Sperm found on her thighs.' She shrugs. 'No match in the system but if and when we have a suspect it could be useful. No DNA without an explanation in Sam's case unfortunately.'

'Right, good.' Jackie turns back to Seb. 'The affair guy?'

'Most likely, taking into account what Katie has told us, we also know that Sam was "seeing" someone she'd spent a few days with.'

'Her phone?' Her eyes turn to Finn.

'Proving tricky but we should be into her WhatsApp account and other social media shortly. Katie has given us a couple of possible passwords.'

'We'll ask her parents if they might be able to help with access too,' Seb says.

She nods. 'I'll hold another conference on the evening news, investigation ongoing and an appeal for any witnesses again. Do not mention any possibility of a linked crime outside of us.'

'Right.'

Jackie stands, grabbing her coat and sliding it on. 'I'll go prepare to feed the vultures then, Seb any info back to me and if you need anything shout.'

'Yes ma'am.'

—

Lucy's face looks impassive, sympathetic, giving nothing away. However, Seb sees her hands curled into each other in her lap. They are in the Smiths' hotel room. Well, the sort of living area. They've rented a suite, which is wise. Seb supposes they'll be here for a while. He would be if it were him. He pushes that thought away; he has many like it. He's sure most policemen and women do. Especially ones who are parents. He knows more than most the many horrors that can befall children. That can befall anyone because crime is often indiscriminate.

Carolyn Smith is glaring at Seb as though she hates him. Perhaps she does. Perhaps he would too, in her shoes.

'She wouldn't do that,' she says, spitting the words out so that they land between them, hard, angry, a declaration of a war it's not worth fighting. Seb doesn't respond. Carolyn looks at her husband who reaches out, his long arm curling round her shoulder, pulling his wife to him as she crumbles.

Anger, Seb always thinks, is the noise that fear makes. But what of fear for the Smiths? When the thing that scares the shit out of most parents has already happened, how could it get worse? Like this. These awful things they need to be told because if it doesn't come from him now, it will come from a newspaper or a pushy journalist who wants only the story and cares not one bit about their feelings.

'She wouldn't.' Carolyn says again but this time to her husband, her damp eyes searching out his.

'I don't think the policeman is lying love.'

She turns to face them. 'Who is he?'

'That's what we're working to find out,' Seb says. Tone soft, even, heart thumping in his chest. So many things about this job are hard. The sheer weight of the crimes, petty, stupid, banal, life-changing. All the bad news he has to deliver. The reactions he can't help but absorb to some degree. He'll feel it today then he'll push it aside. He'll have to.

'Do you think he—' Adam Smith pauses, licks his lips. 'Was the one who…'

'We're not sure. But we'd like to talk to him.'

'It's usually a partner isn't it?' he says. 'They say that, don't they, and the statistics are awful.' They are. Absolutely shocking: two women a week in the UK are murdered at the hands of men who proclaim to love them. It's like a disease, domestic terrorism so everyday it has become the norm. Men who hate the women who care for them, for their children. Seb sees it day in and day out. He sees it in its early stages: the calls to arguments. He's seen women defend men who keep them in a reign of terror. He's seen women try and leave and not make it. He doesn't know the answers but he sees the problem; you'd have to be blind not to.

'It can be,' Seb says, 'but we have no evidence to suggest that's the case here.'

'You have no evidence,' Carolyn snaps.

Seb doesn't respond. Doesn't tell her that they do, that his small, dedicated team are at the station sifting through everything, that Martina rushed the autopsy and will be doggedly chasing results. That it has only been twenty-four hours. Hours which to the Smiths must feel like a lifetime.

'I'm sorry to have to bring this to you,' Seb says. Adam nods, his arm still round Carolyn. 'We need to get into her phone and at the moment, that's proving difficult. We wondered if you might have any idea what password she might have used?'

'Actually, yes,' Carolyn says. 'She used my birthday for most things, I told her recently she ought to change it but…' Carolyn shrugs, 'I also thought it was quite sweet.'

She gives Seb the six- and eight-digit versions, which Lucy sends immediately to Finn at the station. He says to the Smiths, 'As soon as we have any information, we'll be in touch.'

'Okay.'

Outside the hotel, Lucy murmurs, 'That was awful.'

'Yeah,' Seb agrees. He checks his phone. 'On the upside the passcode works, Finn is in and sifting through recent messages. He's also going over the call log.'

'Oh good.'

'It is, yeah. Let's get back.'

–

'I need caffeine,' Lucy says as she and Seb step back into the station.

'We all do,' says Harry.

'Why don't you two go and see to that then,' Seb says. 'Get a chance to stretch your legs as well, yeah?' They had managed to gain access to Hannah's WhatsApp messages before but not via her phone and recent messages hadn't been stored to the desktop version. The last messages they had had were over two months out of date, so getting the password and into the actual phone is brilliant.

'Yeah, sounds good to me.' Harry is already standing. Lucy asks what Finn and Seb want and they are gone.

'I'm in,' Finn says. 'Hallelujah!'

'Great, give us all access yeah?'

Finn does a few things. Seb watches the younger man, perfectly at ease with technologies that seem to move faster than he can keep up with. At just thirty-two, Seb isn't exactly an old git, but having been a dad since he was eighteen he does wonder if he's more middle-aged than his peers. Charlie had always said he was boring. It had been a large part of her reasoning for cheating on him. He could understand it to a degree, too. They didn't have the chance to be young, not like most people did. A baby at eighteen put a stop to that. Though, to him, Charlie's life never looked like much fun.

He pushes the thoughts of his ex-wife aside, wishing he didn't have them but suspecting he always would. He'd told Faye this, expecting her to be upset by it. Maybe he was even looking to give her an easy way out. Instead, she'd taken his hands in hers, squeezed them and said, 'Of course you think about her, Seb. I'm sure you still have love for her on some level. She's the mother of your amazing child, after all.'

If he was a man prone to crying, he thinks, he probably would have burst into tears then. Instead, he'd managed to murmur, 'Yeah, I guess.' Glad it was out in the open and glad too that she wasn't put off. Even if having a relationship and investing in a woman felt like an enormous risk.

'Here you are guv,' Harry says, placing a large Americano in front of Seb. What he really wants is a filter coffee, but they seem to be well out of fashion now. He adds an extra sugar to knock off some of the strength and still winces slightly when he takes his first sip.

Lucy is standing behind Finn, who is scrolling through Hannah Smith's updated WhatsApp history. She murmurs, 'JC.'

'You coming over all religious on us?' Harry asks, grinning.

She swats him. 'Behave. The mystery guy that Katie was talking about is saved as JC.'

'Yes,' says Seb, who is also scrolling through messages. 'The last time he was in touch was by text saying he'd had a wonderful night, and looked forward to seeing her soon.'

'Sent when?' From Harry.

'About half an hour before her suspected time of death.'

'He could have caught up to her,' Seb says.

'Could have,' Finn agrees. 'Or he might not have known a thing about it.'

'Anything since?'

'He called her, the next morning,' Finn says.

'Might have just been covering his tracks.' From Lucy. Most people know now that phones, emails and various messengers leave a traceable trail.

'Might have. Let's get into her voicemails,' Seb tells Finn.

'Alright, might take a minute though.'

'Look at this,' Lucy says, waving Seb over to stare at her screen.

He squints at it, reading messages within a chat. It's between Katie and Hannah.

> Honestly, Katie every time I turned around I caught glimpses of the same person. A woman I think, light brown hair.

> So you think someone's following you?

> Yeah, well, I don't know. It's just a feeling.

> And you're sure it was a woman?

> Yeah I'd say so.

> Could it be his wife?

> What, no, she doesn't know anything.

> She might have found out.

> And you'd love that right?

No response from Katie. An hour later Hannah messages, *Sorry.*

> Maybe we shouldn't talk about him.

> Right.

> We'll never see eye to eye and I don't want to argue.

> Me neither.

That's the end of the chat for that day. The next set of messages are mundane ones about an electricity bill.

'Katie said they'd agreed not to talk about it, didn't she?' Lucy asks Seb.

'She did, yeah, but didn't mention Hannah being followed. Any other hits on messages regarding this?'

She searches '*followed*', '*following*'.

'Not that specific.'

Seb nods. 'Right, we'd better go and talk to Katie again then.'

CHAPTER NINE

STEVIE

I'm early. I left first thing as I really can't bear to watch Angela move, which she's apparently doing today because – why wait? I wonder if I'll miss her at all and if we might stay in touch. I imagine, realistically, we'll dissolve into Facebook Friends at the very most. Occasionally a memory will pop up prompting one or the other of us to remember the 'good old days'. But I doubt her heart will be in it any more than mine.

I'm in a cafe round the corner from school and I order a latte, adding a doughnut at the last minute. The caffeine picks me up a bit and the sugar, as always, hits me in all the good places. I'm contemplating getting another one when someone says, 'Stevie, hi?'

I look up to see Ben Cowley standing over me.

'Ben, hey,' I say, my heart starting to beat a little faster. So many times I've fantasised that he was my brother-in-law; about his parents welcoming me into the fold. The family I had never had who were so happy and so normal. He's my age, a year younger than James, and I remember him from school and from the few times I'd visited James at home. He'd been shy, awkward. I suppose your average teenage boy.

'May I?' he points to the chair opposite me.

'Oh, yeah, sure.' I feel a flutter of nerves as he sits down. He looks a lot like his brother. Both tall, dark hair. James is broader though, better built and with sharper features. Ben looks softer, like a watered-down version. He'd be very good looking by anyone's standards, but next to James he is relegated to just handsome. Not his fault, of course. And maybe not even an issue for him. I have learnt over the years that most people don't give the same level of intense overthinking to such things as I do.

'Still at Beacon Hill?' The little primary school I teach at where once upon a time, Ben, James and I had all attended.

'Still there.'

'Must be so rewarding.'

'It is,' I say automatically, because that is what is expected from teachers. It's vocational, we are told endlessly. I do like my job, in fairness. I am immensely proud that I did well enough in school and went on to university despite the most challenging of circumstances. But I went into it because I figured I'd always have a job I hadn't known then how much I'd love it but I do. The respectability of it also means something to me, especially after dark, lonely weekends with missing hours. Monday morning rolls around and I am Miss Gordon. Trusted, respectable, sane.

'You were just back from university last time I saw you?' he says.

'Yeah that's right.' James had been doing his Masters here while living with his mum and dad. I'd been in my first year of teacher training.

'I went into business with James.'

I know this of course. I've sifted through James's company accounts on more than one occasion. 'Oh, cool, what do you do?'

'We broker energy deals for various companies.'

'Cool,' I say again.

He wrinkles his nose. 'It's not really though, is it?'

That does make me smile. 'But hopefully it pays?'

'It does pay the bills, yes,' he agrees.

'And how is James?' I say, as my pulse quickens, lightning fast, making my face flush. I lean forward to take a sip of my now too-cold latte.

'Oh you know.' He waves his hand. And I do know, obviously. I've pretty much made it my full-time job to know what he's been up to for the past three years.

'He got married, I heard?'

'Yeah. Zoe. She's nice.'

'That's great,' I say, the word coming out funny and slightly too high pitched.

'I mean obviously she's not a patch on you.' He's smiling and adds a wink.

I laugh and that comes out wrong too, like I'm verging on hysteria, which I am. James is married to Zoe. James was sleeping with Hannah Smith. Hannah Smith is dead. She was found in Thames Park's deep woodland. I woke up with damp and muddy clothes. Could it have been blood rather than soil making them stiff? I'd never know because I washed them.

'Stevie?'

'Sorry.' I blink at him. 'I missed that.'

'I, uh, was saying how's your mum doing now?'

'Oh. She's a lot better these days.' I smile, wishing it were true. 'Actually.' I glance at the clock on the wall.

'I'm in danger of being late.' I stand, hitching my bag up on my shoulder.

'So nice to see you,' he says, standing up and leaning in for a hug, which is nice if slightly awkward.

'Yeah, you too.'

'Maybe we could grab a drink or something? Have a proper catch-up.'

'Um.'

He widens his grin. 'Promise not to talk about my dull job.' Which makes me laugh.

'Yeah, alright then.'

'Cool, what are your digits?'

CHAPTER TEN

SEB

They are sitting in the cafeteria at Katie Hardwick's office. She has her hands wrapped around a large mug. Her eyes are wide. She is very well put together and as Seb sneaks looks around him he can see most of the people here seem to be fairly young and everything has a veneer of hipster. From the beanbag area to the fuzzball table set up in the corner. A digital comms agency; he can imagine Tilly somewhere like this.

'I remember the messages, about the man,' Katie says. 'I'd forgotten all about the bit about her being followed, to be honest.'

'What preceded that message? Can you remember that?'

'Um.' She chews on her lower lip. 'I was at work, so was she. It was after her lunch break.'

'Did you talk about it again?'

'No.' She shakes her head. 'I wish I had now, though.'

Seb looks at Lucy, who says, 'It's understandable that you avoided that topic, Katie. I'd have been inclined to do the same.'

'Really?'

'You found a way to maintain your friendship and you also told her honestly what you felt. If you didn't care, you wouldn't have.'

Katie nods. 'That's it exactly.' Her eyes fill with tears. Lucy pulls a packet of tissues from her bag and holds it out to Katie.

'Thank you.' She smiles.

'This must be very difficult.'

'It is. I almost phoned in sick but then had the thought of sitting at home without knowing she'd walk through the door at any minute.' A sob escapes like a hiccup. She dabs underneath her eyes and the tissue comes away with little black smudges on it. 'I just miss her so much.' She looks up from Seb to Lucy. 'Please catch whoever did this.'

'We intend to,' Seb says, thinking of the uncomfortable image of Sam Carmichael laid out flat at the back of a playing field. Almost two years ago and no justice for her, not yet. He hopes it is the same person, then he can get justice for two families, two sets of friends. Two women taken before their time.

Most murders are isolated incidents, but maybe this one wasn't and, if that is the case, they can expect more victims before the perpetrator is caught.

CHAPTER ELEVEN

STEVIE

I leave work as soon as my class do. I don't take the exercise books for today, promising myself I'll catch up before the end of the week. I'm having trouble focusing. My phone beeps: a message from an unknown number.

> Hey it's Joel from Monday night x

Joel. Dark hair, tall, the smell of lemons, my skin pressed against damp woodland. A memory flashes him grinning at the bar, eyes taking me in. 'Why you drinking alone, beautiful?'

Joel, who it seems I gave my number to. I slide my phone back into my bag. I'll answer later, or not, when I've had time to think.

I walk the short distance to my mum's house, my second visit in as many days. I let myself in with the key she leaves in a lockbox by her door. The code is my birthday, which I keep telling her is easily broken and she just shrugs and tells me, 'It's the date that changed everything.' For better or worse she never says and it's a wasps' nest I have no desire to poke.

'Hi Mum,' I call out as I walk in, hit immediately by the peculiar smell I always associate with her. A combination of heavy floral perfume, slightly soured milk and cigarettes.

She doesn't answer me, nor does she get up. I find her in the living room, eyes glued to a soap opera. She points at the TV then presses a finger to her lips. Be quiet, is the message.

I head into the kitchen and methodically check her cupboards. Tinned foods, most within date or near enough. Some suspect cheese in the fridge that I bag up into the food recycling, which is overflowing along with all the other bins. She lives in a tiny house, sheltered accommodation, but she has managed to pack enough stuff inside it to fill a bloody mansion. Every single surface is covered. Stacks of newspapers, yellowing and frayed at the edges. Ornaments balanced precariously and covered with a thin film of dust. I gave up attempting to tidy years ago but just a few seconds in here can make my head feel itchy. It takes me back to sleeping curled in a ball on the tiny end slither of a bed where there were old coats, letters, brown boxes stuffed with god knows what and mice ferreting around the floor.

I take a deep breath and start emptying the bins, taking the bags out onto what is overall a reasonably pleasant little estate. Her neighbour, Martha, is getting out of her car and lifts a hand to me. 'Okay, kiddo?' she bellows as she always does.

'Okay here.'

'Helping her declutter?'

'I wish,' I say, forcing my voice to remain normal, cheerful. My mother is pretty much the youngest person here and the olds that surround her treat her like a sweet eccentric introvert. They don't know she came here fresh from psychiatric care. It was meant to be temporary, just until she got back on her feet, but years on she's showing no signs of doing that. If anything, she has deteriorated. In the last two years, she's stopped leaving the house altogether and, aside from me and her brother, Tom, I don't think she's spoken to many people either.

'Ah well,' Martha says, cheerful and hearty. I imagine her as a young woman; she'd have been strapping, I think. She is still a big woman now, broad-backed, wide shoulders and hips, firm hands that always seem to be busy, the complete opposite of my mother who is like a tiny, delicate bird. Martha bakes and often presses Tupperware containers of lovely sugary goodies into my hands when she sees me leaving. She also gives some to Mum, who I expect smiles sweetly and says thank you but always puts them straight in the bin. She doesn't eat food other people have cooked 'just in case'. In case of what I've never been entirely sure. 'I guess she likes things the way they are,' Martha says, still smiling.

'Yep.'

'School okay?'

'It is.'

'Marvellous job you're all doing.'

'Thanks Martha,' I say and mean it.

'Have a good visit with Mum.'

'Oh, I will,' I lie.

—

'Stevie don't be throwing away any of my things.'

'I'm not, Mum. I was taking the bins out.'

'That's all?'

'That's all,' I say, heading into the living room. She is in the one completely clear chair in the room. A high-backed green velvet thing that could do with a wash but which she insists is absolutely fine. She, herself, is immaculately dressed in tailored slacks and a silky cream blouse. Hair perfect, make-up done. She watches me looking around for a space. I finally move several packets of seeds for various flowers and fruits along on the small brown leather sofa and sit down. 'You look well,' I tell her.

'Do I?' she says, patting the bottom of her perfectly curled-under hair.

'You do. Are you feeling it?'

She lets out a laugh like a loud bark. 'Pass me them.' She waves a hand at the pile on the coffee table to my left where her cigarettes, lighter and toppling ashtray sit. I pass it all to her, saying, 'You need to empty that.'

'Why? You've just put out the bins.'

'Okay,' I say, not here for a fight. I don't have the energy right now. All I can think about is that woman, Hannah Smith, dead in the middle of Thames Park. I picture her bright red hair spread out around her, mingling and clashing with the vibrant purple bluebells.

'I would have emptied it and tidied up if you'd said you were coming,' Mum says.

'I did message, Mum, and I come at least once a week,' I tell her through gritted teeth.

'Could be months for me, the way time acts when you're in my position.'

'Yeah. I know,' I say. Adding, 'Sorry.' Though it is not my fault that she doesn't do anything. It isn't my fault that she's here.

She sighs, lighting a cigarette, inhaling. As she pulls it away I see the red ring left by her lipstick. It's a shade called Fire Engine. A silence settles on us, broken only by the sound of her inhaling and exhaling. If I closed my eyes, I could be ten years old again. I blink as the smoke stings them now. 'Shall I open a window?'

'Sure, if you like.'

I crack it open, breathing in thin slivers of fresher air. I smoke occasionally myself, but I tend to do it only in the evenings as I sit out on the balcony, watching James through cheap theatre binoculars.

'Work's going well for you then?' Mum asks as I sit down, having to, again, sweep aside the debris which seems to have invaded the small space I'd left.

'Not too bad, yeah. Though the Head thinks we might get an OFSTED inspection soon, which will be stressful.'

'Oh.' She stubs the fag out on the towering pile. I notice her hands shake slightly. She is on a wild cocktail of drugs. I may have been known to occasionally slip a few of her sleeping tablets into my bag in the past. She's given more than any individual should be in charge of. A nurse had once commented on it and how irresponsible it seemed, especially given her past. She might hurt herself, the silly, innocent woman had said.

I'd said, 'Yes, I'll speak to her doctors.' Trying to ignore the delicious tingle it evoked to think of her OD'd and no longer here. The weight of responsibility lifted from me.

The silence returns. She stares at me, smoke rising around her.

Eventually, she says, 'Tom said he'd spoken to you?' and I feel a thin spike of pain and panic.

Tom is the only adult in my life I have been able to rely on. I trust him, I do, and understand that he has a separate relationship with my mother. 'I'm not condoning what she did Stevie, but she's my sister and I can't abandon her,' he often said. I wouldn't want him to, either. One of the best things about Tom turning up back from America, where he'd spent close to a decade working, had been having someone to share Mum's care with. Another set of shoulders to lug around the heavy weight that came with being related to her. He did and he does and I'm grateful. But I don't want to discuss him with her. She has a habit, my mum, of telling me things that make no sense and that are probably untrue, but which will stick in my brain like stringy spinach between my teeth.

'How are the new pills?'

'Do I have new pills?'

I frown. 'Yes, in the pill pots in the kitchen.' I put them in little compartments labelled by day. 'You have been taking them?'

'Yes, Stevie, if they are in the pot I have been taking them.'

'That's good, Mum.'

She smiles brightly, eyes shining, pupils dilated. 'I am a good girl.'

I look away out the window. *Childlike*, one of her shrinks had said about her, and that was true. She looked like a middle-aged woman but when she spoke she could sound six years old. Not only is my mother the only link I have to my childhood, she's also not a bad person, she's a damaged person and that is why I've never been able to let her go entirely. 'You are,' I lie. 'You're very good.'

CHAPTER TWELVE

SEB

Leigh Valley is geographically close to Thamespark but definitely feels more like a Surrey village than a London borough. They drive along a small high street that conjures up the word quaint. 'Chocolate-box pretty,' Seb says to Lucy, who wrinkles her nose at him.

'Dull as dishwater, you mean.'

Seb laughs. They pull into a small car park at the back of Leigh Valley's station and head in. The heat has subsided slightly but Seb still feels the closeness of it, and it's only the end of April. He wonders if they'll have a melting summer to come or whether it will just rain sleet grey like it had last year. He's not sure which one he'd prefer. When temperatures rise, so do tempers, which tends to make his day-to-day work harder.

He flashes a badge at a small woman sitting on reception. She says, 'Here for DI Marks?'

'Yes,' Seb confirms.

'I'll give him a call.'

A moment later, a broad-shouldered man with red hair and an even redder beard comes out. 'Thanks Celia,' he says to the woman on reception. Then he puts his hand out to Seb and Lucy. 'Mind talking in the cafe?'

'Not at all,' Seb says.

'Called out to a domestic last night.' DI Marks sighs. 'Was there until the small hours and on the bright and early shift this morning, so caffeine is definitely in order.'

They all get coffees, with Lucy opting for a caramel shot in a latte, which makes Seb shake his head. She ignores him. DI Marks squints at her. 'Do I know you?'

'I don't think so,' she says and Seb sees a flush of red creep up her neck. Interesting; Lucy is usually very hard to embarrass.

'Surname?'

'Quinn,' she murmurs.

'Quinn.' Still frowning. 'Related to Oliver Quinn?'

'My dad,' Lucy says, looking away before Seb can catch her eye.

DI Marks nods. 'Glad to see you ended up on the right side of things, despite everything.'

Lucy nods but doesn't respond. Seb wonders what on earth DI Marks is on about.

'How's Mum doing?'

'Yeah, good thanks.'

'Say hello from me. Good woman, as I recall. Far too good for your dad.'

'Yes,' Lucy agrees.

Seb knows that Lucy is one of five children, a number of dependants he can barely comprehend. He knows too that her mum had raised them single-handedly and that Lucy didn't see much of her dad. But it seems there is perhaps more to the story.

They sit down. DI Marks takes a lug of coffee and makes a wet *ahh* sound. 'I'm getting too old for this.'

'The job?' Seb asks.

'Yes, and late nights in general.' Marks grins. 'Wait till you're my age, son.'

Seb smiles back.

'But,' Marks says, 'you're not here about my aching old bones.'

'No. We're here about Sam Carmichael.'

DI Marks sighs. 'A terrible thing.'

'No one caught?'

'No, and if you ask me the investigation was shut down far too soon.'

'Oh?'

'Yes. I mean, on one hand I get it, her line of work was dangerous, but no one is asking for that. Plus, I said at the time the culprit was a nutter.' Seb smothers another smile at that. 'I also remember telling our fairly rubbish DSI that we'd see more of the same, but did he listen? Did he heck.'

'Why did you think that?' Seb asks.

'Well, it was brutal and it felt personal to me. We found her, poor little thing, blanket up to her neck, eyes shut. Dr Mathewson said that had been done after death. It was weird. Know what I mean?'

'I think I do actually,' Seb says. He takes the images of Hannah Smith out from his bag, laying them between him and Marks.

Marks shakes his head. 'Poor kid.'

'She was twenty-one.'

Marks waves a hand. 'Barely an adult, whole life ahead, gone.' He clicks his fingers. 'Just like that.' He leans back shaking his head and Seb finds he likes the man. 'You think it's the same guy?'

'Martina Mathewson does.'

'Same cause of death, you said?'

'Yes.'

'Did your vic have anything missing?'

'Missing?' Seb asks.

'Sam had a necklace, cheap thing really but sentimental value. Her mother was not much better off than Sam was, I'm sorry to say, and hadn't raised the girl herself. Sam was in and out of care but the necklace was from her gran. She never took it off.'

'It was gone?'

'Yup.'

'A trophy,' Seb murmurs.

DI Marks nods. 'That's what we thought.'

'You interviewed a lecturer from the university?'

'Ah yes, Colin Aftermore.'

'What did you think?'

'He was definitely capable but had an iron-clad alibi.'

'Oh?'

'Yep, he was arrested for curb-crawling in London at the time of her death.'

'Ah.'

'Had it in him though. She had an ex, but he was away at the time.'

'The man she'd spent a few nights with?'

'Ah, the phone messages?'

'Right.' This is what had jumped out to Seb from the case notes. Messages swapped between Sam and a mystery man.

'Couldn't trace him sadly and no one at the club knew who he was. It didn't matter, case got closed.'

'That soon?'

'Not officially, but we were told to move on, likely a trick gone wrong.'

'Huh,' Seb says.

'Yeah, told you the boss was an eejit. We've a better one now.'

'That's good.'

'It is.' Marks yawns. 'And I wish I could help you more but…' He shrugs.

—

Seb knocks on Jackie's office door.

'What?'

'Hey.' He pokes his head round.

'Solved that murder yet?'

'It's only been thirty-six hours.'

'That's a no, then.'

'Can I come in?'

'Mmhmm,' she says. 'Sit down Seb; you're making the place look untidy.'

He sits, feeling, as he always does in her office, at a disadvantage. The chair opposite her desk is ever so slightly smaller than the rest of the chairs. It means he looks like a giant in a child's classroom, his legs bent awkwardly whilst she towers over him from the other side of the desk, wearing her trademark glare.

She looks at him through narrowed eyes. 'You've got something?'

'Yes. We went to Leigh Valley.'

'Right.'

'Spoke to DI Marks. The victim had a necklace and it was missing.'

'She probably sold it, judging by her rap sheet: drug addict, after cash, an endless cycle, as you and I both know.'

'It was cheap, from Argos. She'd had it since she was small, a gift from her gran. Her mum also confirmed she'd had it on when she saw her.'

'Which was when?'

'The day before the murder.'

'How does this connect with Hannah?'

'I checked in again with Mr and Mrs Smith, asked if anything wasn't in with her personal belongings that they expected to be. Her dad said, actually yes. A small gold ring she wore on her pinkie finger.'

Jackie stares without speaking. Seb looks back, unwavering.

'You want me to link the murders publicly.' She sighs.

Seb has learnt that this is generally her first response to any request, even perfectly reasonable ones like this. He says, 'She had also been seeing someone.'

'Oh?'

'Sounded like they met in her club.'

'Name?'

'Just J, and no not the same number as Hannah's.'

'And Hannah's mystery man?'

'He's saved with the initials JC.'

'Her parents definitely don't know who he is?'

'No. Nor her flatmate. I doubt she confided in anyone else but if she did, we'll find out.'

'Can't blame her, everyone's a critic in these situations.'

'Right.'

'Best find JC then.'

'So I can work it as a dual case?'

'Tentatively.'

'And you'll appeal for leads in both murders?'

'Sure.' Jackie's eyes are narrowed, glare all encompassing.

Seb grins. 'Thank you, ma'am.'

She huffs as though he is asking for a great personal favour rather than reasonable assistance with a murder investigation.

CHAPTER THIRTEEN

STEVIE

'How did that make you feel?' Michael Ross, my therapist, asks me. A question he has posed so many times it would be comical, if not for the issues we were led to discuss. I'm telling him about Mum and her incessant hoarding. My overwhelming urge to clean up or run.

'Like I was twelve years old again, the same way I always feel when I'm around her.'

'Yes,' he says, not unkindly. It is the place we revisit all the time. It is the point at which doctors and social services started to be concerned for me, where I almost died. Just before Mum and I were split up for good.

'Also, I want to just get all of her stuff and put it in a skip, have it carted away without her knowing.'

'Mmm.'

'I'm not going to do it, though,' I say, realising as soon as the words are out that I sound petulant and sulky, which I am. I always am when I see Michael as we usually have a session after I visit Mum. It was at his suggestion. So that I can decompress before getting on with the rest of the week.

'But you still think your visits are beneficial.'

My leg is jiggling slightly and I see Michael's eyes flick to it. I tense the muscles, forcing it to be still. 'No one else goes, she'd be lost,' I say, though I'm not sure if that's strictly true. I have a feeling Tom may pop in from time to time. Certainly, they speak on the phone. That bothers me more than it should, more than is fair, I suspect. I don't tell Michael this; any mention of Tom leads to prodding about my mother's family of origin and all I know is Tom grew up to be fine and she grew up to be, well, her. I don't want to feel sympathy for her and always feel that's where Michael is trying to go. I may be wrong on that of course, but I'm still not going to go there.

'I meant are the visits beneficial for you?'

Another topic we circle back to often. A question with no answer. I hate seeing her, hate the way being around her makes me feel utterly desolate, but I hate the guilt of not going even more. I shrug. 'I can't not go.'

'I understand the way you feel,' he says in his moderated, trained voice. I offer him a forced smile in response. Though he does in no way know how I feel. I've Googled the shit out of him and I have strong evidence that he has in fact led a pleasant enough, trouble-free life. On his Facebook page there are pictures of him and his reasonably attractive wife with their reasonably cute baby in a reasonably nice house. There are snaps of his wedding day, his graduation. Plenty of photos with his parents and hers. Someone like him cannot even begin to comprehend what it might be like to be utterly alone in the world, or alone but for a demented lunatic who spent my childhood playing life-or-death games based on paranoid delusions.

'She's my whole family,' I say, for the millionth time.

He nods. 'I get it.' Another lie. My leg starts up again. I shift and cross them. 'You have Tom though, too?'

'Yes.'

'How is he?'

73

I smile. 'Yes good, we're planning to meet soon.'

'That's good.'

I nod agreement.

'Will he see your mother too?'

I shrug, averting my eyes, not wanting him to see the flush I can feel heating my face. 'Maybe, she is his sister.'

'Of course. Though I would understand if that was a little uncomfortable for you.'

'Not at all. I get it,' I say, feeding him back his own line, waiting for my skin to cool down, for the anger to slide away. When I'm sure my voice will come out again, I tell him, 'So we're awaiting an OFSTED inspection.'

'I didn't think schools got told in advance.'

'Yeah, no, they don't. But you hear rumours, or our head has anyway.'

'How do you feel about it?'

'Okay. I mean, they are always horrible but…' I shrug. Again. I'm doing a lot of shrugging today. 'It will be fine.'

'That's a good attitude to have.'

'Yeah.'

'Any news about Angela?'

'Oh, yeah. I was right.'

'She's moving out?'

'Mmhmm.'

'Are you okay about it?'

'I mean, I could use the rent. But it's been annoying never knowing when Mark might be there. I'm happy for her,' I add, fooling neither of us.

'Because she's met someone?'

'Yes. It's good, isn't it?'

'Not for you, because of the rent.'

I sigh, pick at a straggly hole in the knee of my jeans, the edges of the denim soft and frayed. 'Did you see that woman, murdered in the park?'

His eyes widen in surprise before his face settles back to neutral. 'I saw something in the paper. That's near where you live?'

I nod. 'Yeah, awful right?'

'Has it upset you?'

'I mean, someone was killed,' I say going for humour, which falls flat. 'It's pretty horrific, she was probably just walking home.'

'It got to you?'

'I don't know. I guess.' I look out the window. The day is lingering on as evening draws in. Nights are getting shorter; summer is on its way.

He leaves silence which seems to stretch out around us and makes me drowsy.

'I'm tired,' I murmur.

'Insomnia again?'

I nod.

'What's been on your mind at night?'

'Angela, money, Mum. The usual.' I don't add the truth. I miss my ex who probably never even thinks about me. I watch his every move and often plan my weekends and evenings around him, his wife or his mistress.

Mistress. Hannah, the girl with the fiery hair. Dead now.

'The usual?'

'Yeah, same old.'

'Are you having nightmares again?'

My leg jumps again; I switch them over. 'I always have them,' I say because I do. But really, if they are memories, are they even nightmares?

'About when you were a child?'

'Yes,' I say. I have memory problems. Apparently, it's not unusual for people who experience traumatic events at a young age. There are huge grey patches that span years of my life, interspersed with sharp, prickly memories; like small shards of glass inside a shoe, they stab at me.

'Are more things coming back to you, Stevie?'

'I don't know,' I say. 'I, uh, drank a bit too much Monday night.'

'Ah.' He leans forward slightly. My alcohol consumption is always a nice juicy topic. 'What happened?'

'I don't know.'

'You blacked out?'

'Yes.'

'Were you at home?'

'When I started,' I say and I can almost feel myself settled on my balcony, feet bare and pressed to the warm concrete, binoculars pressed to my eyes, vodka making everything slippery. Hannah showing up, distinctive and beautiful. The door opening, James's big smile like a Cheshire Cat.

'You went out?'

'I think so,' I say, thinking of my slightly hard to touch, crusty dress, the red-tinged water as I washed my hair. The man who smells of lemons. The texts that keep pinging up on my phone, *Want to meet?* Do I? Want is a funny word.

'What type of person would do that?' I ask.

Michael frowns. 'Do what?'

'Kill someone,' I say. 'The girl in the park.'

'Someone who is very unwell,' he says. I know this, of course I do. I know that mothers with pretty faces and beautiful clothes can be deadly. That evil looks benign.

76

Unwell. I am unwell. It's in my notes, the ones likely in a neatly ordered file on Michael's computer just metres away from me now.

'It's upsetting you?' Michael says.

'It's an upsetting thing.'

'It is.' He pauses, which means he's choosing his words carefully. 'But sadly this sort of thing happens a lot.'

'Not here,' I say, which is true. It's a busy suburb, as suburbs go, but it has a low crime rate compared to the city.

'You identify with the victim?'

I shrug. 'She's younger than me.' But, we had both slept with the same man. I don't say this, though I am itching to, just to see his reaction. But then I'd have to go into the details of what he had once deemed my 'unhealthy obsession' with James Cowley.

'Still,' he says.

'Yeah, I guess I do a bit.' I'll give him that though, what always surprised me about James was his distinct lack of a specific 'type'. Hannah, Zoe and I were all quite different, looks wise at least.

The buzzer goes and Michael gives me his head tilt smile. 'End of the session for this week.'

I stand, relieved to be leaving, and murmur thanks. Leaving feeling ever so slightly worse than when I arrived.

James, I think, was probably the last person to see Hannah alive. She walked home through the woods where I had gone for an illicit sexual encounter with a man whose name I'd forgotten and whose smell I had not. Did James hurt Hannah? Did they argue? Did he walk her home? Did I see her? Did the man I'd been with?

It would be good, in this kind of situation, to have someone to discuss this with, someone to run things past.

It would be good if I could be honest with another human being, but I can't. Not even my therapist. I learnt years ago that whilst people always say they want the truth, few really do, because the truth can be an ugly thing.

CHAPTER FOURTEEN

SEB

Last night, Seb and Tilly had had a few choice words about her being out on school nights. She'd looked at him as though he was insane for suggesting she needed to be in before dark.

'It's because I was with Kai,' she'd said, accusation making her words spiky.

'I didn't say that.'

'Whatever.' She rose from the table, leaving half a plate of a bolognaise he'd cobbled together and which, if not a patch on Val's, wasn't half bad.

'Don't you want your dinner?' he'd asked.

'Not hungry,' had been the response that was flung at him as she left the room stomping up the stairs and slamming the door to her room shut so hard that the house shook.

So that had been last night.

He finds he's almost holding his breath as he knocks on her door to say goodbye. 'Tilly. Tills?'

Nothing and now he's also starting to feel irritated. 'I'm coming in,' he half yells, pushing the door open slightly. 'I'm going to poke my head round the door, okay?'

'Whatever.'

He looks round and forces a smile. She glares back at him.

'What?' She's sitting up in her bed, hair mussed, face crumpled with sleep.

'You're awake then?'

'Obviously.'

'School soon?'

'K, cool.' She's already turning over and lying back down, phone sliding out of her hand and onto her wooden floorboards with a clatter that makes him wince.

'You'll get up in time?'

'Sure,' she says in the least convincing way ever.

Seb goes downstairs, pours another coffee, glancing over his notes for the day ahead and waiting for signs of movement. Half seven. She's still not down for breakfast or in the shower. Long gone are the days when she'd be up and come in search of him for a morning hug.

'Is she in bed still?' Val asks as she comes into the kitchen already showered and dressed.

'Yes, I think so.'

She tuts. 'Have you not been up?'

'I have. She said she was getting up.'

Val purses her lips in a thin line and heads upstairs, coming down a second later with Tilly in hot pursuit frowning at him.

'You let me go back to sleep?' she says, voice heavy with accusation. Then, 'Thanks for getting me up Nan. I'll shower in five minutes then.'

'What about breakfast?' Seb asks.

'Probably won't have time now, will I.' She's gone again.

'Why did she come down if she's not having food?' Seb asks Val with wonder.

She smiles. 'Just to tell you off for something that isn't your fault.'

'Great.'

'She's not a morning person.'

'No.'

'Plus hormones,' Val says, the mantra they all have on repeat.

'Go on then, you head into the station, I'll drop her if she isn't ready.'

'You don't have to.'

'I know.' She smiles. 'Go.'

'Thanks Val,' he says giving her a peck on the cheek as he goes.

—

As he settles into the car, Seb calls Faye. He's taken to calling her during his drive on the days he doesn't see her.

'Hey handsome.'

He finds himself blushing like an idiot. 'Hey yourself.'

'You on your way in?'

'I am. Where are you?'

'Sadly, I'm already at the prison.'

He frowns. 'That's early.'

'Yeah, I know. One of the kids had an episode.'

'Matt?'

'Yes.' She sighs.

'I'm sorry,' he tells her.

'Me too. It's a terrible environment for him. He's re-traumatised here every day.'

'He'll be moved soon?'

'Yes. I'm pushing for it to be today and honestly won't be leaving here until he is. They can't keep using these places like holding pens.'

'I know,' he says because he does. He often thinks everything in Britain needs reform, but prisons really are crying out for it. Especially young offenders' units. 'He's got you to advocate.'

'He does and I will. How's Tills?'

'Grumpy.'

'Huh.'

'We argued after dinner. She said I don't like Kai.'

'You don't.'

'But I haven't said it.'

'Follow her lead, Seb. Remember the older you get the more you're parenting by consent. Don't crowd her.'

He sighs.

Her tone softens. 'Easy for me to say as I don't have kids, but from a clinical perspective.'

'No, you're right, and besides that, you're great with her.'

'She makes it easy by being ace, which I'm sure is in no small part down to having a superstar dad.'

'Thanks Faye.'

She laughs. 'What for?'

'I don't know, being you.'

'Ah, you're not so bad yourself.'

'Ha.'

'How's the case going?'

'Well, actually I wanted to run something past you.'

'Okay.'

'It looks like Hannah's death may be linked to that other murder.'

'Also posed?'

'Yes, sort of, and killed in the same way.'

'Local?'

'Leigh Valley.'

'Was she also a student?'

'No, a stripper.'

Faye pauses. Seb imagines her leaning her head to one side, long red hair dancing around her waist. 'Different demographics.'

'Yes.'

'Hannah's death will draw more attention?'

'Sadly, yes. The public will see Hannah as a more sympathetic victim, and I suspect we'll be under more pressure to solve it. The guy running Sam's case did a good job, but no leads really, lots of fairly unpleasant encounters and what looked like a growing coke habit that she'd started subsidising through other means.'

'Right,' Faye says. 'Any links other than the method?'

'Actually yes, messages with a guy she'd seen more than once. Didn't read like a customer.'

'Did anyone who knew her say she was in a relationship?'

'Nope, there was an ex who was ruled out, abroad when she was killed.'

'So maybe the same married man?'

'Exactly. Saved as J. Hannah's guy JC.'

'That's a link, tenuous though.'

'It is. Both messages come from burner phones too, so we're having trouble tracing them.'

'Different numbers?'

'Of course, just to muddy the waters. There's another thing.'

'Okay.'

'We think he might have taken items.'

'From the victims?'

'Yeah, like trophies?'

'Been watching *Criminal Minds*?'

'Only with you,' he says, finding a smile spread across his face. Faye loves the show, even as she picks holes in much of its pop psychology. 'That is a thing though isn't it?' He's thinking back to his degree in criminology. A fascinating subject oftentimes without much real-world application. 'I remember it coming up in serial killer cases at uni. Though two victims isn't a serial,' he adds quickly.

'Not yet, no.'

'That's my fear.'

'It's grounded and yes, it's a thing, a symptom of a particularly disturbed mind. What did he take?'

'Jewellery.'

'Expensive?'

'Not in either case.'

'So a pointless theft in and of itself.'

'Right,' he agrees, 'but when you put it together?'

'I think there's a good chance it's the same person Seb. It's not usual to take things from victims and for it to happen twice in such a short space of time in roughly the same area with the same method of killing. It's a strong link.'

'I figured it might be,' he says. 'Thanks, for your insight.'

'Oh, no worries, always here for your pathological murder needs.'

He's smiling again. 'I'm at the station.'

CHAPTER FIFTEEN

STEVIE

Every Thursday morning, my first period is blocked out and my TA oversees my class. It's meant to be when I do my marking, but I do most of that Sunday and Monday night if needed. I'm not marking. I am, in fact, at my local gym with many other women doing a Pilates class.

'Hold the C curve,' the glossily pretty instructor says, and I see the woman in front of me starting to tremble as I am, too. Building a strong inner core is not for the faint-hearted. Nor, I think not for the first time, for the pathetically hungover. In my defence, I only had a few glasses of wine, but I did drink fast, plus I added a sleeping pill, which always means the first few hours of the day are like wading through treacle.

'Very good and release.' A collective sigh of relief. 'Thank you all so much. Same time next week.'

'Killer.' A voice from next to me.

I turn and smile agreement. 'I know, right. How's your week been Zoe?' I ask James's wife.

'Oh, you know. Nothing too exciting.'

'You were away?'

'Yes. Good of you to remember,' she says. I had the days she was gone blanked out in my calendar and made a point to keep an especially close eye on James and Hannah. I now wish I hadn't. I guess ignorance really is bliss.

'Was it okay?'

'Yes, I mean we secured the account so yay.' She does a fist pump.

I say, 'Hooray,' back. Then, 'Did you hear about that woman?'

She frowns. 'Who?'

'In the park, murdered.'

'God, yes I did actually. I was just saying to James this morning how terrible it is. Though I'd never walk through there at night, would you?'

I am used to this. Casual victim blaming. I do it myself often enough. Especially in regards to my own fragile childhood situation. Why hadn't I told someone sooner? Not a friend, I didn't have any of those. I never attended school often enough to strike up bonds. But a teacher or one of the endless doctors.

'No,' I lie. I often come home through the park. Often walk dark alleys at night. I often, I suppose, tempt fate. I'm not suicidal; it even says so in my fat psych file. I am careless and sometimes I wonder if actually it's almost the same thing. I am also not deemed a risk to myself nor to anyone else, including the children left in my care. That particular assessment was especially galling, even as my honey-voiced social worker tried to put it to me lightly: 'We just want to make sure you're up to it, is all.' What she'd meant was, 'Just checking you didn't get the faulty gene.' Or is it wiring? Nature or nurture. The never-ending debate. To which I offer Tom as the case against both and, now, myself and the several classes I've taught, none of whom have met awful ends.

'You're off to class?' Zoe asks.

'I am,' I say, smiling.

'Must be so nice to have a job like that. You know, one that really makes a difference.'

I think of my new increased mortgage payment the stacks of credit card bills which are so daunting I am actively ignoring them. Zoe changed jobs only last year. The role she took was advertised at circa £60,000. James earns well and they bought their house with money gifted to them by their parents for their wedding day. Zoe wrote a Facebook post expressing her gratitude to both pairs the day they got the keys. It was accompanied by a picture of her, slim, shiny in James's arms, holding out the key. Both of them grinning like idiots. A happy day for them that was a knife to my heart.

'Yeah, it's cool. But also nice to hand them back at the end of the day.'

'Ha, yes. Right,' she says, hiking up her yoga mat on her shoulder, 'next week?'

'Yup, see you then.'

—

My phone beeps as I get into the changing rooms. Joel:

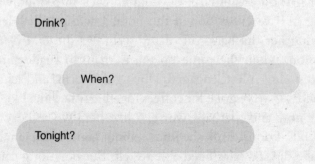

Drink?

When?

Tonight?

I weigh that up against the thought of going home to my empty flat and likely doomscrolling the news. I write, *Yeah OK*.

> Great, eightish, same place?

The Amersham Arms. That means through the park right by James's place, right where Hannah met her untimely end.

Let's meet at the Spoons? Central, well-lit, I can get a bus to and from my door.

> Great look forward to it, xx.

I shower quickly, dressing for work with my head full of too many things. When I first started in this class, I felt nervous, almost giddy with it. To see her close up, in the flesh. This woman I'd watched for so long from afar. We hadn't spoken for the first three weeks. But I noticed she often forgot to bring a hair tie. On week four, I put myself next to her and watched as she tried unskilfully to flick her hair off of her face as we jutted back into downward dog. As we came out of the pose, I whispered, 'Here,' giving her the band off of my wrist. At the end of the session, when she came up to say thanks I made sure I was smiling, alert, engaged. During half terms and school holidays, we've gone for coffees together. I feel like I know her now and, perhaps worse, I like her. We've become friends. I don't think she knows about James and Hannah. If she did, I'd have been able to tell. But how long can it be before she finds out?

CHAPTER SIXTEEN

SEB

Seb smiles his thanks at the woman, eyes skittering around Park Lane, a small street of houses behind Thames Park. Tiny cottages, really, which must be worth a fortune now considering their location. She's the third person he's spoken to and the third one who didn't see or hear anything untoward. The demographic here is a mix of young families and elderly people who, he suspects, have been here for decades and whose houses all seem to be in need of updating. He has spoken to two older women, one of whose husband was dozing peacefully in an easy chair throughout their conversation. The woman, Mrs Gleason, had smiled at the man fondly and said he was deaf as a door post and wouldn't have known if a bomb exploded outside their front door. Seb had also spoken to a young stressed-out mum with three children under five, each demanding different types of attention.

Lucy meets him in the middle of the street. 'Anything?'

'No, you?'

'Nope,' she says.

He glances at his watch. 'Shall we catch up with Harry?'

'Yes,' she says. 'Good idea.'

Harry is in the Amersham Arms. As they walk in, the smell of pub hits Seb and he feels a pang for days gone by. He has recently started going out in the evenings with Faye, sometimes with Tilly too, but they go to restaurants, the cinema, bowling. Neither he nor Faye are big drinkers. He used to come here with Charlie. The only pub in town where she'd get served. Sweet days before she got pregnant, before things got bad. He can remember sitting in the corner table with her, bodies huddled close, oblivious to everyone else.

Lucy is flashing her badge at the barmaid, who says, 'Oh yeah, your colleague is back there with Dean.' Her head inclines to a room behind the bar. 'Come round.'

The room is an office, Seb supposes, though the thought of trying to do any type of admin here amongst barrels and boxes makes his head itch.

'Alright?' A round, red-faced man looks up.

Harry is beside him and stands. 'Hello guv.' Introductions are made and Harry says, 'We might have something.'

'Oh yeah?'

'Yeah. Here.'

The landlord rewinds the pub's footage, which captures the door and the outside and Seb sees a couple leave the pub: a tall man with dark hair, half carrying a woman who is clearly very drunk.

'That's not Hannah,' Seb says.

'No, sorry, bit further on Dean,' Harry says.

'Right you are.' Then, 'That was well past close by the way, those two were right difficult to get rid of.'

'Regulars?'

He shrugs. 'I know the girl, Stephanie maybe? Likes a drink, and a teacher, would you believe?' He raises his eyebrows to Seb as though inebriated teachers are an impossibility.

'Here,' Harry says. 'Stop.'

A tall woman walks into the frame, her flaming red hair instantly recognisable. They watch her walk past the pub and to the bus stop outside. She scans the timetable, pulls out her phone, glancing at it. A man walks up.

'Pause it,' Seb says. 'Can you enlarge it?'

The landlord does so, but the man's face is obstructed, his back to the camera.

'OK, hit play.'

They all watch as Hannah smiles at the man. They talk for a bit and she gestures at the bus timetable. The man shrugs, big powerful shoulders hitching up and down. He's in a dark jumper, fitted trousers and a baseball cap. Hannah laughs, putting a hand out and squeezing his arm.

'She knows him,' Lucy murmurs.

'That's what we thought,' says Harry. The man points in the direction of the park and Hannah nods.

'Could it be the man we saw earlier, leaving?' Lucy asks.

'If it is, he's put a hat on and this man looks... bulkier,' Seb says.

'A bit,' Harry says.

'I wouldn't rule it out. They are a similar height, I'd say.'

'I would too,' Lucy agrees.

'This guy looks like he might be slightly older though?' Harry says.

They rewind the footage, watching the couple leaving, but the camera only really catches the back of the man's head. They flick forward to Hannah, waiting. The other man's face obscured by his hat.

'I think you may be right,' Seb says to Harry. 'He's moving more slowly, at any rate, and I think he is definitely a bit plumper.'

'Still though,' Lucy says, 'can't be certain.'

Seb says, 'No, we need to talk to that couple for sure, and this man.'

They watch as Hannah reaches out, squeezing the man's arm, and then they both make their way towards the woodland, their backs fading into the distance. Hannah never to be seen alive again.

CHAPTER SEVENTEEN

STEVIE

I go home, quickly dropping off my bag and changing from my sensible work dress and flats to a less sensible dress and heels. I freshen up my make-up, run a brush through my hair and head out again. My phone rings as I'm stepping onto the bus and I pick it up with a smile.

'Uncle Tom!' I say and he chuckles, which makes me smile. He's always said the shock of being someone's uncle is one of the first things that's ever made him feel like a grown-up. 'How are you?'

'I'm fine young Stevie, and I'm back home for a few months, at least.' He travels a lot; when he's here, he lives alone, in the very out of the way house which belonged to their parents.

'Well, that is wonderful news,' I say, pushing away the thought that he contacted Mum first. She *is* his sister, despite how I may feel about it, and my feelings are complex and spiky; they have their own relationship. One that, of course, historically hadn't included me.

'How did work go?'

He sighs. 'Oh you know, exceptionally boring.'

I laugh. I don't know exactly what he does; he's always vague about work, reiterating something dull which pays the bills. Tom had come back to the UK shortly after I'd turned eighteen; by that time I'd been housed in the flat that I now own. Free of foster families and terrified on a daily basis. He'd been heartbroken when he discovered what had happened.

He still travels a lot and can be away for months at a time but always seems to end up back here in Thamespark, at a house which had once belonged to his and Mum's parents, my grandparents I suppose, and which Tom inherited. I'd been there once and the place is honestly very run down. There is a picture on his fireplace of him and Mum as children that made me feel sick to look at. He must have been on the verge of his teenage years, my mum barely out of toddlerhood. She was very sweet looking, like a little dolly, her face turned adoringly on her big brother. He'd told me they were very close growing up, despite the age gap. It is hard for me to imagine her before me, of course, as it is for all children and their parents. It is hard to imagine her being young and being well.

'More importantly, dear Stevie, how the devil are you, my girl?' *My girl* makes my heart swell and, I think, it is these type of things I've missed out on by having no father, or no known one anyway.

'I'm okay. My flatmate moved out though.'

'Angela?'

'Yes.'

'In with silly Mark?'

I laugh at this, a topic we've discussed on more than one occasion. 'Yes, in with silly Mark.'

'Well, you're better off rid of the pair of them,' he says.

'You're right,' I say, still smiling, though a jagged spike of fear reminds me that without Angela the coming month's mortgage payment will be a stretch. I push it from my mind. No point worrying about it now.

'And your class?'

'Lovely this year.'

'Likely due to having such a fabulous teacher to learn from.'

'Thanks, Tom,' I say.

'And you're off out somewhere now, sounds like you're on a bus if I'm not mistaken?'

'I am, yes. Just, uh, meeting a friend in town for a drink.' Friend or man I'm not convinced I'll recognise by looks. An image of me walking up to random men with dark hair and smelling to check for lemons comes to mind. It gives me a wave of shame with my uncle on the phone and my illicit one-night stand waiting at my destination.

'Well, that sounds good, and when you're free you'll let me take you to a long lunch?'

'I'd love that,' I say and I would; I always do. When we go out together we are always mistaken for father and daughter and neither of us corrects the assumption.

'Excellent. Now, I've spoken to your mum and will be going to see her this week.'

'She mentioned it,' I murmur. 'Hold on.' I realise we are in town and stand up, then I press the bell and step off. It's warm out here and because of this, town is bustling, even on a Thursday night.

'She sounded a bit manic,' Tom says.

'They've changed her prescription,' I tell him.

'Ah.'

'She's fine though,' I add. 'I mean, as fine as she ever is.'

'I know what you mean.'

The Spoons is up ahead and I feel a flutter of nervous excitement in my belly. 'Sorry, I've got to go, Tom.'

'Right, so I'll see your mum and we'll firm up a date for lunch?'

'Sounds good.'

–

Not recognising him turns out to be a non-issue. I am making my way to the bar when I feel a hand snaking around my middle. I turn, startled, and see him, grinning ear-to-ear, tall, dark-haired, smells like lemons. 'Joel?'

His grin widens. 'You didn't recognise me?'

'Of course I did,' I snap back too quickly. Though I wouldn't have, if we'd met in passing.

He manoeuvres me nearer to the bar, arm still wrapped around me, his fingers pressing into my stomach. He waves at the barman. 'Pint please. Double vodka coke for the lady.'

That annoys me slightly, though I imagine it's what I'd been drinking when we met.

'Thanks,' I say as he presses the drink into my hand, nodding at a table in the corner.

'Shall we sit?'

We settle into the booth and there is a silence that is far from comfortable.

'The thing I don't like about Spoons,' he says, hitching his shoulders up and down, making the muscles there ripple, 'is the lack of music.'

I smile. 'Yeah, no, I know what you mean. It's like an airport departure lounge or something, isn't it?'

That makes him laugh and he laughs properly. I feel myself relax slightly. Weighing up my different approaches to life sober and drunk. Sober, here, now, I'm aware of his size, twice as big as I am easily, muscular. Strong. He could overpower me no problem. Drunk, I'd left a bar with him stumbled into the woods and… well. I think of my back pressed against damp woodland. Anything could have happened. A bad thing did happen, just not to me.

'You look nice,' he says.

'Oh, thanks. I had time to change after work.'

'A teacher, right?'

'Yeah, that's right,' I say, horribly aware I have no idea what he does. I ask, 'How was your day?'

'Oh you know, tiring and dull.'

'Ha, yeah.'

'But plumbing pays well, so.'

'Yeah,' I say. A plumber then, perfectly respectable. I take a big sip of my drink and feel the warmth settle in. 'I, uh, had a bit too much to drink. When we met.'

'Yeah, I figured by the time we left the park, though you seemed fine until then.'

I nod, always surprised that I can be pretty much in a blackout and still be walking, talking, functioning and even 'seem fine'.

'Yeah, no, I was, and then—' I make an exploding hand movement over my head.

'You were shaky getting in the cab, said you didn't want to go home, but you definitely needed to.'

'Yeah must have got in and passed straight out. What time did we get in the cab?' I ask, hoping my assumption that we shared a cab was right.

'Um, I reckon about one. You don't remember?'

'Um, no. God sorry, you must think I'm awful, honestly.' I lie, 'I don't make a habit of that sort of thing.'

He shrugs as if to say whatever, it's cool. Which it's not really.

'You seemed a bit better when you got out. I offered to walk you in, you said no.' Relief floods me; he'd seen me back to my place. I had got out of the cab.

'Yeah, I was fine.' I say, 'Thanks.'

'So who is James then?'

'What?' I ask.

'That's who you said you wanted to go and see when we got in the cab.'

'Oh.'

'Romantic interest?'

'No, nothing like that.'

'Good.' He moves slightly closer, his long arm stretching out behind my back. 'I don't want competition.'

We both got intoI the cab, I made it home, he dropped me at the bottom of my block of flats. I suppose it's possible I waited until he was gone, went back to the park and followed Hannah. Possible but unlikely, which is good. I allow myself to relax and find he's not bad company. After we say goodbye I'm not ruling out the possibility of seeing him again.

CHAPTER EIGHTEEN

SEB

Seb looks up from his desk to find Finn in front of him fidgeting. 'Yes, Finn?'

'James Cowley.'

'Sorry?'

'JC is James Cowley.'

Seb grins. 'Finn, you genius.'

'Harry found an email thread. In fairness, he and Lucy went through most of it.'

'Right.' Seb stands and heads over to the rest of the team.

Lucy looks up from the desk grinning. 'Got him.' She swivels the computer around and Seb quickly reads James Cowley's LinkedIn profile.

'A small energy brokering firm,' Finn says. 'Looks like it's his business. Also listed is a Ben Cowley – that's his brother. They have two salesmen working for them, a paid accountant and an admin assistant. All work mostly from home since the pandemic. Healthy company accounts, better for moving into shared office space. Lives locally.' Finn adds, 'Married, to Zoe Cowley.'

'Gotcha.' Seb says. 'Do we know where he is today?'

'Working at home, I'd say, according to a Facebook update from his wife whose page is public. They're both home today and she's made a fresh pot of coffee after the gym.'

Seb shakes his head. 'The crap people share with all and sundry.'

Lucy laughs. 'You're a dinosaur.'

Seb frowns. 'Honestly though, and dullness levels aside, you and I know how nefariously that info can be used. Most people don't even consider it.'

'True,' Lucy agrees.

'Do you want to go while the wife's there?' Harry asks.

'Yes, it will immediately put him on the back foot. I'm assuming she has no idea about the affair.'

'I'd say not,' Finn says. 'Her socials present the kind of marriage most would envy. Poor woman.'

'Better she knows though,' Seb says slightly more forcefully than he meant to. 'In the long run.' He adds in a softer tone. None of the team know details of him and Charlie, though they may have asked around and found out that Seb's ex-wife was a troubled addict. She had moved from Thamespark about five years ago and was in London now. Mostly sleeping rough. The thought of it still chilled Seb. The pain of it as raw now as it had been then. Zoe will hurt, he knows that from his own experience, but not knowing is worse. Not knowing means you're making choices without all the facts.

He stands, shrugging into his jacket and grabbing his car keys. 'Nice one, Finn.'

'Thank you, guv.'

'Seb,' he says automatically.

'Yes Seb. Sorry guv.'

Lucy laughs as they head out and Seb says, 'He'll never manage it, will he?'

'None of them will. You just have to accept guv.'

'Yeah, I guess.'

–

The house is a neat new build, not much more than a two-up, two-down, but Seb imagines that it probably cost a small fortune nonetheless. It's a stone's throw from the houses, and the pub that he and Lucy had visited earlier. He knocks and a woman with damp hair answers.

'Hello?' she says looking uncertainly from Seb to Lucy.

'Hello, I'm Detective Inspector Sebastian Locke, this is Detective Sergeant Lucy Quinn.' They flash their badges and Zoe frowns.

'We would like to speak to James Cowley please.'

'Oh?'

He gives her a tight smile, certain that he is about to shatter her world apart and now feeling awful for it. Though she can't be ruled out as a suspect, of course. Yet a woman scorned was certainly not a trope Seb bought into, having seen the damage of enough scorned men over time to know their crimes generally outweighed their female counterparts.

'Is he in?'

Zoe falters for a moment and Seb doesn't blame her. 'What… is everything okay?'

'We just want to ask him a few questions at this stage.'

'Who is it, Zoe?' A tall man appears behind her. Dark hair, wide shoulders, Seb notes. 'Hello?' he says to Lucy and Seb, looking from one to the other.

His wife turns to him. 'It's the police. They want to talk to you.'

He moves out onto the doorstep and Seb can see terror in his eyes. 'I, ah…'

'Perhaps you could step out, we'll go to the coffee place at the end of the road?' Seb says. Taking a chance but thinking, actually, they'll likely get more out of him without Zoe present. He'd meant to throw a spanner in the works of their relationship, was planning on using James's evident discomfort to his advantage, but the looming threat of the awkward conversation to come with his wife would be enough.

'You're welcome to come in...' Zoe begins, but James is already grabbing a jacket and sliding his feet into trainers.

'No let's head out. You're working, Zoe.'

'But...'

He gives her a peck on the cheek and practically pushes her back into the house, offering a wide smile that's fooling no one. 'I'll be back before you know it.'

'But...' She tries again and Seb can see the rising panic in her eyes. She'll have had suspicions, surely? About other women, or maybe not. Charlie was a good liar but hadn't bothered to hide anything in the end. James struck Seb as confident, from a few of the Facebook pictures. He was like a Cheshire cat in most of them, arm slung round his pretty wife, on holiday somewhere lovely, embedded in his grinning, tanned family life. Confidence made easy liars, for sure, but this was next level big deal. This was police on the doorstep asking about a murder. This would be hard, if not impossible, to talk his way out of.

Zoe frowns but lets it go, murmuring, 'See you soon.'

As soon as they start walking, James turns to Seb with a snarl, 'Did you have to come to my house?'

Seb says, 'You know why we're here then?'

'Christ, I can guess.' He runs a hand through his hair, making it stick up in all directions. 'These past few days…' He shakes his head. 'It's been a nightmare for me.'

'Worse for Hannah,' Lucy interjects. They continue to walk to the coffee shop in silence as James glares at Lucy. When they arrive, she smiles sweetly and says, 'I'll get some drinks eh?'

'Nothing for me,' James snaps.

Inside, the young woman behind the counter waves at James, giving him a soft smile as he takes his seat. Seb observes, 'Nice place.'

James says nothing. The two men sit in silence while Lucy places her and Seb's coffees down. Offering another smile that is met with a frown.

'So,' Seb says, 'you heard about Hannah?'

The man's face falls. 'Yes. Shit. It's… awful.'

'You were having an affair with her,' Seb states.

James's eyes fill with tears. 'That makes it sound so sordid.'

Seb wonders if he is expecting sympathy. Probably he is and Seb supposes if he isn't the killer Hannah's death would of course be a loss to James and cause him pain. He waits, lets the sounds of the cafe waft around them, then asks, 'When did it start?'

'About four months ago. She was doing an internship thing at a company we have a contract with.'

'Which is?'

'Masterson.'

'The insurance firm?'

'Right,' James says. 'I've been working with them a few years now.'

'How many?'

He shrugs. 'I'd have to check exact dates but since we set up our company three years ago.'

'You're from Thamespark?'

He nods. 'Yeah, my parents are nearby, my brother too. I had a temporary role at Masterson. That ended, I travelled for a bit, met Zo, moved back here and set up a business with my brother. Ben approached Masterson, said we'd find them a better energy deal.'

'And you did?'

'We did, yeah. They were our first client, one of our biggest. I do all the front-facing stuff so I'm in the office from time to time, get invited to drinks and events.'

'When did you start the business?'

'Four years ago. Been doing that ever since.'

'Going well?'

'Yeah, I mean Covid was a bit of a panic, worrying that people might not go back to offices at all, which would make us fairly obsolete, but actually we've mostly stayed working from home, got a few grants to see us through, and the majority of our clients are back, if not to normal then somewhere close enough.'

'And Hannah was doing what?'

'Interning in marketing. She was doing it as an extra year via university.'

'Only twenty-one,' Seb adds. 'Her whole life ahead of her.'

'God. Yeah. It's... awful.'

'You were with her?'

'What?'

'The night she was killed.'

He swallows, picks up a napkin on the table, rolls it between his fingers making the end pointed and firm. 'Monday?'

'She was killed the early hours of Tuesday morning.'

He nods. 'She wouldn't normally have walked back through the park though. There's a bus.'

'From where?'

'Mine, just outside by the pub. Runs until two.' His voice is barely a whisper. Any modicum of sympathy Seb may have felt washes away. If not a killer, this man is definitely a scumbag. He had taken his mistress to his house and let her make her own way home.

'Could you not have dropped her back?'

'I'd, uh, we had had a few drinks.' James shrugs. 'Probably should have called her a cab but I didn't think. Besides, she always seemed so confident and independent. She said to me she had every right to walk where she wanted when she wanted.' A sentiment Seb agrees with, though he knows too well that a lot of areas after dark are unsafe, especially for women, especially in today's awfully polarised environment.

'What time did you kick her out?'

'I didn't, I mean, I would have loved her to stay but...'

'Your wife?'

'Right, due back early Tuesday. She, ah, goes away a lot with work.'

'What does she do?'

'She's a project manager, works for a group of travel companies.'

'Right.'

'It was only meant to be casual, you know, with Hannah. The first time was at a Masterson party, someone's leaving do. We'd been drinking, I offered to walk her home and it just happened.'

'Zoe doesn't know?'

'No. God, it'll destroy her.'

Seb understands the pain of infidelity, how it feels to have your feelings so utterly disregarded by someone who should protect them and treasure them. 'You'll need to tell her.'

'What, why?'

'Did you kill Hannah?'

'No. Of course not.'

'But you don't have an alibi?'

'Well, I was at home, we'd just well... you know.'

'So no one to say you didn't follow her and attack her en route. You'd have had perfect access, eh.'

'But I didn't – why would I?'

Seb shrugs. 'Maybe she wanted to tell your wife?'

'No. She knew the score. I knew the score.'

'Which was?'

'I loved – I love Zoe.'

'But you still cheated?' Met with silence. 'How did you feel about Hannah?'

'I liked her, more than I expected to.'

'When you had sex with her?'

James flinches. 'Yes. I know it all must sound horribly clichéd to you,' he snaps and Seb doesn't respond, because of course it does. James sighs. 'I cared for her. I would never have hurt her.'

'And Sam Carmichael?'

'Sam?' He frowns. 'I don't know a... oh hang on, the stripper.' He sort of laughs. 'What's she got to do with this?'

'You knew her?'

'I mean, I've been to the club, stag dos, seen her. Pretty woman, we've chatted.'

'Chatted?'

'Okay, I've watched her dance, which is her job after all. What's she got to do with anything?'

'You don't follow local news?'

'Not really.'

Seb opens his bag and takes out the photo of Sam laid out in a field, eyes closed, blanket pulled up beneath her chin.

'God is she… when?'

'Almost two years ago,' Seb says.

'I had no idea.' James sounds genuine, but he has given them an even clearer link, and Seb is pretty sure he's J.

'We saw the messages between you two.'

James's face visibly pales.

'You didn't just watch her dance, did you?'

'I'm not answering that.'

'Why?'

'You're…' He waves a hand around. 'Getting at something.'

'What am I getting at?' Seb raises his eyebrows.

'I think I'm done here.' James stands.

'We'll need to speak to your wife too actually. So.' Seb glances at his wristwatch. 'We'll give you an hour to fill her in before we come knocking.'

'You can't be serious?'

'A woman is dead. A young woman with her whole life ahead of her. Two women, if you count Sam, which I do, especially in light of your answers.'

'I didn't do anything.' James's voice is rising.

'You were the last one with Hannah as far as we know and despite your protestations that you cared for her, currently you are our prime suspect.' Seb gives James a steely smile.

CHAPTER NINETEEN

SEB

Seb glances at his watch. 'It's been an hour,' he says to Lucy. 'Long enough for him to tell her.'

Lucy sighs. 'Horrible conversation.'

'He brought it on himself,' Seb says.

Lucy nods. 'I meant for her.'

'Oh, I see, yes, I imagine it was.' He picks up his coffee cup, downing the dregs.

'Do you think he'll have a solicitor there?'

'Not this fast, but it won't take him long.'

'No,' Lucy says.

'Come on, then.' They both stand. Seb puts a few coins on the table for a tip and they head back to the Cowleys' house.

This time it's James who answers the door. Seb flashes him a smile that must be infuriating. He doesn't consider himself a petty person, but he gets a smarmy vibe off James that he dislikes. He strikes Seb as the kind of man used to doing what he wants when he wants, consequence free. His smile fades as he follows James into the living room and sees Zoe's pale, tear-stained faced, knees bent up on the sofa.

'Sit then,' James says, plonking down next to his wife, who moves her body to the other side of the sofa and then stands.

'Tea?' she says.

Seb glances at Lucy, who offers the woman a smile. 'I'll give you a hand, eh?'

James looks like he's about to open his mouth to protest. Seb says, 'Coffee for me please.'

Zoe nods, leaving the room with Lucy trailing behind her. Seb hears a door being closed and the muffled sound of voices from the kitchen. The house is nice enough, if a little bland. Lots of happy couple pictures everywhere. The best of life on display as it is in almost every home he steps into, even the ones hiding the most awful horrors.

'I'm getting the feeling I should probably hire a lawyer or something.'

'That's fine, James. Though, if you have nothing to hide...' Seb trails off. James glares but doesn't push back so Seb goes in with a question, keeping his tone conversational, 'Were you planning on telling her, Zoe?'

'What, no. I was going to end it with Hannah. I meant to on Monday.'

'But you didn't?'

James shakes his head.

'You're sure?' Seb asks. 'Maybe you said it was over and she didn't want to take no for an answer?'

'What?'

Seb shrugs. 'Maybe she was going to tell your wife.'

'No, she wouldn't do that.'

'A woman scorned though, and then Zoe to consider, your life. It would make me feel panicky in that situation, maybe it did you?'

'Don't be stupid. She knew it wasn't a forever deal.'

'Unlike Zoe?'

'I love my wife.'

'But you cheated.'

James sighs. 'I suppose you've never been tempted?'

Seb gives him a tight smile. Until very recently, Charlie was the only woman Seb had been with. Not that he'd been short of offers. The first time Faye spent the night, he'd still felt like it was somehow letting Charlie down, somehow cheating. Absurd, of course.

'I'm not proud of it,' James says. 'But I didn't kill her. I wouldn't…' His voice breaks.

'Where were you?'

'Here.'

'Alone?'

'Yes.'

'Right.'

Zoe and Lucy come back in. Seb takes a sip of his coffee and looks at Lucy, who shakes her head once. She doesn't think Zoe is in the frame. Seb suspects her alibi will be watertight. As she sits down, Seb says to her, 'This must be very upsetting for you.'

She makes a sort of strangled sound somewhere between a laugh and a sob.

'It's not been a good morning, no.'

Lucy says, 'Mrs Cowley was away for work. She left her hotel in Sussex at six a.m.'

'That's early,' Seb says.

'I felt bad, about being away. Wanted to get home and see James.' Her husband reaches out a hand for her and she bats it away. 'I can't do this.' She stands and leaves the room.

Seb and Lucy stand too.

'That it then?' says James. 'Come in, drop a bomb in my life and sod off.'

Seb counts to five in his head, teeth clenched. 'Two women are dead and the bomb in your life was set by you. You'll need to come into the station and give us an official statement. As soon as you can please.'

'I have work to do.'

'I'm sure your clients will understand. If not, I could contact them for you?'

'No.' His shoulders slump like a spoiled child's.

'Right then.'

'I'll be getting a lawyer first,' James says.

'You do that,' Seb tells him.

—

Lucy lets out a loud huff as they get in the car. 'What an idiot,' she says, then quickly adds, 'Sorry.'

'No, don't be. He really is.' They exchange a smile.

'Do you think he did it?' she asks.

Seb shrugs. 'Not sure at this stage but he's connected to not one but two victims.'

'They are linked aren't they?'

'I'd say so, yes, and Martina's fairly certain of it too.'

'God,' Lucy says. 'His poor wife.'

'What was she like?'

'Lovely. Married to a dick and completely unaware of it until today.' Lucy shakes her head. 'So maybe a bit deluded. I didn't like him much, murder aside, did you?'

Seb laughs and she frowns at him. 'I'm sorry but, "murder aside".'

'Ha, well you know what I mean.'

'I do and no, I didn't warm to him and don't think I would have in other circumstances. But I imagine he can be charming and knows what to say. He and Zoe have been together three years, married for two. He must have given her the impression of being a good guy.'

There is a silence in the car, not unpleasant. Seb won't rush to fill these spaces, his stoic ability to wait it out is often a huge advantage in interrogations.

'We'll check her alibi, but it sounds tight,' Seb says.

'Oh yeah. Sickeningly, she went to the hotel gym at five a.m. before she checked out. But I've got the name of the hotel.'

Seb laughs. 'You go to the gym.'

'Not at five a.m. though, and I always ruin it with a pastry in the cafe after.'

'One cancels out the other.'

She laughs. 'Do you think?'

'Depends how hard you work at the gym.'

She sighs. 'I'm doomed.' That gets another chuckle.

Her phone rings. 'Harry,' she tells Seb as she picks up. 'Hi Harry, I'm with Seb. You're on speaker.'

'You two finished at Cowley's?'

'Yeah, heading back now.'

'Okay, I think I might have found something on him.'

'Oh?' Seb says, eyes on the road.

'Yeah, a complaint made against him by a fellow student.'

'What kind of complaint?'

'Details are thin but looks like a sexual assault.'

'Who was the student?'

'One Misha Batt. They were dating at the time.'

'How far did it get?'

'Not far at all; local police looked into it but she ended up not pursuing charges.'

'Would have been difficult to prove,' Lucy murmurs. 'He said, she said.'

'Right.'

'Okay,' Seb says. 'Good work. Send for details from the station that dealt with it and see if you can get in touch with her, yeah? We'll go see her.'

'Will do. Also, DNA is back.'

'Right?'

'We need to get a sample from James. Despite a condom being used, they found semen on Hannah's thighs.'

'It will likely be his.'

'Yes, also some skin under her nails which they are quite sure is from a different person.'

'Hmm,' Seb says, frowning. 'Different DNA under her nails would suggest a struggle with someone else.'

'It would, yeah. There was nothing in the way of DNA with Sam?'

'No.'

'Okay.'

'Finn's trying to drill in on the images from the Amersham Arms?'

'He is but not with much luck.'

'Okay, tell him to keep trying.' Lucy hangs up.

'Maybe it's not James,' Lucy says.

'Maybe not,' Seb agrees, mouth set in a grim line, 'which makes you wonder why all roads lead to him thus far.'

CHAPTER TWENTY

STEVIE

The class are all diligently reading, their little heads bent over carefully chosen books from the library. One week, Michael asked why I'd chosen teaching, and specifically primary-aged children. I'd replied flippantly, 'Well, not to get rich, but I figured it's a respectable way to pay the bills.'

'Respectability is important to you?' he'd asked as I sat rigid trying to appear relaxed.

'To everyone, I assume.'

'Was it important to your mum?'

'Yes. Whatever her flaws,' I'd quipped, 'she always looks amazing. Even now.' And it was true. 'The house itself was disastrous, but we in contrast had to be kept clean, neat and tidy.' I didn't add that that cleanliness had descended into a new kind of madness.

'Are the children in your class clean, neat and tidy?'

'Of course not, they're children.'

'And you keep their space relaxed?'

'I do, yes.'

'A wonderful thing to do considering it wasn't something you yourself got to experience.'

I had made a decision when I started seeing Michael, after years of many other therapists, that I would tell him just enough but never too much. Because of my back-ground and my job, I had agreed with my key worker that I'd continue therapy. I could have cancelled by now but I've always felt if ever I was questioned with regards to my job, seeing Michael would be a good way to point out that I was being responsible and vigilant. I had an act down pat by the time I left care. I knew how to appear suitably scarred; my mother had, after all, been trying to kill me for all of my childhood, while appearing to be doing great, all things considered. That day he found something real embedded behind my bravado, though, and when he poked it, it hurt.

I clear my throat now and all the children's faces look up at once, eager and ready to go.

'Who'd like to start?' I say and several hands shoot up. 'Ronnie, let's begin with you.'

He tells us about a dog on a long adventure. We move to Liv, who's reading about unicorns and rainbows. My morning passes in a pleasant blur of their fertile imagin-ations and discussions about character. Before I know it, it's lunchtime and the children head out to play.

I get my phone while the children are outside, a missed call from Mum, ugh, and a text message from a number I don't recognise. I hit open.

> Stevie, so nice to bump into you, this is my number. Let me know if you fancy that drink anytime soon. Ben

Ben. James's little brother. I stare and stare and stare at it and whilst I'm doing so another message comes through, Joel: *last night was fun!* I feel heat wash over my face.

I'll ignore him, I think. All I wanted to know was how I had got home and when. Now I knew that I had at about one, and that Joel had seen me go in, too, which should be good news, but the fact I'd mentioned going to James's is less good and means there is still doubt as to my whereabouts. I put the phone back into my bag. I shouldn't have it out in the classroom anyway, and I love my job; my job is the one aspect of my life that brings me real joy. The one place I feel less like a loser. Where I don't need my personal life intruding. Even so, I wonder what Mum wants and also hope she is okay. Everyone, I suppose, wants a good relationship with their parents really. Certainly, no one would want to be in my position, but I have at times wondered if we'd be better off not speaking at all.

I'd almost cut her out once for a year, the same year I was with James, when happiness felt like it might be real and, better still, that it might be mine. When I'd told him, trying to keep it breezy and light, that I didn't really have much contact with my mother anymore, he'd asked me the same question people always did: 'What if she died?'

—

We have twenty minutes whilst the children are outside playing. I would happily, and preferably, be using those minutes to sit on my own. I love the children and generally feel at ease in their company. Other grown-ups, though, I often find exhausting and Bethan, whose classroom is next door to mine, is no exception. Though I think she annoys just about everyone a bit, not just me. My phone vibrates. I turn it over whilst Bethan's voice drones on and on. Something about her husband and how wonderful he is, no doubt. She's perched on the edge of my desk, her

116

large bottom pressing onto the stack of marking I've left there. I glance at my phone. Zoe: *The police came to my house, wtaf.*

'I've got to go,' I say, standing up and making Bethan look at me wide-eyed.

'Class starts in like ten minutes.'

'It's my Mum,' I mumble, waving my phone at her. 'I need to call her.' And I leave my own classroom realising only once I have that she should have left, not me. In the staffroom, I find a corner and ring Zoe. It goes straight to voicemail. Oh god.

Bethan walks past me. 'All okay?' I sort of shrug. She reaches out a hand, squeezing my shoulder. 'Can I do anything?'

'No. I'm fine,' I lie as my heart races and my palms start sweating.

She goes.

Hannah Smith was at James's house. I knew that; I saw her go in. I squeeze my eyes shut and try and try to think. To remember what happened next? Joel and I got in a cab and he saw me home. Had I gone out again to James's house as I mentioned to Joel? I know I do that sometimes and luckily have never knocked on the door. I don't think I did. I struggle to believe I'd have made the walk back through the park twice without remembering at least some of it.

My phone rings. I glance at the clock; class will be back in a few minutes, I can't be on my phone in there when it is. I have to keep everything squeaky clean and above board. I decide I can spare a minute and I'm the only one in the staffroom, at least. 'Zoe?'

'Hi.'

'What the hell?'

'I don't know. Sorry, you're at work by now?'

'I'm on break, but need to be quick.' I add, 'I'm glad you messaged.' Thinking of the hours I've put in with her. The exhaustion of striking up a friendship. The surprise I'd felt when, actually, I found I quite liked her. The thrill of embedding myself into James's life when obviously I shouldn't have.

Michael said to me once in a session, 'You know, it's secrets that will keep you sick.' And he was right, of course. Who knew that better than I did? The girl who grew up with the burning stench of secrecy. Secrets that kept me teetering on a thin line between life and death. Often not knowing for sure which one would be best.

'Yes, I know,' I'd said as I held so much in. All of this in. My obsession with James, as he'd put it when I'd said I was finding the relationship hard to get over.

He'd also said, 'Leave it alone, it will pass. There will be other relationships.' It was then I knew he didn't get it. That he never could.

'What did they want?' I ask Zoe now.

'James.'

'Your husband?' I say, as ever super careful to keep any knowledge of him to the minimum she has fed me.

'Yes. He's gone down the road to talk to them.'

'That's weird,' I say, even though I know it is not weird at all. The police are there to ask him about his mistress. The woman who'd been there Monday night. Who was dead by Tuesday morning. A woman he won't want his wife finding out about. I hear the clanging of the bell, children's voices outside subsiding as they step into class lines ready to come back in.

'Are you okay?' I ask.

'I mean, I don't know. I'll wait to see what he has to say, maybe run it past my mum.' Her mum. Of course, Zoe has a lovely family. She looks almost exactly like her mother and often posts pictures of them out for various meals and shopping trips. She's won the lottery of life. Except she hasn't, has she, and she's about to find that out. .

CHAPTER TWENTY-ONE

SEB

Misha Batt works in South London, only an hour away from Thamespark, but as they weave in and out of traffic and around various obstructions, it takes them almost two. She'd asked that they call when they arrive, which Lucy does as they park up.

'Come into the building. I told Jim at reception you'd be coming; he'll take you to our cafe, I'll meet you there.'

They arrive in the work cafe, which is actually quite nice, at the same time as a tall woman with perfectly highlighted hair and a long flowing dress. She nods at them. 'You're the police?'

Seb pulls out his ID.

She waves a hand. 'Sit, sit. Coffees?'

'Please,' both Seb and Lucy say at the same time.

Lucy smiles. 'We had a longer than expected drive.'

Once they are settled with drinks, Seb takes in his surroundings. Arty, he thinks. Lots of cartoony murals on the walls, products on posters with environmentally friendly credentials. Misha follows his gaze. 'Sustainable cleaning products.'

'Your main business?'

'Yep.'

'You're in the advertising department?'

'I am.'

'Is that what you studied at university?'

'No, business, the degree for people with no specific talent who don't know what they want to do.' She smiles.

'A useful degree though,' says Seb, who has become something of an expert on these matters, as Tilly is choosing her GCSEs and thinking about the future. The sheer level of routes and choices give him a headache.

'Yes, it was, and I love my job, so I guess I ended up where I was supposed to be.'

'Was James on your course?'

'Yep. That's how we met.'

'You were dating?'

'We were.' Her voice is strong, confident. Seb is ready to step aside on the questioning if she becomes uncomfortable though, he has found yet another benefit to having a female partner. So many of their investigations inevitably led them to women who'd been mistreated by men. Understandably, those women weren't always comfortable talking directly to him.

'What was he like?'

Misha shrugs. 'Arrogant, which I mistook for confident. Good-looking, superficially extremely charming.'

'Superficially?'

'Yes, or I don't know, maybe that's not fair. I guess after he attacked me, the charm was no longer apparent.'

'Of course,' Seb murmurs, pausing.

Lucy who can read his silences as well as his direct instructions, steps in. 'Was it serious, between you?'

'No, though I must admit I was fairly awed by him.' Misha shrugs again. 'I'd been sheltered, I suppose. My parents were very strict; we lived in a semi-rural area.

James grew up in a London suburb. Well, your suburb. I assume that means he's moved back?'

Seb nods.

She sighs. 'If I met him now, I think I'd have seen the red flags.'

'Which were?'

'He was… dismissive, arrogant. He'd make plans with me then not show up, or worse call me at the end of a night out, insist on coming round.'

'Is that what happened that night?' Lucy asks her. It said in the retracted case notes that he'd turned up drunk in the middle of the night.

'Yes, only he didn't call, just turned up.'

'That was unusual?'

'Yes, the first time he'd done that. I was furious. He woke up my flatmate, but he was fall down drunk so I figured I'd get him into bed and have it out with him in the morning.'

'That's not what happened?' Lucy again.

'No. Well, it was to start with. He passed out, I got into bed next to him. Next thing I know, I woke up to him pawing me. I screamed, hit him, yelled no. My flatmate came in. Between us, we got rid of him. I'd have left it, put it down to a bad experience and gone back to sleep, but Tracy, my flatmate, said it was an assault and I should report it.'

'It was assault,' Lucy says.

'Oh, I know that now. But the police officers who showed up didn't agree with you.'

Seb frowns. 'They didn't take it seriously?'

'Nope, let me know between sighs and eyerolls that "domestics" rarely ended up in anyone being charged. He didn't rape me. He didn't get that far. The fact he had his hands in my underwear and me pinned to the bed, whilst I was asleep and therefore obviously unable to consent, didn't matter, apparently.' She shakes her head. 'I did push for it to be taken further. The police went and spoke to him, I believe. They also suggested maybe I wasn't ready for city life, that perhaps I should go home, mature a bit and come back in a year's time.'

'I'm so sorry that happened,' Lucy says and Seb feels his temper rising. He believes her; of course he does. This kind of attitude, despite great strivings, at least publicly, to change it, was still rife on the Force. Misogyny, laddism. Stupidity.

'You stayed though?' Seb asks.

'Yep, wasn't going to be scared off by that pillock.'

'And the charges?' Seb asks.

'I dropped it. Their shitty advice aside, it would have been difficult to prove and I had a degree to get.'

'Did you see James again?'

'He came round after the police visited his. He was furious. Called me a silly bitch and said he could hardly even remember being at mine, like that was any kind of excuse.' She shakes her head. 'I told him to get fucked. Aside from that, I saw him round campus but we didn't speak again.'

A pause as they all take this information in. Seb wonders if Misha is reliving it. She strikes him as tough and capable, not easily shaken, but he can imagine her younger, less confident, less sure. He hadn't liked James and this makes him like him even less, though it doesn't necessarily make him a murderer.

'Can I ask what this is about?' Misha says.

Seb weighs up what to tell her and settles on, 'We're questioning him in relation to a murder case.'

'You're kidding?' Her eyes widen.

'No.'

'He's a suspect?'

'I can't say any more at the moment,' he tells her. 'But we will be in contact when we can tell you more.'

She nods. 'Yeah, okay. Shit.'

'Are you all right?' Lucy asks her.

'Oh, yeah fine. I mean, really, I got away lightly didn't I? Everyone dates a shitbag or two. I haven't made the same mistake twice.'

–

They get into the car. Lucy growls, 'Urgh.'

'Yes,' Seb agrees, jaw set so hard it aches slightly. He breathes in, willing his muscles to relax.

'You're like concrete,' Faye has told him. 'You hold all your tension in your shoulders.' He'd laughed, but since she'd pointed it out, he had noticed it was true and likely a cause for his fairly frequent tension headaches.

'Remind me what the messages were between him and Sam,' Seb says.

Lucy scrolls through the document on her phone while Seb drives. 'Okay. Here you go:

'*I loved watching you dance.*

'*I loved you seeing me.*

'A week later, her: *that's it then?*

'Him: *we had fun right?*

'*You're an arsehole.*

'That's the end of their messages.'

'He really needs to answer the question of Sam now, whether he wants to or not.'

'Can we bring him in officially?'

'I hope so. Let's go ask Jackie and find out.'

CHAPTER TWENTY-TWO

SEB

Over the phone, Jackie tells Seb and Lucy to check in with the officers involved with the complaint made by Misha. 'You may as well do it while you're there, come back, and aim to bring James in in the morning.'

'Not today?' Seb says. He'd rather just get on with it.

'No, speak to the other officers first; the more you have on him, the more you'll get out of him. I'm due to give a statement shortly. I'm going to tell the press we think this may be connected to Sam's murder and I'm going to appeal for witnesses to come forward in both cases. I'll give another statement tomorrow saying we've brought a suspect in. That means it will go out twice tomorrow, being on the weekend news as well, and more people will see it. I'll appeal for witnesses again, but if you can use the rest of the day to dig up anything else, I'd appreciate it.'

'Yes of course. Harry's gone over to Sam's club too, so he should have something more solid.'

'Good, keep me up to date, yes?'

Seb hangs up.

'We've got loads on him,' Lucy says, and Seb can hear the frustration in her voice. He gets it, he really does.

'We have to tread carefully, that's all.'

'Yeah, I guess.' She's still frowning. 'Let's find the local nick then.' She taps it into Maps and starts driving. The London traffic at midday is far more forgiving; whatever the hold-up had been seems to have cleared and they are there in minutes.

At reception, Seb flashes his badge and his best million-dollar smile. The woman behind the desk has a battle-worn face and a deep ingrained line in her forehead that tells Seb she frowns a lot. She scowls at him now as if to echo his thoughts and he suppresses a smile.

'Why you over this way?' she asks, her voice thick with years of cigarettes. He fleetingly thinks he misses smoking and a memory comes to him, of he and Charlie, young and happy, passing a Marlboro Light between them. He wonders if her voice sounds like gravel yet and tries to push the thought away, wishing she didn't haunt his mind like a vengeful ghost.

He says, 'We have a suspect on a murder case who faced some charges here, while he was studying.'

'Right.' Gravel Voice Frowny now just sounds bored.

'Patrick McFadden took his initial statement; we want to talk to him,' Seb says, speaking plainly.

She picks up the phone on her desk. 'Pat, couple of Surrey officers here for you.' There is, Seb thinks, a sarcastic emphasis on the word 'Surrey'. City cops thinking they just bumble around out there doing bugger all. A stereotype that never changes. The man on the other end of the line must say something amusing because Frowny smirks. Turning back to Seb and Lucy she says, 'Do come round.' With feigned politeness, they follow her through a side door into a large open-plan office, not dissimilar to their own station.

McFadden is a detective now and stands as the sour-faced receptionist walks Seb and Lucy to him. He greets Seb and Lucy with a vague nod and a sigh as they tell him why they're there.

'I hardly even remember it, to be honest,' he says, screwing his face up. Despite no one having smoked in buildings for decades now, Seb thinks somehow it manages to stink of cigarette smoke and greasy food, an odour which quickly puts to bed any smoking-related fantasies. Detective McFadden has reams of paperwork laid out in front of him. Enough to cover most of his desk. Seb recognises all the pieces of an assault case. McFadden sees him looking and gives him an eyeroll, 'paperwork eh, such a ball ache'. Seb gives the man a tight smile. It is a ball ache and really they shouldn't have to do as much as they do whilst also working out there in the community. But poor behaviour and hard-to-find trails have led to it being necessary. Seb does most of his on the computer now; he taught himself how to in the evenings, following various tutorial videos.

'Easier if you do it digitally in the first instance,' Seb says and McFadden frowns. Seb backs off. If the man wants to double his workload that's his own business.

'The complaint was made by Misha Batt. She would have been quite young and very shaken up. The guy's name was James Cowley.'

'Oh yeah, he was her boyfriend though, wasn't it?'

'So you do remember?' Seb says, finding his annoyance at the man growing.

'Yeah, well only because you mention it and because I remember being pissed at the time. A lot of fuss over nothing.'

'She woke up to him assaulting her.'

McFadden stops laying out written statements, interviews and reviews. 'He was her boyfriend,' he repeats. 'She let him in, they were in the same bed for Chrissake.'

'That doesn't make it okay.'

'Yeah well you know as well as I do it's a grey area.'

Seb knows no such thing and feels his jaw tightening. McFadden sniffs hard and Seb can hear the mucus rattling around his nose.

'Did you tell her that at the time?' Lucy asks.

'I did, yeah. Advised her to get on with what she was doing, let it drop.' He shrugs. 'The guy had hardly any memory of it anyways. Six of one, half a dozen of the other and we're stretched now, we were stretched then. People getting stabbed on the streets here, remember.'

'The guy, James Cowley, is our prime suspect in the murder of Hannah Smith.'

McFadden frowns. 'The girl in the park?'

'Yes. James was having an affair with her and was the last person to see her alive.'

'Shit,' McFadden manages, and for the first time since they've spoken to him, Seb sees some glimmer that he actually might care a little bit about the work.

Lucy says, 'He's also been linked to another murder which occurred in the next town over. Same cause of death. He had a sexual relationship with her too.'

'Puts that assault in a new light now, doesn't it,' Seb states.

'It just didn't seem that big a deal.'

'It's the kind of low-level behaviour that might lead to a "big deal" later, though,' Seb says, thinking that a man who had been on the Force as long as McFadden should know this stuff by now; the instinct should be second nature. 'Hannah Smith was twenty-one,' Seb adds, the enormity of a young life taken so cruelly resting in front of McFadden.

McFadden runs a hand over his face. 'That's bad. But, even if the girl had pressed charges, nothing would have come of it. You know that.'

'No, but maybe if James had understood even a little bit that what he did wasn't okay and would at least cause him some inconvenience, he might have thought twice.'

'You really think it's him?'

'He's our prime suspect.'

'Come on.' McFadden turns on his heel. 'I'll get you the file.'

–

They leave with a copy of the file, which really doesn't tell them anything new but is definitely evidence.

They get back to the station at the same time as Harry.

'Alright?' he asks Seb and Lucy.

Lucy yawns. 'Yes, but tired, too much driving.'

'I hear you.'

Lucy scowls at him. 'You went twenty minutes down the road.'

Harry looks like he's about to snap back. Seb puts a hand up. 'It's not a competition. Harry, what did you get?'

'He came in, hung around after, sweet-talked her. She brushed him off but her colleague' – Harry gets his pad out, looking over his notes – 'Joanne Swanson, said Sam only gave him the brush-off so he wouldn't think she was easily won.'

'So she liked him?' Seb says as they head into the station where, Seb thinks, it definitely smells nicer than the borough McFadden is working out of.

'She did, yeah, and he was persistent, took her number, called her two days in a row. On the third day, she had him over and he stayed.'

'How long for?' Seb reaches the coffee machine. He picks up the near-empty pot and holds it out to Lucy, who shakes her head. He pours himself a mug, Harry doesn't do hot drinks, but gets through an alarming number of sickly sweet Monster energy drinks.

'Two nights.'

'Okay, after that?'

'Ghosted her.'

'That's when someone ignores you as if you don't exist,' Lucy says.

'Yes alright Lucy, I'm slightly older than you, not dead.'

'You say that,' she says, 'but you're hardly online are you, so you are out of touch.'

'I'm sane Lucy, which feels more important.'

She grins.

'Anyway,' Seb says, 'as far as her colleagues know that was it?'

'Yeah exactly,' Harry says. 'She was found dead two days later.'

'God,' Lucy says.

'Yeah, awful,' Harry agrees. 'And her mate Joanne was understandably still shaken up about it. She did say something else.'

'Yeah?' Seb picks up his drink, thinking he is exhausted and the weekend isn't looking like there'll be a pause of any kind.

'Yeah, she said she thought she was being followed.'

Seb frowns. 'When?'

'The day she said goodbye to James, said she felt like someone was watching her and she saw a woman walking away. Someone she said she thought she'd seen in the club.'

'And she told Joanne this?'

'She did. They don't get female customers so she stuck out to her.'

'The woman was there when James was?'

'The morning he left, apparently.'

'Description?'

'Sadly not,' Harry says, 'and we won't be getting one now.'

'No.' Seb mulls it over. 'But Hannah said to Katie she felt the same thing, didn't she?'

'She did yeah,' Harry agrees.

'Maybe Zoe wasn't away at all.'

Lucy's eyes widen. 'The hotel haven't got back to us yet but I know she checked out by putting her keycard in the box, which she could have done at any time.'

'She could,' Seb says. 'But she says she went to the hotel gym at five?'

'Yes and we're waiting for them to get back to us.'

'Let's chase that then.'

'Yeah okay, now?'

'I'll do it,' Seb says and Lucy looks relieved. 'You should both go; we'll be working many lates and the weekend, I'm afraid.'

CHAPTER TWENTY-THREE

STEVIE

The children are irritable this afternoon. The days are heating up and as they do so their patience lowers. I opened the back door at half two and we went outside and played so by the time they left they were overall better, even if my anxiety was riding so high it felt like a pinch in my mind. The first thing I do is leave my classroom briefly and call Zoe. Her phone is off. Understandable. I think that by now she probably knows about Hannah. I feel a spike of joy at that. Sharp, ugly and unbidden. What I hadn't really allowed for when I'd started taking her Pilates class was that I might actually like her. But I do. Though not as much as I have missed James. Nothing is ever quite as big as that. If he'd stayed with me, if it was I in Zoe's position now, I think I'd forgive him. I know that without having to dwell on it. I'd forgive him an affair just to feel the way I did back then. In fact, I'd already forgiven him many times in the past. To be part of his world in its easy-going normalness. Would I forgive him murder? The thought is fast and prickly. A horrible thing to even contemplate, as dark as befriending his wife, as following his mistress. Creeping towards the awfulness of my mother. Does it run in the blood? Unintended badness. I blink away tears and take a deep breath. This is a spiral I cannot go down, that I will not go down.

I'm back in my classroom, I have lesson plans to get done. I shake away the awful ruminations and look at the stack of paper and my open laptop. My phone beeps: an alert. A late credit card bill. Payment unsuccessful. I check the account, which is now over my overdraft limit. Shit. Shit.

'Hello?' Bethan's grinning moon face peers around my classroom door.

That decides it. I stand. Gathering the plans, stuffing the endless reams of photocopied tasks into my large leather satchel, using it as padding for my dated, less and less reliable, laptop. I hitch the bag onto my shoulder, forcing a smile. 'I was just leaving.'

'Oh right, not planning today?'

'I thought I'd take it home,' I say through gritted teeth.

'Okie-dokie and good luck.' She gives me a weird hand salute and I make my way past her. She smells of Imperial Leather soap and that clothes softener that's named Fresh Cotton.

I feel musty and fuggy by comparison and suspect I smell of stale sweat and desperation. I no longer have a car, which is annoying and inconvenient. I sold it earlier in the year to pay the last credit card bill. My eyes sting with tears as I remember the brilliant feeling of being free of it. Clean slate, I'd told myself. No more spending binges and no more expensive booze-laden nights out. I'd done okay for a few weeks, over a month even. Then the dread crept in and here I was again. I pretty much earned my outgoings with little left. It only took a few purchases a month to tip me over. Even when I still had Angela's money it seemed to slip through my fingers like water. I despise my mother's hoarding and yet I often find myself buying clothes I don't need, opening my overstuffed wardrobe doors to find things in stacks, tags often still attached, and I spend on doing stuff as well. Nights out at bars I can't afford. It's the same sort of thing isn't it? As my mum. Driven, I suppose, by a hundred different types of fear. Scarcity is always a looming worry.

I walk. The bag thumping my side as I go, the sun beating down from above. Thoughts of Hannah, Zoe and James swirling around in my mind.

I finally arrive and walk in to my mother's tiny stifling house.

'You need to open some windows,' I tell her as the hot smells assault me, the air thick with blue cigarette smoke.

She is sitting prim on the sofa surrounded by stacks of junk in a pretty dress with her bright red lipstick.

I sit back on the green velvet winged armchair that she has owned since I was a child. The arms are balding. Little bits of material stick out and up at jagged angles. 'It's too hot in here,' I tell her.

'Is it?'

'I'll do the washing up,' I say, standing. In the kitchen, I move piles of dishes with various stains and remnants on. The sickly yellow of an egg, syrup of some kind. Congealed milk sour in the bottom of a cereal bowl. Toast crumbs spill from the plate onto the sides. I roll up my sleeves, sink into blankness and start to clean. Piece by piece. Dish by dish. Sides cleared, things dried and put away. One single, clean space now. I open the door to the fridge; nothing much in it but what is there is wildly out of date. I bag it up and take it to the bins, marching past my mother, who sits with her head falling towards her chest. She is asleep, as I suspected she would be. She's on handfuls of pills and any change in them, which she has just had, tends to conk her out for large parts of the day. I watch her inhaling, exhaling.

I imagine picking up one of the ragged scatter cushions from the over-piled couch and pressing it against her face. The image becomes so vivid I can almost feel her squirming beneath me. I inhale sharply and realise the cushion is in my hands and I am mere steps away from her. I stand frozen, waiting for my pulse to slow. I have hours of Monday night turning to Tuesday morning missing. In that time, Hannah died. I hated her, envied her; I was filled with thoughts of her. Would I? Certainly I do things I wouldn't normally when I'm drunk. Alcohol and spending are my two costly weaknesses.

I walk to my mum's bedroom, open the drawers alongside her bed and pull out the burgundy card holder. I photograph her three different bankcards, front and back, and then I take one last look at her as I slip out into the evening air. Finally cooler as dusk creeps in and the day fades away.

–

I call Zoe again once I'm in. No response. I send a text: *Hope all okay? Thinking of you x.*

I pull out my laptop, which groans and splutters to life. I open various accounts and clear my credit card bill in payments of no more than £300 a time, using my mother's three accounts. Then I do a massive Tesco shop to be delivered after work tomorrow and order clothes. By the time I am finished I am almost giddy with excitement. The thrill of it; I'm owed, I tell myself. And one thing I have learnt over the years is that my mother never, ever seems to run out of money. Nor does she seem to notice my not-infrequent use of it. Or if she does, she doesn't say. Sometimes, I like to think the latter. That on some level she is sorry and wants me to be okay. That my stealing is just our own, unique enactment of familial support. I go round, do some washing up, check on her. She helps me out occasionally when I'm struggling. It's unlikely this is the case though.

My phone beeps and I stare at it in panic. Maybe this is the time I'll be caught. Perhaps she'll involve the police. Perhaps I will get arrested, lose my job…

I pick up my phone. Ben again.

'About that drink… or dinner if you have time?'

'Sure,' I say, the relief making me reckless. 'Friday any good?'

'Yes, let's do Côte at eight?'

'See you then!'

'Can't wait.'

Friday, a whole day away. Enough time surely for him to know something about his brother who is being questioned in relation to a murder case. I have less than half a finger's worth of vodka left. I drink it standing on the balcony. My eyes are glued to James's house where the curtains are drawn. I imagine he and Zoe arguing. Tears flowing, recriminations flying. He'll be devastated, of course, and I'll be there. Somehow, I'll find a way. This, I feel, is my time. I allow the fantasy to float and expand around me and, as always, I am taken back first to school where his attention felt like a lifesaver in a stormy sea and then to the summer when he was mine. I was a newly qualified teacher, dazed and immensely proud every single day I went to work. I was absolutely laser-focused on making a good future for myself. I would build a life, one I loved. I cut out drinking, tried to eat at least twice a day, ran three times a week, kept my spending in check with the mantra I learnt from Michael: *things won't fix you, it's temporary relief, fleeting so fast it's gone before you can catch it.* Then I saw him again, the first boy I ever kissed, who I had been head over heels in love with. James had smiled, had been delighted to see me, happy to pick up where we'd left off and anything seemed possible. All the best versions of me felt like they were almost, almost within reach. If I can get him back, earn his trust… and what better way than being there for him during a crisis. Maybe this time I can grab fast enough, hard enough to make it real and to make it last.

I go inside, Hannah Smith's image flashes up on the TV screen. Souring my fantasy because James was with her the night she died, and James, despite his philandering, wanted to keep Zoe.

The woman, DSI Jackie Ferris, is giving a statement. She is suggesting they have a suspect and that that suspect had been linked to the death of another woman. Sam Carmichael. I sit down, a chill creeping through me. James was a cheat I already knew that. I'd seen him more than once with other women; there was an ex from university he'd met for drinks in London, the stripper who worked a few towns over. He'd been with her for two nights in a row another week Zoe had been away. Her name was Sam – oh god, her name was Sam. But being unfaithful was a far cry from being a murderer, wasn't it?

CHAPTER TWENTY-FOUR

SEB

The hotel had Zoe as checking into the gym first thing, as she'd said she had, though she'd checked in electronically and there was no one on the desk at that time. They need to talk to her, Seb thinks. But they need to speak to her husband again first.

Seb gets home and feels the inside of his head itching with the day's work. He'd called James on the way back to the station and told him he needed to come to the station first thing tomorrow morning. He'd panicked, argued, mentioned work he'd missed during the week and now needed to catch up on. Seb said he could come in willingly or they'd go and collect him with a warrant. The thought of Cowley sitting at home sweating it out actually brought him some small measure of satisfaction. He knew too that the man would be even more rattled by the morning, and that rattled meant mistakes, which he hoped would work to his benefit.

He pushes his front door open and is greeted with the sound of laughter coming from the kitchen. He hangs his coat, takes off his shoes and goes in. Sitting at the table are Val, Tilly and Faye, who looks up at him with a grin.

'Faye,' he says, 'I wasn't expecting you.'

She stands, heads over to him and plants a kiss on his cheek. He feels his face heat up. 'Nope and I do need to go. I just dropped some magazines off to Tilly and now she's telling me I'm horribly old fashioned for buying things in print.' Faye scrunches up her nose and Seb feels his stomach flip-flop. Exactly the same way it used to with Charlie, but with Faye he is spared the side order of acid-inducing anxiety.

'Magazines?'

'My dress,' says Tilly, as though he is especially stupid, 'for the cast party.'

'We had that?'

Tilly had done set design for a school production of *Romeo and Juliet*. Kai had played Romeo and this is where Tilly had developed her massive crush on the lad who was in the year above.

Tilly sighs. 'The proper party, no parents.'

'No parents?' Seb feels his pulse quicken.

Val says, 'It's at Kai's place, his parents actually will be there but seemingly they have a large property so they'll be overseeing but not infringing.'

'Is that a smart idea?' Seb says and is rewarded with an eyeroll from Tilly.

'You said I could go,' she tells him.

'Did I?'

'You did,' says Val. 'She asked weeks ago.'

'I thought you meant the other party, after the show.'

Tilly shrugs. 'For a policeman you should maybe listen more closely.'

He opens his mouth to respond but finds himself speechless, which for some reason sends Tilly into a fit of giggles.

'Dad, you look like a goldfish.' She does an unflattering impression. Now Val and Faye are hiding smirks. He frowns as Tilly heads over, grabbing a stack of magazines from the table. She gives him a quick hug. 'It will be fine, Dad. You can pick me up as long as you don't come in, obviously.'

'Right,' he says as she walks out of the room yelling, 'Thanks Faye.' And leaving him bewildered.

Faye is looking at him narrow-eyed. 'You okay?'

'I guess,' he says. 'I mean, aside from agreeing with plans I don't really approve of.'

'She's growing up,' Val says, to which Seb continues to frown.

'I've got to go.' Faye glances at her watch. She hosts a therapy group on Friday nights. 'See you tomorrow though?'

'Yeah, great,' Seb says.

Once she's gone, Val gestures to him to sit at the table. 'You've not eaten?'

'No.'

She heats him a plate of food, squeezes his shoulder and says, 'I'm going to watch my shows, I doubt you'll see Tilly again this evening.'

'Okay.' He eats and realises he wishes Faye was still here; that in fact he finds himself wishing for that more and more often.

CHAPTER TWENTY-FIVE

STEVIE

I don't sleep well and give up trying at about four a.m. I make coffee, drink two cups and sit out on the balcony. Despite the warm days, the early hours are chilly, a reminder that summer is yet to come despite appearances, that spring is here but winter is still nipping at its heels. I watch the sun come up and feel... nothing really.

At seven I'm on my balcony knowing I need to leave soon to get to school on time and honestly feeling like I'd rather just go back to bed. Glad that it's Friday at least, I get a text from Joel asking when I'm free. I ignore it, though a single delicious spike of excitement gets through when I see his name. He's after sex of course. Easy, uncomplicated sex. I'm not into him, so haven't been the one chasing, and they always love that for whatever reason. After James broke my heart the second time, I went over almost every interaction again and again. I re-read messages between us, seeing with the benefit of shitty hindsight how he'd started to pull away and I had responded by crowding in.

I'm meeting Ben later for dinner and the thought of it makes me feel uneasy. Everything is falling in; all of the odd bits of my life I keep separate are crashing towards each other. James, Zoe. Now Ben. Hannah Smith dead in the park. The news report linking her death to Sam

Carmichael, the beautiful dancer from a club two towns over. I'd seen James with her, she was all glamour and shine. Zoe was objectively better looking but Sam had that thing, pure sex on display, every bit of her made up, and I guessed she'd be free und uninhibited in bed too.

I see the front door to James's open; Zoe goes to her car, opening the door and getting something out.

I call her and she picks up on the second ring.

'Hello.' Her voice sounds thick with tears and I feel a stab of unexpected sympathy for her. The odd split that I get whenever we interact. Half of me hates her, this girl that James chose to marry after I was happily cast aside, the other half of me understands that in another world, a different version of events, we'd have been *real* friends. Proper friends. I would have been the pal Zoe thinks she's got rather than the one I made up. It makes me feel horribly sad and utterly broken. Who would do this? Who would behave in this way?

A madwoman of course. Like mother like daughter…

'Are you okay Zo?'

'God, not really no.'

'The police were there?'

'Yes.' Her voice is small, like the children I teach when they are unsettled. She suddenly sounds impossibly young, this woman who I am so jealous of, so envious of that sometimes I can hardly breathe. 'It's not just that he's been having an affair.'

Silence, my heart beats thump thump thump. The long red hair in my handbag, the feel of it coarse and wiry between my fingers. Her bare and freckled shoulders. The deep voice that had been a surprise. Melodic almost. My dress hardened and blood in streaks on my ankles. Joel who smelt of lemons pressing me down, the weight of his bulky body above me, the missing hours of the night Hannah Smith never made it home.

'Oh god,' I manage. 'I'm so sorry.'

'The, the… woman well she…' There is a pause, a break where I hear muffled, incoherent sobs. 'She's dead.'

'Oh my god,' I say and imagine I am hearing it for the first time. Though I don't have to imagine at all, not really. Each time I'm hit with it, it is a fresh wave of horror.

Dead.

Hannah Smith.

Gorgeous, young, vibrant, happy Hannah Smith. The woman who'd cemented my real affection for Zoe. Because suddenly I knew mine wouldn't be the only heart that James ever broke.

'Are you, I mean obviously you're not all right, but…'

'It's awful.'

'Is he… did they…'

'He's here. He has to go in to the station and he spent most of yesterday afternoon talking to a lawyer, for goodness' sake. Stevie I can hardly even look at him.'

'But you don't think… I mean, it can't have been him?'

She lets out a painful sound, somewhere between a strained laugh and a scoff. 'I would have said he was a good man, that he would never cheat. What do I know Stevie?'

'I mean…' But my voice trails off. James isn't a killer, is all I think. The word killer flashing across my mind in lurid red letters. An image of my mother leaning over me when I was small, in bed sweating, puking, shaking. Her lips pressing to my forehead.

'Poor baby,' she'd murmured and I'd felt so glad, so grateful for her concern, her love. *Killer.* Perhaps they never look like monsters. I stand, turning and catch sight of my reflection in the glass door. I look sweet and kind. I look like Miss Gordon, 1A's teacher, and I am. I am her but I am other things too. Things I wish I wasn't.

'I don't know,' I tell Zoe. Because you can never really know everything about anyone, not one hundred per cent. No one can. 'I hope not,' I tell her, and it's true, though the alternative keeps whispering in the back of my mind.

Killer.

'I've got to go,' Zoe says, her voice a whisper, 'I'll call soon.'

'Okay. Take care.'

Could you be born bad? A thought I've played with more than once. One I pick up and give time to over and over again. My beautiful, wicked mother. Her blood running through my veins like a curse.

CHAPTER TWENTY-SIX

SEB

James Cowley looks like a reprimanded, sulky child. His face is set in a deep scowl but his jiggling right knee gives away his nerves. Lucy has bought him a crap machine coffee. She and Seb have one each, too, and Seb takes almost a full minute, taking a sip of his drink, checking the recorder and lining up his black pen alongside his small notepad. It is just for show; Lucy will be the one taking notes. It's all part of Seb's preparation and he has seen suspects crumble before he's even spoken a word. Not so for James Cowley, whose frown deepens. He is, Seb thinks, barely containing incandescent rage. Beside him is his lawyer, a man in a suit that says he gets paid a lot.

Finally, Seb smiles at James, an eerie kind of grin that shows teeth but deliberately doesn't meet his eyes. He records relevant details prior to the interview, gives James's name, pauses for his lawyer to add his, gives his own and Lucy's along with the time and date. He reads James his rights. As he speaks, Seb watches small beads of sweat break out on the suspect's forehead. It's often the way. Everyone recognises some version of this bit, after all everyone has seen a cop show or two in their time. Most people think they'd be unaffected, if innocent anyway, but

Seb is yet to see someone devoid of reaction when being questioned at the station in an interrogation room. He pauses again, takes a long sip of his coffee. James swipes a large, meaty hand across his brow quickly; the beads are smeared but not gone. 'Hi James.'

'Isn't this a bit OTT?' he asks, his voice slightly too loud but unwavering. Seb marvels at the confidence of him, even if it is bravado. He is their sole suspect in what has fast become a high-profile double murder case. He is at his local police station being questioned about it. He is, he thinks, desperate not to show them any fear but they can see it, hidden beneath the loud words, apparent in his fidgeting, the slight tremor in his fingers as he reaches for his cup then thinks better of it, pulling away. He clasps his hands together as a pair in front of him. This small airless room can play havoc with the mind. It is set up intentionally to do just that. It is a place no one wants to be.

'You think that us interviewing you, the last person to have seen a murder victim, is over the top?' Seb says, smile gone now, his dark eyes flashing, his words slow and forceful.

'N… no,' James stutters. Seb keeps his steely gaze on James.

'Allegedly the last person to have seen her,' his lawyer points out.

Lucy is taking notes. There is no need, not really as they'll have the entire conversation recorded, but it is how she and Seb work, the patterns they have slipped in to together. When Seb leaves silences all you can hear is the scratch scratch scratch of Lucy writing. True to his word, he's been teaching her shorthand and he knows she is studying it in her spare time too. Watching videos, going through the little book. James's eyes flick to her as she stops writing. She looks up and smiles. He grimaces.

'I liked Hannah. More than liked, had feelings for her. Why would I hurt her?'

'So your wife didn't find out,' Seb states the obvious.

'Well, she wouldn't have found out would she, if Hannah was still alive?'

'Unless she'd decided to tell her of course,' Seb says.

'She wouldn't have.' Seb doesn't point out the thinness of only having James's word for this. He's sure the lawyer will explain it to him.

'Who knew?'

'Knew what?'

'About you and Hannah.'

'My brother, Ben.'

'What did he think about it?'

James shrugs. 'I don't know exactly but he saw us having lunch together.' He looks like a petulant child Seb thinks. Annoyed that he's here, annoyed that his brother caught him misbehaving.

'He gets along with Zoe?'

'All of my family get along with her. She's a nice person.'

'Hurting at the moment, I'd imagine.'

'Well, you definitely ruined her week.'

Seb smiles his shark smile. 'I'd say you did that, James.' He makes a *pfft* sound.

'We'll need to talk to Ben.'

'What on earth for?'

'He's connected to you, our primary suspect.'

'Suspect.' James spits the word out with venom. 'That's laughable isn't it?'

'Not really laughable at all, James, and it's not just for this murder either.'

'My client has nothing to do with the other case you've been reporting on,' the lawyer says.

Seb pauses, reaches into the box file by his right leg, pulls out a picture of Sam Carmichael. 'She is another of James's exes though.'

'My client has assured me she wasn't his girlfriend and that their encounter was brief and casual.'

'Still,' Seb says, 'you can see how it looks from our point of view.'

The lawyer smiles. 'How it looks isn't relevant until you have strong evidence to back up your accusations.'

Seb stays quiet for five seconds, ten, twenty, and then, 'Tell us about Misha Batt?'

The colour drains from James's face so fast it's almost funny.

'W…what?'

Seb smiles his shark grin again. 'Did you think we wouldn't check?'

'She dropped the complaint. It was nothing.'

'Not to her,' Lucy interjects.

'What's this?' the lawyer says and Seb can only imagine how irritated the man must be, how annoyed he'd be in his shoes. He's paid to help James and James is barely helping himself.

'Um,' James says.

Seb says, 'You probably should have mentioned this to your lawyer, James.'

The lawyer looks at him. James tells him, 'It was a fuss about nothing.'

And to Seb, 'I was drunk.'

'Prisons are full of people who committed crimes under the influence, Mr Cowley. It's not a defence.'

'Yeah, people who committed crimes, for god's sake. I booty-called the girl I was seeing after a few too many, hardly a crime.'

'She says she woke up to you assaulting her.'

'God.' The word comes out loud and irritated. 'It was bloody years ago, a misunderstanding. A mistake at worst. Misha could handle herself; still can, I suspect.'

'So what, she was asking for it?' Lucy says.

'You don't need to answer that,' the lawyer says, but James is indignant.

'There was no "it",' James says exasperated now and, Seb thinks, he genuinely believes this.

'Still,' Seb says, 'you can see how it might look, considering.'

'Considering?'

'Why you're sitting here now. Under suspicion for murdering not one but two women you were sexually involved with; a complaint in the past from another woman you were sexually involved with.'

'I'm not some kind of predator. Look at me, for goodness' sake: I don't have to go out and take it, women tend to like me well enough.' His voice is rising, his thin veneer of cool dissipating with every word. He is, Seb surmises, a bully, though he himself has no idea of it.

'Look, I've had enough of this.' James stands up. 'I'm out of here.'

'Sit down, James.'

James looks to his lawyer who says, 'We'd like to conclude this interview now, please.'

'I didn't do it,' he says and his voice is whiny.

'Your full cooperation is noted,' Seb tells him, 'and certainly goes in your favour.'

'My client has come in in good faith exactly because of this,' the lawyer says.

Seb turns to James. 'We need a DNA sample from you.'

'What?' He looks to his lawyer who says, 'Best to go along with this, all things considered.' James's face flashes red.

'So go and see our colleague out on reception. She'll take you where you need to go and then you are free to leave.' It's a reminder to the man that he is not running this show. That he is not in charge here.

The lawyer stands too, gathering up his thin file, likely pleased to be escaping this room and the bombed interview.

'Don't go too far,' Seb says.

'What does that mean?'

'Exactly that. We'll be in touch.'

James makes a big show of stropping out.

CHAPTER TWENTY-SEVEN

STEVIE

It feels weird getting ready for a… date? Of sorts, I suppose. It's not like I don't see guys, but usually my liaisons are casual and short-lived. I usually skip this bit, the preparing with a long-term view. I wouldn't have seen Joel again if I hadn't needed information about that night. My modus operandi is casual drunken hook-ups; I dress up, go to a bar and find a guy. I don't bring people back to mine, I rarely give my real name or my phone number and I either sneak out or leave amicably at the first opportunity, waking up in my own bed. Always, always, I am comparing these casual encounters to the real connection I had with James. My boyfriend whilst I languished in foster care with a perfectly nice family who genuinely wanted the best for me. When I went to school every day, ate well, studied hard and felt wretched for feeling so much better whilst my mother was in an institution. James had taken my mind off of her then; James had seemed like the final piece in the puzzle of 'normal'. When we'd reconnected the year after I graduated and began to work towards qualified teacher status, it had felt like he was there again at just the right time. Part of a fantastic and hopeful start to my adult life.

And now I'm going to meet Ben, his brother. This has a different kind of risk and I find, as I dress with care, shower using my favourite shampoo, spray myself in perfume which arrived along with my Zara clothes, that I have butterflies, anticipation and fear mingling into one.

'A few drinks,' we'd agreed in the end, after I'd said I might not be able to do dinner. Eating in front of other people remains one of my least favourite things to do, my mother had poisoned me, of course, adding bleach and other cleaning products to my food in an attempt to 'cleanse me'. I suppose because of this the thought of sitting through a meal all dressed up and nervous filled me with dread, so a bar is preferable.

I take so long getting ready that time seems to slip away and I realise with ten minutes to spare that I'm likely to be late.

—

I make it just five minutes after we'd agreed to meet and see Ben standing at the bar deep in conversation with the barmaid. I feel a flash of misplaced jealousy and am taken back to turning up to meet James many times, and finding him in conversation with young women. No one was spared the web of his flirtatious joy and he'd talk to pretty much any female who stepped in his path.

This date, I think, is new-level madness. I shouldn't be here and I'm contemplating doing the right thing for once and just leaving when Ben turns round and sees me. His smile widens and he waves. Too late now. I head over and when I get there he leans down, kisses my cheek and steps back, taking me in. 'You look great,' he says.

'Oh,' I manage, eyes flicking to the barmaid, who is watching us. 'Thanks.'

'This is my pal Jinny; Jinny this is Stevie who I was telling you about.'

'Cool name,' the girl says with a big smile.

'Thanks,' I say, having been told some variation of this my entire life. I'd hated my name when I was a thin, hungry, awkward kid. I can still remember the taunts on the playground from the other children who were adept at sensing weakness, discomfort, and difference and exploiting it: 'Stevie's got a boy's name, Stevie's got a boy's name.' I see variations of the same type of bullying all the time in my own little class. I know and understand that kids can be cruel, just as adults can but with no filter. By the time I hit secondary school, I had learnt to be quiet and small, to not attract attention to myself, even when Mum was away and I was placed in foster care. I made sure I was clean, neat and agreeable and then once I started dating James I became almost popular by association.

'What can I get you?' Ben asks.

'Vodka tonic would be great.'

He orders drinks. Jinny brings them over with a 'great to meet you' to me and a 'see you soon' to Ben. We head to an outside table, a balcony overlooking the green riverbank below, the water shining in the distance. The Thames cuts through this bit of Thamespark and bars and restaurants, keen to exploit the pretty spot, have set up so we can sit outside during the thin sliver of beautiful weather sipping drinks while our shoulders pink up and we watch little sailing boats go by. It's a nice town in places, pretty and with easy access to London. I can see why people want to live here, though I've often wondered if I should leave. Start anew somewhere else because everywhere I turn here memories find me.

I settle in a metal chair. The slats of the chair are warm as they touch the top of my thighs. I take a sip of my drink, the ice pressing against my lips, welcome and cool. As I put the glass down I realise Ben is watching me intently. 'What?' I say, worrying that I've got lipstick on my teeth or an errant bogey I've not noticed.

'Just looking at you.'

'Okay,' I say, an eyebrow raised in question.

'I mean, you're nice to look at.' His face flushes red. 'Sorry, that was...'

I find his awkwardness suddenly endearing and reach across the table for his hand, squeezing his fingers in mine. 'Thanks.'

He grins and I think, *he is* handsome, and he is sweet and here I am, embroiled in his brother's life still, though he knows nothing of it. Am I on this date under false pretences? Of course I am; almost every aspect of my life is built on lies or omissions of some kind. I'm so mired in twisted truth and dishonesty, even I struggle to keep up. And here's Ben, this super sweet version of James, and here I am, a crazy cow with an unclear agenda. My phone buzzes and I peek a look. A message from Zoe. Ben's sister-in-law. I turn the phone over, zip up my handbag and say to Ben, 'This place is nice.'

'Oh, yeah. I'm here quite a lot. We have an office just down the road.'

'We?'

'We, me and James, we work together.'

'Oh yes, I think you said. How is that for you? Don't they say never work with friends or family?'

He laughs. 'I thought it was animals or children but there may be some truth in it. It's mostly fine to be honest; we have quite different functions. But, between you and I, it is a bit stressful at the moment.'

'Oh?' I pick up my vodka tonic, taking a sip, slipping a thin shard of melted ice between my lips. This is what I'm here for isn't it? The insider info.

'Yeah, he's, uh, well he's got some marital trouble.'

'Oh that sounds ominous.'

'Yeah, I probably shouldn't say but he cheated on his wife.'

'Shit.' I manage to sound suitably shocked, widening my eyes in surprise as my heart kicks up a bit faster.

'Probably not a surprise to you. I mean, you know what he's like.'

I blink, once, twice. That perfect idyllic school term spent with James which ended by text and resulted in him and Vicky Gibson announcing their love for each other mere days later. Four years ago, the summer we'd spent reconnecting. I don't tend to ponder on the less good bits, like turning up at his place and finding a random girl leaving one Sunday. James assuring me it meant nothing, he'd had a few too many, me running down the drive in tears, Ben being the one who followed and checked to see if I was okay.

'Yeah, I mean we weren't married or anything.' I go for a playful smile as if none of it matters, my broken heart worn lightly.

'No, but still, I know you were pretty into him.'

I wave a hand. 'It was fine, and ages ago. Sorry for his wife though.'

'Yeah, she's great too.' Ben shakes his head. 'I hate to say it, he's my brother and everything, but he's honestly a bit of a dick.'

I make a sort of murmuring agreement sound.

'You don't have siblings do you?'

'No,' I say, surprised he remembers. 'Was just me and my mum growing up.'

'That's right and you don't speak to her?'

'I didn't for a while,' I say, with a shrug. 'We're in contact again now though.'

'Families, eh,' he says with a sigh.

'Your folks were pretty nice as I recall?'

'Outwardly, sure.'

'Oh?' My interest picks up at that. I'd always seen them as picture-perfect, super nice.

'My dad can be an arsehole.'

'Really?' I say, surprised again. His dad was charm personified, I'd felt.

'Yeah, let's just say as far as James goes, the apple didn't fall far from the tree.'

'Ah.' When I think back, his dad had had that sort of lingering eye. Certainly, he'd given me a good once-over. 'That must have been tough growing up.'

'Yeah, he cheated on my mum a few times. She turned a blind eye mostly but his last affair was with a friend of hers.' He shakes his head.

'God, that sucks. What did she do?'

'My mum?'

'Yeah.'

'Told him to finish it, cut out her friend and pretended like nothing had gone wrong.'

'Wow.'

'I know,' he says, anger giving his words extra heat. 'She should have left the first time.'

'Maybe she loves him.'

'Maybe, but still.'

His phone sitting on the table between us buzzes to life. He grabs it. 'Do you mind?' he asks me.

I wave a hand, watching him pick up, downing the remnants of my drink.

He's frowning. 'When's she going?' A pause. A sigh. 'Well what did you expect?' I can hear a raised voice at the other end of the call. It's James; he sounds stressed. 'I'm out,' Ben says, listens, sighs again. 'Yeah okay.' Another pause. 'Bye.'

He turns to me.

'You've got to go?'

'Sorry. I don't want to.'

'It's cool,' I say.

'Let me drop you home?'

'I can walk.'

'No,' he says quick and firm. 'Let me, so I know you're safe?'

'Yeah, okay.'

We chat about nothing in particular on the drive to my flat and I find myself enjoying his company, laughing, and when he leans across the seats, pressing his lips to mine it's... nice.

I watch him drive away, waving and out of the corner of my eye I see movement. When I turn to catch it there's no one there. I walk round to the side of my block. On the floor is a still-smouldering cigarette butt but no sign of the smoker. I hurry inside, taking the stairs two at a time. I get into my flat and bolt the door behind me.

CHAPTER TWENTY-EIGHT

SEB

They'd gone out not just to say they suspected the murders were linked but to say they were now quite certain and that they had a suspect in for questioning. They upped the appeal for witnesses on both the lunchtime and evening news and it had been crazy trying to field calls, most of which were useless but a few that they'd be following up. They'd warned Zoe in advance and asked her to come into the station in the afternoon after her husband had been in.

Zoe Cowley sits in the small room at the station, back ramrod straight, eyes red-rimmed. She looks, Seb thinks, like she's aged five years in the few days since they last saw her. Lucy got her a cup of tea from the machine and her hands are clasped round it now. Her nails are painted though slightly chipped; Seb reckons she's a woman who is normally immaculately turned out. Her clothes are expensive and her hair is well cut but today it is greasy and unwashed. They'd had confirmation from the hotel she'd stayed at that she had been in the gym shortly after she checked in. She was on CCTV in the cafe afterwards, so there was no way she killed Hannah Smith, though Seb hadn't ruled her out as the person either woman thought was following her.

'Thanks for coming in, Mrs Cowley, and on a Saturday too. It really is much appreciated,' Seb says.

'Zoe,' she says.

He nods. 'Zoe then.' He supposes that right now being Mrs Cowley probably isn't ideal.

'I've checked into a hotel.' She turns her wide damp eyes to Seb. 'I don't want to go home. I can't even look at him.'

'I'm sorry, this must be awful.'

'It is.' She looks away, eyes trailing around the room. It is a horrible little space that no one really wants to end up in and this is the nicest of all the private rooms in the station. It has sofas instead of hard-backed chairs nailed to the floor. It even has a window which is where Zoe's eyes linger now, taking in the sunlight slipping in and making them all slightly too hot for comfort.

'Thank you for the warning, about the news yesterday.'

Seb nods.

She says, 'I assume dancer was code for stripper?'

'Sam was an exotic dancer, yes.'

'She knew my husband?'

Seb forces himself to keep eye contact. 'We believe James had a sexual relationship with her.'

She says, 'When?'

'Two years ago, they spent two nights together during April.'

He slides a photo of Sam across the table. Not the cruel pale-faced version of her dead and covered, but one her friend at the club had provided, of her smiling at the camera. 'You never met her?'

'No.' Zoe's eyes are glued to the image. Tears spring up in them.

Seb pulls the picture away. 'I'm sorry, this must be very difficult.'

She gives him a faint smile. 'We got married that March, so we were newlyweds. No, I've not met her and like an idiot never suspected a thing, though of course now I'm looking back and wondering. I'm away a lot. He and Ben have their own business and therefore can take time out whenever they like really. It never occurred to me to check up on him. If you don't have trust after all…' The words trail off. Her eyes flick to the tiny window, which is too high to see out of and offers scant and ineffectual light. Seb wishes she wasn't here. Wishes she didn't have to be.

'I understand.' Seb pauses. 'Do you know many of his exes?'

She frowns. 'No, none.'

'Has he ever mentioned them?'

'I mean, not in great detail. It always sounded like he was a bit of a player, to be honest. He said he was seeing some girl before he went travelling and we met. Nothing serious but I do recall that he said she got a bit clingy and it ended with her quite upset. I was his first long-term settled relationship, I think. Always took a sort of pride in that. Laughable now, eh? Me thinking I was the one who tamed him.' She grimaces at her own words.

'Do you know the name of the girl he was seeing then?'

'No. God, he said yesterday that you lot were blowing everything out of proportion. Even when caught, he didn't choose to be honest.' Zoe leans forward, pressing a hand to her mouth.

Seb waits, hating to have to be the one who delivered this news. James should have told her immediately about Sam; she shouldn't have had to hear about it in a hurried phone call from a detective. The man is a pathetic coward; Seb had seen that first hand. But, was he a killer?

'Did you ever notice any behaviour changes from James?'

'Not then. All I remember is being blissfully happy.' She pauses and shakes her head as tears fall down her face. She pulls a tissue from her handbag and blows her nose. 'I've thought about Hannah though and, with her, I think I did notice a change. He was being especially nice.'

'In what way?'

'Very attentive, lots of gifts. He'd even brought up the idea of children again.'

'Were you planning a family?'

'Not exactly, but we'd always said early thirties, which is where we are nearing now, I suppose. We thought we'd have children eventually but it's so expensive isn't it?'

'Yes,' Seb agrees. As a father of one, he knows without Val's help, he wouldn't have been able to buy a place, nor would he be able to do his job and the hours it entails. A couple now has to earn a fortune just to cover childcare. 'So he'd raised it again, recently?'

'Yes, which is mad isn't it, because he was sleeping with someone else.' Zoe lifts the teacup to her mouth and takes a sip, wincing slightly. 'God that's hot.'

'Shall I get you some more milk?' Lucy asks, pausing from taking notes.

'No, it's... I'm not even thirsty really. It's fine, thanks.'

'How did James seem, that morning when you got back?' Seb asks.

She sighs. 'He was... jumpy.'

'Jumpy?'

'Yes, nervous somehow.'

'Did you ask him why?'

'I did yes. He said he'd had a to-do with Ben about work.'

'Did you believe him?'

'Yes, they often bicker.' She shrugs. 'One of the downsides to working with family, I imagine.'

'Do they get on well?'

'Yes, mostly. Though James is his dad's favourite, which causes a few issues. Ben is a mummy's boy, or so James puts it. Normal stuff I guess. I think their dad had an affair years ago which caused a lot of problems, as you can imagine.' She chuckles. 'Like father, like son, maybe.' The sad smile dies on her face.

'So you never met Hannah nor Sam? Never knew of them until now?'

'No, detective, and I never suspected a thing, which somehow makes it seem even worse.'

'People show us what they want us to see,' says Seb.

Zoe was away at the time of the murder, now all confirmed by CCTV: she has an iron-clad alibi and Seb believes what she's saying. Plus, he sympathises. Having been in the same situation himself and with a child to consider, he knows all too well the pain of infidelity and the lasting effects it leaves on you, like scars on skin. Zoe is currently in shock but, eventually, that will wane and she'll get wary, just like he did. It had taken him years to trust another woman, years to let someone in, and even now, he finds he can still be consumed by fear. Even now, he is taking things so slowly he worries he may lose Faye due to lack of momentum. He pushes the thoughts away and focuses on the situation in front of him. Zoe has it worse because her husband isn't just a cheat but the prime suspect in a murder case.

'Did James ever discuss a woman he dated at university called Misha Batt?'

She frowns. 'No, why?'

Seb glances at Lucy, who immediately picks up the signal and says, 'Misha reported him to the police.'

'Reported him for what?'

'An assault.'

'Assault?'

'Yes.'

'Who is she?'

'A girl he was seeing, casually.'

'They were dating?'

'They were. He turned up at her place late one night. She says she woke up to him assaulting her.'

'God.' Zoe shunts forward, knocking the cup, which falters but remains upright, steam still coming off of the top. Her already pained face looks even worse.

'I'm sorry,' Lucy says and Seb knows she means it. He's sorry too, though he could tell in seconds that James was a bit of a dick and Zoe doesn't strike him as stupid. Love can be blind, he supposes. Charlie probably looked exactly like the nightmare she turned out to be but that wasn't what he'd seen when they met.

'He didn't mention it then?' Seb steps back in.

'No, it seems, detective, that there are many things he failed to tell me about.'

'Yes.'

'This doesn't look good for him, does it?'

'No.'

She nods.

'Do you think he has it in him?'

'To kill someone?'

'Yes.'

'I have no idea right now what he is and isn't capable of.' Which wasn't *no.* Although, she was hurting and therefore biased. She sighs as if reading Seb's thoughts. 'Honestly, the cheating is a shock, detective, but looking back I can see that I was perhaps naïve. The assault charge is an even bigger shock, or at least a different kind of one.'

'Yes,' Seb agrees.

'But a murderer? I'm not sure he has *that* in him.'

'I understand,' Seb says, then asks, 'Will you be remaining at the hotel?'

'What?' She frowns. 'Oh, I see. No, not for long, maybe another night. I'm going to have to swallow my pride and call my parents today, I suppose.'

'Where are they?'

'In Reading. Not far. I'll go home, pack, get my car. I had to cab it to the hotel last night; I'd had rather too much to drink.'

'Understandable,' Lucy murmurs.

'Yes, but it didn't make me feel any better. It never does, does it?'

'No,' Lucy agrees. Zoe gives her a weak smile.

'If you need anything else...' she says as she stands, ready to leave, the too-hot tea sitting untouched on the table.

'We'll get in touch.'

'Thanks, I guess.'

CHAPTER TWENTY-NINE

STEVIE

'Thank you for meeting me,' I tell Tom, who has ordered more food than either of us will probably be able to manage.

'A pleasure my dear. I nipped into your mum's and saw you'd somehow managed to clean her kitchen?'

'Yes.' I reach for the napkin on the table, picking idly at a corner. 'I don't know how she lives like that.'

Tom shakes his head. 'No, I know. I've managed to persuade her to let a crew of cleaners in.'

'Oh?' I ask, my heart hammering at the thought. I take her money when I need to but I repay her by cleaning parts of the house. If Tom has the place cleaned, how will I balance out my theft?

'Yes, it's unhygienic and a hazard to her health and yours too when you're round there.'

'I don't go that often,' I tell him, tearing the corner of the tissue off and rolling it into a little ball, 'which probably makes me sound like a dreadful daughter.'

'Stevie, you're very good to go at all,' he says, so earnestly that it makes my eyes water.

I smother the imminent tears by going for a chuckle that comes out like a cough and say, 'She is my mother.'

'She is, and lucky to have such an understanding daughter.'

I'm saved from answering by a waitress with a laden tray. Tom, I discovered soon after we connected, likes to eat. His face lights up now as he contemplates all of the food being put on the table between us. A fruit platter, pastries, a pot of coffee, small finger sandwiches. 'Let's grab brunch,' he'd said when he called me this morning at just after nine. I was tired, run ragged after an unrestful night where I had replayed the evening with Ben and tried to imagine what, exactly was going on in James's house. The message from Zoe I received during our drinks had just said she was going to a hotel.

I'd called her when I got in, no answer, called her again this morning. Still no answer.

'How's work?' Tom asks, yanking me from my fairly dire musings and the paranoid feeling that everything was about to come toppling down around me. It was James who called Ben while we were grabbing drinks. Zoe had left him. I know this because of the message. I am an invisible, tenuous link between all three of them and none of them know.

I fill Tom in on what the children are doing at school; he beams at me, asking questions, laughing at my impressions. I find myself laughing too and enjoying the company and the food, though mentally I am weighing up each morsel as my mother would do if she were sitting here, deciding what looks over processed.

'You've done ever so well Stevie,' he says.

'I don't know about that,' I tell him because I don't, not really. Outwardly, I seem fine, mostly. But I have endless debt cycles, periods where I drink too much, what I know is an unhealthy obsession with my ex. One that has led me to wondering in the small dark hours after midnight if that obsession makes me capable of murder?

'I do,' he says. 'After what you've been through.' He shakes his head. Tom carries a lot of guilt about my childhood. He'd been away for most of it and never suspected I was unsafe; why would he? My mother's obsessions with eating and cleansing, her weird manic periods where she'd poison me to 'flush me out'. She knew it was wrong or why would she have lied to doctors and nurses? Just as I know it is wrong to befriend my ex's wife, to go on a date with his brother. To follow his mistresses and not go immediately to the police when her name flashed up on the six o'clock news.

'I'm okay,' I tell Tom, 'and it's nice to have you.'

'I feel the same way.' He flashes me a smile. He is not a physically demonstrative man but his smiles warm me up. His pride gives me hope that maybe, just maybe I'm not all bad. Maybe I can even get to be happy again if I just try hard enough.

'So, when are the cleaners going in?'

'Two days' time,' he says.

'Will you be there?'

'Oh yes, I'll have to be. I'm going to try and take her out.'

'It'll never happen,' I tell him, pouring us both fresh cups of coffee from the pot on the table, adding milk and sugar to mine. 'She hasn't left the house in about eighteen months, I don't think.' She did used to walk down to the shops and back at least. Lockdown, though, had sealed her indoors fate.

'It will,' Tom says and sounds so sure. I forget, of course, that they had had a lifetime together before I even existed. Shared a childhood which I knew only snippets about.

One which Tom has said was unpleasant. I knew their mother had had terrible OCD. Finding that out had led to me reconnecting with my mum. Not that it excused anything, but I felt some compassion for her. I knew what it was like to grow up in instability, to have your days tinged with madness before you were old enough to know what sanity was. Tom, though, had turned out fine. Better than fine even, but as he said, he got out first, before his father left, leaving poor Maddie, my mother, unprotected.

I smile at him, relaxed by his confidence, allowing myself the fleeting charade of being looked after if only for the time it takes to have brunch.

'So,' he says, 'met anyone special yet?'

A favourite topic. Tom is one of the few people who knows how much my breakup with James hurt. I'd told him the whole sorry tale when he found me in floods of tears at my place after James left the country.

I shake my head. 'I mean, I had a sort of date last night.'

'Sort of?'

'Okay a date.'

'How did it go?'

'Okay actually.'

'And how are you feeling about the undeserving ex?'

That does make me smile, though the smile fades fast. 'Actually, I heard he's being questioned by the police.'

'You're kidding?'

'No,' I tell him wide-eyed. 'Seems he was having an affair and the woman, his mistress has been… well, murdered.'

He screws his face up. 'Not the killing in Thames Park?'

I nod, picking up my large, round coffee cup and drinking, hiding my face, which I know has flushed as red as Hannah's beautiful hair. 'It's been linked to another murder as well, some stripper from two towns over, and, I'm sorry to say, another woman James was involved with.'

'How do you know this?' he asks.

'Oh, well, I, uh, bumped into his brother.'

'I see,' he says and is that… suspicion I hear in his voice? Despite meeting Tom so late in my life, despite not having years of history, I often find he can read me when others can't.

'Awful, eh.'

'Yes, very, and yet another reason to be thankful you escaped.' Another favourite theme of Tom's is that I'm too good for James anyway.

I smile. 'Yes.'

Tom offers to drive me home but I tell him I'll walk. I leave the little bistro and wander through Thamespark's town centre. It's busy on a Saturday as always and I watch harassed mums pushing buggies, gaggles of teenagers with too loud voices, bored partners sat on benches outside shops scrolling through phones. I bump into a set of parents from school, Christian's mum and dad; he is with them excitedly saying, 'Miss, miss!' and I feel that spark, the slither of happiness. I had done something right. I may not be a completely good person but I am a good teacher. The children like me, and I them. They thrive in my class and I know prospective parents are often hoping their little ones end up with me.

My phone rings as I get to the town's outskirts and head along the river towards my flat. I snatch it up so fast I almost lose my grip and say, 'Zoe.'

'Hey, sorry I missed your calls.'

'No, that's fine. You have a lot to deal with.'

'Yes.' The word comes out on a sigh full of sadness. It's how I'd felt, way back when I'd found out James had been sleeping around. He hadn't even been sorry really, had said quite cheerfully in fact, 'I'll understand if you want to kick me to the curb.' I hadn't wanted that, hadn't done that, but two short months later he did it for us both anyway.

I'd told Michael about the cheating, the breakup and how much I loved him still. Michael had been silent for a moment then said, 'Do you feel like he treated you well?'

'No,' I'd said, but the word was wary, unsure. 'But, I was lucky to get a man like that in the first place. I was really lucky he chose me all those years back at school when I was a social leper.'

'A man like what?' he'd said, his smooth voice slipping under my skin like pins.

'Well, you know...'

'I don't. Tell me.'

'Normal,' I'd half-whispered. Because that's what James represented to me: normality. I saw him, his family, his smooth movement through life, and I wanted that too. I thought perhaps I could even obtain it, with him.

'How are things?' I ask Zoe now, a stab of pain at this tangled web I find myself in.

'Awful. I've been at the police station all morning.'

'Shit, and at a weekend.'

'Yeah, I know. I stayed in a hotel last night, I can't bear to look at him.'

I pause, watching a procession of birds float by on the river. Geese, unbothered, unruffled. 'It's shit, I'm sorry,' I tell her and I am. Sorry she's having to go through this, sorry that the friend she thinks gets it, who she can rely on, is a fraud too, just like her husband. She is, I tell myself, better off without us both.

'What are you going to do?'

'I'm going to stay another night in the hotel. I'm just leaving our house; I came to pick up some bits and my car. He's out so I guess he felt well enough to go to football.'

'Do you think?'

'Yes, his kit's gone.'

'Maybe it's distracting him, to stay busy?'

'Maybe he just doesn't give a shit.'

'I'm sure that's not true,' I murmur.

'Either way, tomorrow I'll head up to my parents for a bit.'

'Okay, can I help?'

'No, but thanks.'

'What for?'

'For being there for me.'

'It's the least I can do,' I manage, almost choking on the words.

'No, seriously, you've been great. I mean you've only known me from class?'

'Yes but you're my friend.'

'I probably shouldn't have dumped all this on you, it's just we'd had class and…'

'No, you've nothing to apologise for,' I say, guilt making my blood drop by degrees and my stomach churn with acid. 'Please don't.'

'Okay but thanks, really.'

I hang up and see movement out of the corner of my eye. A flash of something there and gone. I'm near the river's edge and behind me are tall trees, back beyond them tennis courts. I step towards the trees peering around one and onto the footpath, empty as far as I can see, but I feel

171

the hairs on the back of my neck stand up, my heartbeat picking up pace.

Michael calls it fight or flight. A state I lived in for so long I'm especially attuned to it. Children with mums like mine grow up in a state of hyper vigilance. I am used to feeling around for atmospheres, pre-empting anger, sadness, madness and danger. I wait now, breath held to see if anyone appears. I hear voices to my left, turn quickly and see a small family, man, woman, child, a large lolloping dog running a few steps ahead, panting. They waft past me, all offering 'hellos' and 'good afternoons' which I give back. Best smile, teacher face on. The Stevie I so want to be, in stark contrast to the liar, bad friend and conniving version I have been for most of today.

I hurry home unable to shake the sense of being followed.

CHAPTER THIRTY

SEB

Ben had said to come along to their office; despite it being a Sunday, he is at work. They arrive at the address to find a small building at the back of the high street in Thamespark, still central enough to be impressive. The door is open, but it's a stiflingly hot day and as they step into what looks to be a front of house area, Seb thinks it may be hotter inside than out. There is a long desk, a small table and a two-seater sofa. On the table are various glossy business mags promoting well-known energy companies. Seb feels like the little structure may hold the heat instead of doing anything to cool it.

'Hello?' he calls out.

'Hey, press the button to the left of the door and head in,' a voice booms.

They go through a door and Seb is relieved to find this part is air-conditioned.

'It's like an oven in reception, eh?'

'It's pretty hot,' Lucy says. Seb finds himself looking at a man who is so like James Cowley he would have known they were brothers without being told.

'Awful for Marie, our receptionist,' Ben says. 'She's not in at weekends anyway but she's mostly working from home for the foreseeable. We share this space now with another firm.'

'Probably best for her in the heat.'

'Yeah, I think so. One of the few good things about the pandemic, eh, we had to make that possible.'

'Yes,' Lucy says, giving him a quick smile.

Seb introduces himself and Lucy, both flashing badges and bringing his attention back to focus on the matter in hand, the reason they are there. Ben gestures to chairs around a long table sitting in front of a large whiteboard that he's evidently been filling in. He sees Lucy looking. 'Energy price comparisons,' he says by way of explanation.

'Commercial prices have gone up as well?'

'Yep, which from our point of view isn't the worst thing.'

'No,' Lucy says. Seb suspects she is pushing aside bitter thoughts of her own bill, like everyone else.

'Sorry,' Ben says now, 'that's probably really insensitive considering how much people are being affected by this.'

Despite looking similar, Seb thinks, Ben is definitely softer than James. He doesn't have the same arrogant swagger.

'Do you know why we're here?' Seb asks, as all Lucy had said when he set the meeting was they wanted to discuss a case linked with his family.

'Yeah, James has filled me in.'

'Did you know Hannah?'

'Nope.' He emphasises this with a head shake. 'I had no idea at all that he was currently embroiled in an affair.'

'Currently?' Lucy says, looking up from her notes.

'Has he cheated on Zoe before?' Seb, of course, knows he has but he wants Ben's take on it.

'I mean, not that I know of with one hundred per cent certainty.'

'But you suspect?'

He nods. 'Yeah.'

'What makes you think so?'

'James is James.' He shrugs as if that in itself is explanation enough.

'What does that mean?'

'He's ah… you know, a womaniser.'

'But Zoe didn't know this?'

'No, and when they first got hitched even I thought he'd changed his ways.'

'Now, you don't think so?'

'No, well Hannah Smith kind of proves that, eh?'

'And you think she may not have been the only one?'

Ben shrugs again but doesn't answer.

'Do you have names of any other women he might have had relations with?'

'No. Not since Zoe.'

'But you've had your suspicions?'

'I've smelt perfume on him, covered a few times when he's been "away for business",' he says, putting this in air quotes. 'I think I saw him and Hannah having lunch didn't know it was her until I've thought about it since though. And byond that no hard evidence as such, and like I said initially he was pretty smitten with Zoe.'

'So these things are more recent?'

'Yeah, I guess. Actually, no, that's not entirely true. There was a, uh… dancer. We were on a stag night for our friend, Dave. What was her name…'

'Sam?' Seb asks.

Ben clicks his fingers. 'Right. Oh, you know about her?'

'Haven't you watched the news reports?'

'Not really.'

'She was murdered two years ago.'

'What the hell.' Ben's eyes widen. 'Who by?'

'We don't know yet, but we suspect it's by the same person who killed Hannah.'

'Shit,' Ben says.

'Their only connection, as far as we know, is James.'

'Shit,' he says again. 'He's a cheat but… I mean… he's not a killer?' It comes out like a question and he looks from Seb to Lucy and back again. He shakes his head. 'God.'

'Are you close?' Seb asks. 'To your brother?'

'We have the business so we see each other every day.' Seb doesn't respond, letting the silence draw out the words which Ben had left unsaid. 'No, probably not close exactly. But we're family and as well as working together we go home for lunch at least once a month, sometimes more.'

'You all get along, as a family?'

'Yeah, mainly. I'd say I get on better with my mum, James is tight with Dad but they're similar people.'

'In what respect?'

'Oh, most respects really.'

'Including womanising?'

'Sadly, yes,' he says. Seb sees his jaw tightening as he speaks.

'Tough for your mum?'

'Tough for all of us but especially Mum, yes.'

'And James was always like this in relationships?'

Ben nods. 'Pretty much. The worst part is he attracts really cool women too.'

'Oh?'

'Yeah, this one girl he was seeing, Stevie, was really great. They dated years ago when we were in school and even then she was lovely. When he moved back home they started up again. She was absolutely besotted with him and he was awful to her.'

'Are they still in touch?'

'Oh, no but I bumped into her recently. We went for a drink Friday night actually.'

'Do you think James would mind?'

'No, he called while I was with her and I had to leave to go to his. I mentioned it, he hardly remembered who she was.'

'Right. What's her surname?'

Ben gives it, Seb scribbling it down.

'Why did you have to go over to his Friday night?'

'Zoe left,' Ben says with a sigh.

'How did he seem about it?'

'Oh man, gutted to be honest. He was also really drunk. I had to call Mum. She's taken him back to theirs for the weekend. Zoe told him she won't be back anytime soon...' He shrugs. 'Not looking good.'

'How far do you think James would have gone to stop her finding out?'

'I don't think he'd have killed anyone over it,' Ben says fast and Seb believes that he believes it.

'Do you know a complaint was made against him, while he was at university?'

'I vaguely remember. I know my dad went up there, went to the police with James. Said it was a lot of fuss over nothing though.'

'A girl your brother was seeing woke up to him assaulting her.'

'Shit, seriously?'

'Your dad didn't tell you that?'

'I mean, I was sitting A levels; like I said, I vaguely recall the incident but… shit, this looks bad for him?'

'It doesn't look good.'

Seb wraps up the interview; he doesn't think Ben knows anything else. He says get in touch if they need anything else from him and Seb promises to do so.

In the car, Lucy says, 'They're not close at all. I don't think Ben likes his brother very much.'

'No, me neither. I'd say there was a fair bit of jealousy there too, wouldn't you?'

'The bit about him pulling great women despite being a dick?'

'Yes. I also think it's a bit odd that he'd take his brother's ex out for a drink, isn't it?'

'Yeah, it is a bit.'

'Stevie Gordon,' Seb murmurs. 'Call back to the station. Let's get Harry and Finn to check her out.'

–

'Hey Tills,' Seb says. As he steps into the house, she is right by the door.

'Hey Dad.' Tilly pauses long enough to give him a quick hug and, he thinks he could stay right here and be happy, his job paling into insignificance against this role. But she's pulling away, slipping her feet into her tatty Air Force Ones.

'Are you going out?' he says.

'Yeah, going to meet Kai in town.'

He forces himself to smile. 'Great.'

She gives him a crooked smile back. 'Bye Dad.'

'Bye,' he says to the front door as it closes. Leaving the strong smell of her behind. Floral shampoo, hairspray and some perfume that Faye got her and which she now uses judiciously. The sweet scent of Tilly. He stands savouring it for a moment knowing one day, probably far too soon, it won't be here at all and he'll miss it, miss *her* like mad.

In the kitchen, Val and Faye are at the table, coffee cups producing another great smell, both women laughing. It is nice to be home.

'Sebastian.' Val gives him a warm grin.

'Hey, Tilly's gone to meet Kai?'

'She has, yes.'

'What are they doing?'

Val shrugs. Faye says, 'Cinema, apparently.'

'Oh,' says Seb.

Faye chuckles. Seb frowns. She stands and comes over to him, wrapping her long arms around his body, nestling in so close that her red hair tickles his nose. 'They'll be fine,' she tells him.

'Sit down, I'll get you a coffee, then I'm off out myself,' says Val.

'Do you want a lift?' Seb asks, stifling a yawn.

'No, it's a lovely day and the evenings are getting lighter. I have my bus pass, Sebastian, thank you though.' She puts a cup in front of him and heads out of the kitchen, leaving just him and Faye.

'Hey you,' Faye says softly, and Seb feels his stomach flip-flop.

'Hey yourself.'

'A busy weekend?'

'Yeah, I'm so sorry, it's this case.'

'You don't need to apologise for your job, or anything else. I had to go in to the prison today anyway.'

'Daniel?'

'Yep, finally got him transferred out.'

179

'That is good news.'

'Yeah, I mean it's better than where he was but, god Seb, the poor kid, he's so broken, you know.'

He picks her fingers up and squeezes her hand to his. Faye keeps hold of Seb's hand, standing up and dragging at him to do the same. 'Looks like we have the house to ourselves.'

'Oh, yes it does.' He grins, work seeping away and out of his mind, at least for now.

CHAPTER THIRTY-ONE

STEVIE

It's Sunday night, I'm dozing on the sofa when my phone rings, pulling me from sleep so fast it makes me gasp. I'd been having a bad dream, that I was lost and looking for my mum but everywhere I turned there was a monster instead. Even my dreams are textbook.

'Hello,' I say before I look at the phone.

'Stevie.' Her voice sounds thick, like dense, muddy sludge.

'Zoe?'

'Yeah.'

'Are you okay?' The room comes into focus and I settle out of the dream and back into the here and now.

'Not really.' She sounds like she's crying.

'Is it... has anything happened?'

'Other than my cheating husband possibly being a murderer as well as an adulterer?' Her words slip and slide. She is drunk, I realise.

'Yeah that's enough, hey.'

I can hear her sobbing. 'Where are you?' I ask.

'Hotel.'

'Which one?'

She gives me the address, I tell her I'm coming and then I hang up, brush my teeth, check my face and leave.

I order an Uber to meet me at the bottom of my block of flats and watch its painfully slow progress on my phone. Twice I look over my shoulder, startled, irrationally afraid. It's so dark. I spend all winter longing for the drawn-out nights where the sun stays up, then when it's here I just wish the days would end. Tonight I'm grateful not to be standing alone, waiting in the pitch black. I'm haunted by thoughts of Hannah's walk home, no streetlights, with what, maybe a phone torch held out in front of her? I'm about to do a 'fake' loud voice phone call when my Uber blinks into 'imminent arrival'.

I get in the car, releasing a breath I hadn't known I was holding.

'Stevie?'

'That's right.'

'Park top hotel?' he asks, catching my eye in the mirror.

'Yes,' I say, certain that I see that flash again, out of the corner of my eye, red and… what is it? There is something familiar about the colour. Something I can't quite put my finger on yet.

I wonder if Hannah had ever felt me, walking along behind her in supermarkets, between work and the flat she shared with her equally plummy, young and pretty friend. I'd followed Sam too, after I saw James leaving the club with her. I'd got very drunk that night and called Uncle Tom sobbing incoherently. He'd come round, listened and not judged. I'd felt embarrassed in the morning but he'd been lovely. 'We're family Stevie. I'm happy to be here to help when I can.'

Tears sting my eyes at the enormity of everything, the awfulness of it. Two young women dead, *and blood on your clothes*, my mind whispers. I push that thought away. I'd been with Joel; he'd pretty much confirmed that I got home. I've been ignoring his messages, though, not wanting a repeat, not wanting anything more from him, despite his persistence.

I'm not a killer, I'm not violent. I am not, I think, my mother.

–

The Uber driver leaves me in the car park after a silent drive where my head tried to replay all the places I'd seen Hannah, not in the park, I don't have any recollection of seeing her there.

I didn't do it. I didn't kill her, I know I didn't, and I can't believe James would either. Her flatmate must have been ruled out, her colleagues too. There was a guy she had occasional fag breaks with, I wonder if he's been questioned? I wonder at what point I'm going to have to come forward and tell my weird inexplicable tale to police? The thought fills me with dread but mentally I'm preparing for it because everything is closing in now. The carefully managed parts of my subterfuge are getting closer to each other and so I need to think about what I might say. What might be useful and what might take the heat off of me.

I would tell them about the work guy. Hannah wasn't really a smoker, one of those take it or leave it types, but I'd seen her on the odd Friday outside, sparking a cigarette, laughing at his jokes. He fancied her, I could see that clear as day. She wasn't interested. She only had eyes for James. I understand that, of course. His magnetic pull. Though I'm beginning to understand that that pull comes with a drip feed of poison too and I feel a flash of unexpected anger towards him, like fire in my chest. I never wanted to be a deceptive, dishonest person. I never wanted to be a bad friend. Yet here I am.

I see Zoe's car parked up, an ostentatious Tesla, the new status symbol of those with disposable income. I'd admired it the first time she drove it to the gym. She'd offered me a lift to work, which I declined because I kept some details to myself, where I lived and where I worked, for example. She knows I am a teacher but I've never told her at what school. In my mind, I think I'd felt like I was compartmentalising. Zoe exists in my Pilates class. We message each other outside of class but it has grown over time and I realised that actually, she wasn't from Thamespark, didn't know that many people here, and my friendship mattered to her. Just as hers had come to matter to me. It suited her though, the car. Women like her should have everything, all the accessories of a successful life.

It's a nice hotel too. I smile at the receptionist as I pass. Zoe is at the bar sitting on a high stool, shoulders slumped inwards as if she is crumpling into herself, and who could blame her? Is it worse to have had everything go well before you realise the world can be shit, or worse to have always known? She turns and sees me, lifting a hand.

I head over, hoiking myself up onto the stool next to hers. 'Hey.'

'Hey Stevie. Thanks for coming.'

'Of course,' I tell her. 'What are friends for?' I'm surprised I don't choke on the words. Friend. I'm not much of one, am I? The problem is, I'd started out hating her, for existing, for being so happy, for having him. I had no game plan at the beginning. I saw a post on his Facebook saying he'd moved into that house on that road. I'd realised I could literally see it from my balcony and it had felt like a sign. I'd blundered on, watching their picture-perfect life, eaten up with an envy so strong some days it made me feel physically sick. I knew he'd gone home with Sam, of course, so not quite as perfect as Zoe thought it was, but that had seemed a one-off. A meaningless physical encounter. Hannah had been different.

'Drink?' she asks. 'On me. Or James, actually.' She pulls a credit card from her bag and waves it at me with a crooked grin.

'Vodka tonic.' I'd gone to that Pilates class full of my festering, green-eyed resentment and that had kept me going back, week after week until I realised it had been three months and, actually, I liked her. I'd told her I didn't do social media but our friendship was always a risk, of course. Though, if James had found out it was me, would it have mattered? Oh, *a girl I dated at school and for a second years ago* would have been his take, I suspect. To me, he was the boy who took my virginity, the first person I fell in love with. He was a solid anchor in a teenage sea of uncertainty and when we'd reconnected I'd let myself believe that maybe, just maybe, I could have good things too.

If he ever twigged about me and Zoe, I didn't know about it. I had a fake profile set up for stalking him. Now we are here and I'm torn; I want her to leave him, to leave here. I want to swoop in and be the one to see him through it all. Or at least I had wanted that. Now I'm doubting it, doubting him, and I also want her to be okay. I feel wretched that she's hurt and pissed off that James has done this to her.

The barman settles my drink in front of me and I take a long, deep slug. 'What's happening?' I ask Zoe.

'Nothing new.' Her words are slurry, her eyes wide and glassy.

'What did your mum say?'

She throws me a bitter smile. 'She said why did I let his head be turned.'

'Jesus.'

'Yeah.' She looks at her own drink, a large glass of white wine, picks it up and raises it to her lips. Her hands tremor.

'I, uh, thought you were close?'

She shrugs. 'We are as long as everything is going well. She'll take this as a personal failure, her daughter getting divorced.'

'You're getting a divorce?' I say, trying to take in this new information about her mum, not the perfect mother-daughter relationship after all. And the mention of divorce which should make me happy but just makes me feel like maggots are squirming in my bowels, ready to burst out and spread my wretched poison all over the place.

'What else can I do?' she says and I can hear real, agonising pain in her voice.

'Could you forgive him, do you think?'

'God, I don't know. I don't think so. The dancer, stripper, whatever, was literally weeks after our honeymoon. He took Hannah to our house. To our bed.' She pauses, the barman is at the other end of the long shiny chrome bar talking to a customer. I can't make out the words but hear the friendly murmur back and forth. I wonder if he is a regular? Do hotel bars have such things? These places, purpose-built for anonymity.

'You don't think he killed them though, surely?'

She sighs. 'The police said he was reported for assault.'

'What?' My blood drops by several degrees. Assault?

'Yeah, at university. A girl he was seeing. He turned up at hers drunk.' She shrugs.

'God,' I say, my heart hammering, thinking of all the Friday and Saturday nights I'd spent indoors, shaved, made-up, ready and waiting at my flat hoping he'd call me or turn up at the end of the night. I was always pitifully, pathetically grateful when he did. Could I imagine him stepping over the line in an inebriated state? Yes, I think I could. It occurs to me that my version of him is not real. I am in love with a fantasy, something that doesn't exist. Perhaps overactive imagination runs in our family. My mother with her endless fears of germs and conspiracies. Me with my wishful thinking making indifference feel like love. It is too much; these thoughts are too agonising. I shake my head as if that can dislodge them, take them all away. I could tell her. Zoe. I could come clean. She'd end the friendship, of course, but at least she'd know. Instead, I ask, 'Did he ever do anything like that with you?'

'What? No, I'd never have put up with him booty-calling me at midnight.'

'Yeah, no, I get that.' I reach for my drink as a flush of shame warms my cheeks. I am the sad girl who will open the door after midnight. I ask her, 'Will you be okay at your parents'?'

'Yeah, Mum will calm down. My dad's cool, told me to run a mile.' She smiles. I think of Tom saying the same thing. We are not so very different it seems, Zoe and I. Not when you boil it all down, and that somehow makes the stabbing guilt worse. Lies will fester, dishonesty will shape you, irritate your mind and make you sorry you ever started.

We drink a lot more. At some point, I leave, though I don't know when. But I wake up on my sofa fully clothed and feeling shit and horrified because it's Monday.

CHAPTER THIRTY-TWO

SEB

The sun is rising as Seb is halfway around a three-mile circuit of Thames Park and he passes a gaggle of street drinkers, up early or perhaps yet to turn in. They are huddled around a bench. One woman flat on her back, her already red face turned towards the sun. He suspects she'll regret that later when her skin is crisped and peeling. Or maybe she won't feel a thing because that's what this lifestyle does. He scans the faces of the others in the group. Three men, another woman. None of them Charlie, which sends relief through him. He knows she's mainly in London these days. Her record has grown over the years and her name often comes up in the system.

He forces the thoughts from his mind, focused on one foot in front of the other while his mind flutters over the details of the case. It isn't Zoe who had committed the murders and he has a niggling feeling it wasn't James either. He understood well enough that the most obvious suspect was ordinarily the right one and if it had just been Hannah, he would have been quite sure it was James not wanting Zoe to find out. But he doubts Sam would have threatened to tell his wife; certainly, there was no evidence of that in the few exchanged messages. Nor were there any showing friction between James and Hannah, as far as Seb could see. James was a scumbag, no doubt about that, but Seb is starting to think he isn't their killer.

He found Ben's flash of jealousy interesting and the man in the video with Hannah could have been Ben or James; both looked alike and were tall. They couldn't see the colour of the man's hair in the footage, as he'd been wearing a hat, and it was possible he was slightly paunchier than both James and Ben… was it possible it was someone else entirely?

–

Seb is home, showered and sitting at the table with Val, Faye and Tilly. They are currently discussing Tilly's GCSE options. Seb has put his phone on silent and told the team he may be in slightly later as this has to be done. She can't decide between design and creative media. For Seb, it's glaringly obvious that design is Tilly's thing, plus the course now encompasses digital design and a lot of what is included in media. But he has learnt that what she really wants during these discussions is for the grown-ups to be a sounding board. She will, however, take questions from Faye. Largely, Seb thinks, because Faye has a way of framing them that sound like interest rather than steering. The discussion is over much faster than he'd anticipated and, actually, it *had* mainly been between Faye and Tilly. The outcome is Tilly will do design and Faye had asked the right questions to get her there.

Tilly leaves, Seb turns his phone back on to sound and it immediately rings. 'It's Lucy.'

'Go take it,' Faye says. 'We need to clean up anyway.'

Seb heads into the garden, closing the bifold doors behind him.

'Lucy, hi, everything okay?'

'Not really. Zoe Cowley has been in a car crash.'

'What, when?'

'First thing this morning. She was on her way to Reading, to her mum and dad's.'

'Is she okay?'

'No and worse still, it looks like her brakes might have been tampered with.'

'You're kidding?' His brain runs over this, turning it this way and that. 'How do you know?'

'Traffic police called out looked under the bonnet, usual procedure, saw a cable looked dodgy called in scene of crime officers. Deliberately cut they said.'

'Where was James?'

'At his parents', in bed nursing a hangover judging by the state of him, but the cable could have been cut before this morning. The guys have said the car might have managed a few short local journeys. She got into trouble on the motorway, hence why it's so bad.'

'Where are you?'

'At the hospital. He's here.'

'How does he seem?'

'Flustered, messed up. He looks a state, can smell the alcohol on him.'

'Her parents?'

'On their way now. James's parents are with him and I have to say his mother is a gigantic pain in the arse.'

'Oh?'

'Yeah, thinks we're picking on her precious son.'

'You've spoken to him?'

'I asked where he was last night and today.'

'He said at his parents?'

'Yes, Zoe left Friday actually, but has been at a hotel for the past few nights.'

'And the car?'

'Brake cables tampered with for definite as I've said. Zoe left the car there Friday and went for it Saturday. It was fine then or at least didn't malfunction, which fits as the car would have been fine for up to twenty miles but not much more. Finn and Harry are at the station. Harry's talking to local mechanics so we can get a clearer picture.'

'I'm on my way.'

'See you soon.'

CHAPTER THIRTY-THREE

STEVIE

I woke up to my alarm blaring at six o'clock. I am on my sofa, fully clothed. I have vague recollections of helping Zoe up two flights of stairs to her hotel room before us both realising there was a lift. This had caused much giggling. My next memory is Zoe sobbing and me pouring us drinks from the mini-bar fridge in her room which, judging by the pounding in my head, was most definitely ill-advised!

It's almost seven. I've drunk half a pot of coffee, taken two paracetamols and an ibuprofen and I still feel like shit. I have the children's cheerily wrapped workbooks on a stack on the table in my living room. It's Monday, these need to be marked; they should have been going back with them all today. I pack them into my satchel, willing the painkillers to kick in, wincing every time I move my head too fast.

My phone rings, making me jump. It's Mum. I watch her name flash for a few seconds before I finally make a grab for it.

'Mum, hi.'

'You sound tired,' she says.

'Yeah, I was up late marking,' I say, wishing this were true. It would certainly be better than *I was busy playing the role of loving friend to a woman I had sworn to hate and who I've come to care for.* My mother wouldn't understand anyway. No, maybe she would, hurting people who trust her by accident is, of course, her speciality. Her intentions hadn't been bad, she'd genuinely believed there was poison in certain foods and tap water. When she fed me bleach she'd done so thinking it would help, would clean me out.

'Tom said he saw you,' she says.

'Yes, we had brunch.'

'That sounds nice.' Her voice is floaty, the words falling into each other like dominoes cascading.

'You could have come along,' I say.

'You know I can't leave the house.'

'You *won't* leave the house. Not quite the same thing, is it?' I feel the flash of anger born of frustration which has plagued me for years where my mother is concerned.

'He said you're well.'

'I am.' I think of all the myriad ways that isn't true. 'You agreed to having the house cleaned?'

She sighs. 'I have because he's rented me a storage unit. He assures me he won't throw anything away. The place could do with a tidy up and a bit of decluttering. Did you hear about the girl, in the park?'

My blood seems to drop by various degrees. 'W...what?' Did Tom tell her about James, about this case? More of the precariously balanced cards seem to tumble. My face heats up at the thought of such an overt betrayal. I know he tells Mum when he sees me and gives her surface info but I assume a certain understanding and a decent level of need–to–know between him and his sister.

'How do you know about it?' I ask her.

'I do read the papers, Stevie, and I own a television.'

'Yeah, no, of course,' I say as my pulse slows and the adrenaline settles down, reminding me that I have the headache from hell. I look at my face in the mirror, could be worse. I grab my bag and coat, heading out the door; it's warm already, despite being so early.

'You don't walk through the park do you?'

'Not at night.'

'Okay, good.' I feel an ache at that, the worry in her voice. Ill, not bad, Michael is fond of reminding me.

'Are you, um, are you okay?' I splutter. 'In the house, I mean.'

'Yes, safer than I would be wandering around Thames Park, it seems.'

'Well, yes,' I agree. I get my mother's agoraphobia. Understand it more than I care to admit. I too can suffer from a strong temptation to just lock the door, perhaps crawl back into bed with the covers pulled over my head and shut out the world. With all its noises, people, and exhausting conversations. Michael always says this is a normal response to severe trauma. Fight or flight is exhausting and I can go into survival mode at the drop of a hat, and over the smallest things. I sail through life expecting the worst because I know all too well what can happen.

My mother has issues too. Though their root cause is a mystery to me, one I'd love to unravel. I've prodded Tom a few times but he simply told me their parents were lovely people at heart but not without troubles; there was their mother's OCD for a start and their dad had left when Mum was very young. I know Tom remained in contact with both of them until they died, though they, my grandparents I suppose, never spoke to each other again.

One of my mum's diagnoses is psychosis and I can see that now, looking back, certainly that's where everything started. There'd be times, weeks, months, a whole year even occasionally, where she was fine. Then she'd start sleeping less and doing random things, cleaning at two in the morning, stashing piles of papers and post that she believed couldn't be thrown away for fear of malevolent repercussions. It's what drove her Munchausen by proxy. It's what complicated the criminal aspects of her case. During the times when she was in a cycle of harming me, she was also in psychosis.

I knew when Tom came back to England and we became close that he loved my mother, 'despite all her wrongdoings'. But I still hated the thought of them both talking about me. I understood it, though, because I loved her too. I have many fond memories of her from when I was small. I know she loves me and I had found having no contact with her more painful than visiting. I wasn't sure why.

'You will take care?' Mum says now. 'Tom said you were fairly sensible about taxis and whatnot.'

'Is that ah… is that all he said?'

'About the girl?'

'Yes.'

'Pretty much.' A pause and then we both speak at once. 'You go,' I say.

'Be careful, was all.'

'Oh.' I find tears spring to my eyes. 'Yeah, of course.'

–

My phone pings as I step off the bus. I pull it out of my pocket, the headache finally subsiding thanks to the painkillers.

Ben: *Sorry about Friday, I'm working just by your school, can I buy you breakfast?*

Oh, yes please! I say. I've got an hour before I start and as it looks like I'll be using all of my spare time to go through marking; I may as well eat first.

CHAPTER THIRTY-FOUR

SEB

Seb hates hospitals. He's pretty sure no one actively likes them, but for him they hold some of his worst memories. This hospital in particular. He walks through A&E and can remember many occasions where he burst through the doors with Charlie in all kinds of states. The first time she overdosed wasn't even the worst. That time, at least, he had held out hope while he waited for her stomach to be pumped, for her to wake up so they could talk. So she could take in the shock and start to get better. What he hadn't expected was her grim-faced rage. She was, Seb had felt, just sorry she'd lived. He feels as if he's being haunted by her as he walks through the wide rubber-floored corridors, as if his past might reach out and grab for him in a second. It's not now, he reminds himself, taking deep breaths full of the odours of bleach and disinfectant so strong he can taste them on the tip of his tongue.

ICU is up two floors and he leaves the lift following the green signs which say they'll take him there. It's an area cut off from a lot of the hospital but joined to a surgical suite. He sees Lucy frowning at the coffee machine.

'Hey,' he says.

'Hey yourself. This looks like pish,' she says scowling at the machine.

'Go downstairs, there's a Starbucks.'

'You sure?'

'Yes.'

Lucy tilts her head towards a desk where nurses in mute-coloured Crocs are standing around talking in hushed tones. 'They know you're coming.'

'Right.'

'James, his parents and also Ben are in the family waiting room.'

'Thanks.'

'I won't be long.'

'It's fine, really.'

'Thanks. Do you want anything?'

'Not yet, let me get the lay of the land, eh?'

'Yeah, alright. Text if you change your mind, I'll likely be in the queue for a while.'

Once Lucy is gone Seb heads over to the gaggle of nurses and doctors, flashing his badge. A tall woman with dark hair scraped under a surgical cap and a white coat stands and says, 'Here about Zoe Cowley?'

'I am, yes. How's she doing?'

'Until she wakes up, which she may not at all, we can't assess her fully.'

'Okay, how likely is she to wake up?'

'Not very.'

'I see.'

'One of your scene of crime officers is here. I put him in a separate room, I'll take you to him?'

'Please,' Seb says. They walk down the corridor to a small room.

It's an SOC that Seb has met before; he stands, holding out a hand to Seb. 'Hello guv.'

'Marcus?' Seb asks.

The younger, smaller man grins. 'Good memory.'

'Pays in this job.'

'Well, yes.'

'Where's the rest of your team?'

'Some are at the crash site, but we've had the car towed now and they'll be following on back to the station.'

'Thamespark?'

'Yes, happened this end of the motorway.'

'And the brakes were definitely tampered with?'

'Yup. A real amateur job. Tears and cracks in the hoses can occur naturally but whoever did this had hacked straight through several cables.' Marcus shrugs. 'It's like they Googled how to stuff car brakes and just ran with it.'

'And that information is readily available?'

Marcus grins. 'All information is now available if you have patience and decent search terms.'

'Yeah I guess,' Seb says. It's true, but annoying. And worrying that reckless people had access to more info than was good for them. Teenagers too. He'd realised recently that at thirty-two he was probably part of the last generation who would have to spend big chunks of time looking things up and using actual books occasionally. And even he had grown up with a lot more digital life than people ten years his senior. The world had probably always moved fast, but since 2000 the rate was ferocious.

'You think they'd already been cut when she drove from her house to the hotel?'

'Yes, which would have been possible with that damage; it took a few miles for the final cable to snap.'

'So they could have been tampered with on her own drive?'

'Yep, or at the hotel, though we'll know that for sure because, lucky for us, the car park has a camera on it and we've got yesterday's footage. Could even have been done a while before that; seemingly she doesn't use the car that much. She normally drives to a Pilates class but walked the last few weeks.'

'Great.'

'It's not an exact science, but I can be fairly certain it was done in the last week.'

'Oh?'

'No dust build-up on the lead, which had been wiped clean.'

'Huh,' Seb says. His frown softens. 'So after our victim was killed.'

'Lucy said there'd been another two women?'

'Yes, both linked to Zoe's husband, James, both romantically involved.'

'He's your main suspect, the husband?'

'He's our only suspect so far though. I'm not sure what his motive for this could be. Either way, the dust thing helps timeline wise. Thanks.'

Marcus nods. 'It's the mundane things sometimes, isn't it?'

'I guess it is.'

'We'll be going over the entire vehicle piece by piece. I'll try and narrow down as much as I can.'

'Okay, let me know the outcome?'

'Of course. If that's all, I'll leave and get on with it?'

'Yes, do and thanks for waiting.'

'No problem.'

Seb's doubts about James as the perpetrator grow. If he has done this, it is sheer self-harm, and Seb feels that James is a man who wants to keep his life as hassle-free as possible. His mind goes over everything. The couple leaving the pub before Hannah appeared in frame. The man who could have been James but seemed bigger and had a hat on; he was the last person she spoke to, who was he? Could he have been the man with the other woman, earlier in the footage? Seb wasn't ruling it out. He couldn't rule anything out at this stage, but they needed a break and soon, because three deaths would make a serial killer and serial killers don't tend to stop of their own accord.

CHAPTER THIRTY-FIVE

STEVIE

'You look gorgeous.'

'Oh,' I say, feeling a grin creep over my face despite the wasps' nest of unhelpful thoughts that are swarming in and out of my mind. 'Thanks, I don't feel it.' Which is the honest truth. I feel like shit warmed up. Last night's too many vodkas feel thick and clogged on my skin, as if the alcohol is fermenting in my pores. But I've showered, styled my hair and used eye drops to take away the redness. I probably do look okay, overall. I notice as each year progresses, though, that hangovers are getting harder to deal with.

'Big Sunday night?' Ben asks.

'I mean, not big but I, uh, met a friend for a few brews which turned into more than was perhaps advisable. Let's just say not huge but bigger than expected, and lining my stomach beforehand would have been a good idea.'

'Ah,' he says. 'Let's get some grub in you now, then eh?'

We're at a little cafe five minutes away from school. It's got nice, subdued lighting; long floor-to-ceiling windows with black faded glass show the Thames out there in the background. But I hate eating with people, to be honest. Even at home with Angela I'd preferred it when we did mealtimes separately. It's leftover weirdness of course, from my mother's obsessions and preoccupations. A thing I've never felt comfortable enough to explain to anyone other than my therapists. And even there I edit what I say. It is hard to describe real hunger unless you've known it yourself; hard to put into words what it's like to know, or at least strongly suspect, food you're being offered is laced with something less than desirable, and to eat it anyway. When I was very small, we ate only healthy things and that was fine. Then Mum got it into her head that some of the food in supermarkets was poisoned. This resulted in trips to A&E when she would feed me so much saltwater I'd be throwing up for hours. Almost always I'd be released without treatment. I don't know exactly how that moved on to bleach and rat poison, but it did. And she'd wait until I was good and sick before seeking help. Initially, she told doctors it was the processed food they were giving me at school. When they finally worked out I was ingesting poison she started ranting about poisons and toxins in the water; her psychosis became apparent and that was that. I was taken away, she was hospitalised. But I'd had years of erratic behaviour, of learning to binge and purge. Years of faulty training to try and unlearn; something I haven't managed entirely. My relationship to food, let's say, remains erratic.

'The toasties are good here,' Ben tells me and just the thought of cooked rubbery cheese and heavy bread makes me feel sick.

'I think I'll just get toast. You're right, I am a bit delicate this morning.'

'Fair enough. Mind if I go for a full English?'

'Not at all.'

The food comes. Outside the street is quiet; it's not even eight yet.

Ben is doing impressions of a particularly difficult and super posh COO that he has to deal with at work fairly often. I laugh so hard it kicks off my headache again. I wince slightly.

He tilts his head. 'That bad, huh?'

'I, uh, don't normally overindulge,' I lie. I'm not an everyday drinker, I'm not even that frequent a drinker, but when I do start, more often than not, it leads to binges which can go on and on and floor me mentally, physically, emotionally. Michael is always quick to remind me that blackout drinking isn't a normal state to be in. I am always quick to wave away his concerns and downplay any and all tricky situations I get into.

I could, I think, stop seeing him now. It was a condition with my key worker when I left care at eighteen that I would have ongoing therapy. 'People who have gone through what you did, Stevie, don't recover overnight.' I'd kept it up so no one could say I hadn't dealt with my past. But it's been more than a decade, and I lie to him frequently. I often wonder if I am as well as I'll ever be. A thought that can fill me with dread if I let it.

'It's what weekends are for, eh,' Ben says.

'Maybe but not Sundays.'

'Nah, maybe not.'

'How was your Sunday?' I ask.

He sighs. 'Went to my 'rents' place for lunch.'

'Are you at your parents' often?' I ask. I know that Zoe and James go at least fortnightly.

'Yes, at least once a month sometimes every other week. We're all pretty close I guess.'

'That's nice,' I say.

'Well, it wasn't nice yesterday, after everything with James.'

'God yeah, must be rough.'

'It is. He's less of a dick when Zoe's around, I have to say.'

'You think he's a dick?' I ask. He's said that more than once. He's one of many people who have said it recently. I think, perhaps, they all have a point.

'He can be, yeah.'

'You get on, though?' Every time I broach this, I've noticed he sort of dodges a real answer.

'We get on well enough.' He takes a bite of a hash brown, chewing slowly. I nibble at my toast and find it far too dry. If he wasn't here, I'd spit it out. Instead, I swill it down with my now cold peppermint tea.

'We're very different, James and I,' Ben adds.

'Oh?'

'What he did to you...' He shakes his head. I feel the usual flush of shame heat my face at the thought of it. James's words, which felt like tiny precise stab wounds: 'Just a bit of fun, eh.' The man I'd loved so much that I had planned a whole fantasy future around him. A fantasy I'd watched him bring to life with Zoe. Only look at how that has soured. Look at the state she's in.

'Ah,' I say, 'it was years ago. Water under the bridge isn't it.'

'Still, it must have hurt.'

'It wasn't my best,' I acquiesce, honestly wishing at this point he'd just leave it. It's weird enough for me that I'm here with him, for reasons he has no idea about. But simply the fact that I dated his brother once probably makes this whole thing fairly strange.

He opens his mouth about to say something else when his phone, resting to the left of his plate, buzzes to life. He looks at it, frowning. 'It's my mum, do you mind?'

'No, of course.'

–

He leaves immediately after receiving the news. I pull out my phone, call work, tell them I'm sick, then I half walk, half run out of the cafe, my overfull satchel bashing on my back with each step.

I'm almost home, my head thrumming with a million thoughts. They cycle in and out of my mind like demented fish.

The brakes on Zoe's car failed shortly after she hit the motorway. She has been in a headlong collision with another car, as she lost control of the wheel.

I picture her veering wildly. I imagine the terror she must have felt for herself, of course, and for everyone else on the road too.

She sped across lanes and lost control. The other car slowed but not enough and she shunted and bounced across to the hard shoulder where she lost consciousness, slipping into a coma.

Now she was lying in a hospital bed, unresponsive, the Cowleys crowding around her and the police in attendance too. Ben had gone straightaway, apologising for having to leave so abruptly. 'Don't be daft,' I'd said and somehow when I spoke I sounded normal.

I'd spent most of last night with Zoe. She was hurt, seriously hurt. I was probably the last person to have seen her, wasn't I? That was bad on all kinds of levels. Really horribly, awfully bad.

How long, I think, as I turn the key to my flat wishing I could hide from this – how long until the police find out I was the last person to see her alive? How long before they connect me and James? How long before they find out I followed Hannah and Sam?

How long before this life I'd felt wasn't enough is suddenly and irrevocably snatched away from me?

CHAPTER THIRTY-SIX

SEB

Lucy is back, carrying a drink in a see-through plastic cup that is larger than her face and appears to have various layers. Seb looks at it dubiously. 'Jealous?' she asks.

'What is it?'

'Caramel frappe.'

'I thought you wanted coffee.'

'It is coffee,' she says very slowly, in a way that makes him think of Tilly.

'Right.'

She laughs. 'Bet you don't do bubble tea either?'

'Overpriced and weird.'

'But your daughter loves it, right?'

'Can't get enough.' Seb sighs.

'Middle age is looming, eh.'

'Oi.' He suppresses a smile. His old gittery is a running joke amongst his colleagues and, he thinks, between Faye and Tilly. He probably was a more mature thirty-two-year-old, but being a teen dad will do that to you, if you're doing it right. 'That tea has tapioca in it.' He screws up his nose.

'Yeah.' She sips noisily through a wide paper straw which Seb suspects will be soggy and unusable in seconds.

'We should all be using metal straws,' he tells her.

209

'Yes, I think you're right, but people will forget to bring them.'

He shrugs. 'It worked with shopping bags.'

'That's true,' Lucy relents. 'Maybe there is hope for the human race after all.'

'You have to hope, Lucy.'

'If not, I guess we'll either burn to death on a scorched earth or AI will bomb us out of existence.'

'Cheerful.'

Another shrug. 'But, maybe realistic.'

The doctor, a tall woman with dark hair and a serious face, is headed down the hall towards them. Seb nods at her while Lucy attempts to surreptitiously wipe a cream tash off of her face.

'Hello doctor.'

'Detective. I've just been in speaking with her family, or her family-in-law, I think.'

'That's right,' Seb says. 'Her parents are heading here from Reading now.' He cannot imagine how that journey is going but it must be awful to be even an hour away. 'Any change?'

'No, none and I'm afraid she's in a coma.'

'Outcome?'

'Not great,' she says evenly.

'Her family have been told this?'

'Her husband has as he is her next of kin. He's in there with her now.'

'Okay, thanks,' Seb says.

–

Seb pauses at the door to Zoe's room. It's quiet on this ward and he can hear the whoosh in and out of the machine that is currently breathing for Zoe. James is sitting next to his wife, her hand, stuffed full of needles and tubes, held in his. The man looks exhausted, red-eyed and panicked. His previously coiffed hair is a mess. The change in just a few days is astonishing. But stress will do that. All he needs to do is work out what James's stress is. Is it a murderer's remorse? Or a grieving husband's fear?

He clears his throat and James turns blank, glassy eyes to the door. 'Oh,' he says. 'You're here.'

'I am, yes.' The family haven't been told yet that there is foul play suspected. Seb will break the news, but he wants to see James's reactions and state of mind before he does so.

'Loads of your people seem to be crawling about. Traffic cops, they said.'

Seb moves into the room, pulling up a chair from the corner and settling in front of James. His eyes move back to his wife.

'It's my fault,' James says, his voice small.

'Oh?'

'If she hadn't been driving to Reading…' Not a confession to murder then, though Seb suspects this kind of guilt could eat away at you, especially as time passes. If Zoe doesn't wake up and if James didn't do this, which Seb is leaning towards as likely, he will have to live knowing the last exchanges with his wife were bitter and hurt.

Lucy pokes her head around the door. 'Alright guv.'

'Shall we step outside?' Seb says to James, going for an informal off-the-record chat. He doesn't want to have it in front of Zoe; who knows what she might be able to hear. 'Lucy can stay in here, keep an eye.'

'Okay.' James stands, arms hanging heavily at his sides. He looks back at his wife once, pain twisting his features.

Seb manoeuvres him to a set of four chairs in what he assumes is a waiting area. Two facing each other. He takes one side, gestures at James to take the other.

'When did you see her last?' Seb asks, keeping his voice moderate.

'Friday.' Three days ago.

'Where?'

'At home. We...' He pauses and his breath hitches slightly. Seb takes in the wobble in his slumped shoulders; he is a caricature of defeat and Seb believes he is affected by seeing Zoe here, in a bed diminished and in danger. But, he is also a possible murderer. A fact that Seb is keeping in the forefront of his mind. 'We argued,' James says.

'About?'

'Hannah, Sam, everything.' His voice is barely a whisper.

'How was it left?'

'That she hated my guts, and that I might well be a killer for all she knows.' James rubs the hand across his face. 'That, that made me cross. Though, I'd probably no right to it.'

'What did you say?'

'I said if that's how she felt we probably were better apart.'

'I see.'

James turns wide, desperate eyes on Seb now. 'I didn't mean it.'

Seb doesn't respond. He's not here to offer this man comfort, though he feels for him on a basic, human level. Knows very well how grief and regret can pick away at you. *Should haves, could haves, would haves* is how Faye refers to it. When Seb was telling her one night how he always felt like he'd let Charlie down, when he'd chosen their daughter over her, Faye had said that humans were the only species who felt guilt over and over again. 'It's crippling,' she'd told him, 'and it achieves nothing.' That had made a kind of sense. Much of what she said did. He'd been wary of getting into another relationship, wary of letting someone in, but each day that passes with Faye seems to get better.

'So you were angry with her?' Seb says.

'God, I don't know.' James runs his hand through his hair, which seems to be a nervous tic of his. 'Angry at the situation, at myself mainly.' He sighs.

'Was your relationship with Hannah your first long-term affair?'

James nods, looking absolutely defeated.

'How many other women were there?'

'I mean, a few days with Sam. *She* approached *me*, I might add. Zoe was away. I knew she'd never find out so… you know how it is.' James shrugs.

'I don't, no.'

James looks at Seb and gives him a grim smile. 'Like that, eh? Men like you who never get tempted. Like my brother Ben, whiter than white to the point that it's sickening.'

'It's sickening that not all men cheat on their wives?'

'That's not what I…' He falters. 'It may be hard for you to believe, detective, but I do love my wife and yes there's been the odd night here and there where things have occurred, but prior to Hannah no one I ever saw for long.' He says this as if it's some sort of achievement and Seb marvels, not for the first time, at how genuinely awful some people can be.

'So you love your wife, but on Friday you were angry with her?'

213

'I didn't want her to leave. Didn't think there was any need to tear down everything we'd built together over nothing.'

'So, Hannah was nothing.'

'Yes, no, that's not exactly what I meant. But I wouldn't have left Zoe for her if that's what you're getting at.'

'Did Hannah want you to?'

'We didn't discuss it.'

'Right, but she might have told Zoe?'

'She wouldn't have,' James rushes in.

'How can you be so sure?'

'She, uh, wouldn't have wanted to be thought of like that.'

'As someone's mistress?'

'Yes.'

'So you would have ended it?'

'I imagine so.'

'You imagine, but don't know for sure.'

'Well I was planning to do it. I knew it had gone too far.'

'Is that what happened that night James? Maybe you tried to end it? Maybe she fought you on it, threatened to tell Zoe?'

'No. For god's sake, no. You with this bloody… theory. She left happy. We'd had a nice time, hence me not breaking up with her. Why are you doing this now?'

'Zoe's crash wasn't an accident.'

James stares at Seb, jaw ajar, eyes open wide.

CHAPTER THIRTY-SEVEN

STEVIE

The minutes tick by, each one seeming to take far longer than I'd like. I sit on the sofa paralysed by fear, frozen into doing absolutely nothing. I wait an hour and decide I can probably take two more paracetamols, my raging headache chasing me like a spectre. The headache I have from the drinking last night with Zoe. My friend. The tears come and my hands shake as I unscrew the child lock. I spill drops of water from the glass, which land on the bare skin of my arms. I dab at it with kitchen roll, wiping my face, forcing my breath to calm down and elongate. I try hard to settle on the sofa, switching on the TV, turning to news channels.

Nothing is being reported about Zoe's accident, yet. No knocks at my door, yet. But, they will be coming, won't they? The police. They'll discover I was with her last night. Then they'll dig and find out I'm James's ex. I'll deny knowing about the connection. It's literally all I can do at this stage. Or maybe I could say once I realised it felt too awkward to mention and, also, what James and I had was nothing. That's true for him, of course, so he'll back me up.

I sink back into the sofa, pull out my phone and message Ben, *Are you okay?*

> Not really. Zoe's in a bad way.

> I'm so sorry; this must be awful for all of you.

I feel my own stab of concern for my friend, which I cannot, of course, relay to Ben.

> Yes, her parents are on their way.

> Let me know if I can help.

> Thanks, you are brilliant x.

I turn my phone over and feel a gasp starting in my chest. My head buzzes with a million stinking thoughts and I am overwhelmed. I squeeze my eyes shut, leaning forward.

> You are brilliant x

I'm not though, am I? I'm awful.

Terrible.

Repugnant.

I'm a wolf in sheep's clothing. I'm a lie. I am not what I pretend to be at all. I am no better than my own mother who made my mind wobble with all of her fictitious lunacy. Am I worse still, as I can't even plead insanity?

Not like her; she was out of control, yes, but it wasn't her fault. She has a mind that plays tricks on her, that takes reality and twists it until she no longer has any grasp at all on facts or truth. I'd convinced myself of something. I'd convinced myself James was the love of my life. But I knew really, didn't I, that he didn't feel the same. I saw the evidence, understood it on some level, and ignored it anyway. I have not acted with the best of intentions as my mother did when she tried frequently to wash me from the inside out. I just wanted him, and I was willing to go to any lengths to try to make it happen.

I shake my head as if it can wash away the thoughts and sit numb while they build up to an almost unbearable cacophony in my head. Each way this situation could play out spools in my mind's eye. No possible outcome seems good.

CHAPTER THIRTY-EIGHT

SEB

'We want to see their reactions.'

'They aren't all under suspicion though, are they?' Lucy asks Seb.

'What? No, of course not. But if any of them think James might be the culprit, or capable even, we might get a knowing look or a telling glance.'

'Yeah, okay,' Lucy says, then, 'Are you doubting him guv?'

He sighs. 'I don't think he'd have done this.'

'No, I think you have a point.'

'And if he didn't do this, well the chances of two murderers targeting the same group of women...'

'Women involved with James Cowley?'

'Right,' Seb agrees. 'He's the link, we know that much.'

'We do, yes. So how do you want to play it, with the families?'

'I'll give a quick intro and then I want you to do the talking, okay?'

'And you'll watch them?'

'Yes.'

'Right then, and do bear in mind that, despite James being unlikeable, her parents are here, and the rest of the Cowley family might be alright, too.'

'Yes. God, her poor parents.'

'Gently please. Let's respect their grief.'

'Yes,' she says, her face setting into serious lines.

'Ready?'

'Ready.'

They head down the corridor, the entire hospital like a furnace. Despite plenty of open windows, the building seems to trap the heat in. By the time they get to the small family room, Seb can feel sweat beading on his forehead. He pauses to press a tissue over his face then opens the door, stepping in ahead of Lucy.

Five faces turn to look up at him. A woman so like her daughter he immediately knows this is Zoe's mother. Next to her a man, ashen-faced with an arm over his wife's shoulder. Ben sits next to a stiff-looking woman with impeccable hair, clutching a Dior bag, and slightly further down the same sofa is James. Dishevelled and undone.

'Hello, for those of you I've not met, I'm DI Locke.'

'Fancy you turning up here in these circumstances,' the woman with the perfect hair and upright back says, her lips joined in an annoyed button of disapproval.

'Mrs Cowley?'

She nods, looks away.

'I'm sorry to meet you like this, of course, but I can assure you we wouldn't be intruding at this time if we didn't have to.' He pauses for one beat, two. 'My sergeant here will talk you all through what's going on and hopefully you'll understand why we are here, now.' He turns to the other couple. 'You must be Zoe's parents?'

The woman nods, her mouth wobbling. The man looks dazed as if he has been caught in some dreadfully surreal and awful film. Which, Seb knows, is how it must feel to him. 'This must be a very difficult time so we'll try and keep everything succinct. This is my sergeant, Lucy Quinn.'

Lucy steps forward. James shifts uncomfortably; Seb sees his eyes drawn to the door. Seb thinks he hasn't told his family yet, about it not being an accident; if he had, they'd have known why there was such a strong police presence. Seb is no longer convinced he's their killer but he is almost one hundred per cent certain that James is a coward.

Lucy starts speaking. 'As you know, Zoe's car crashed on the motorway earlier today. What you may not know yet is that the brakes on Zoe's car had been tampered with.'

Seb studies each face, moving his eyes quickly between everyone. Mrs Cowley is glaring at her son, James. Ben has moved slightly closer to his mother, putting an arm out behind her shoulders. He also throws a hard look at James and says, 'What the hell.' Zoe's mother has started crying. Awful silent tears that peel away mascara and leave grey trails down her cheeks.

Zoe's father is open-mouthed. 'She... what... why would anyone do something like that?'

Seb steps forward again. 'That, Mr Gerard, is what we are working diligently to find out. What I can tell you is that we think this incident may be connected to the two murders we are already investigating.' Zoe had told them she'd filled her parents in on what was happening, but still, his words hit like a bomb.

Mrs Gerard stands up, turning to James. 'Your bloody little tarts. You, you're the suspect, you're the link.'

Her husband stands behind her, placing his hands on her shoulders. 'Ann,' he says, his voice carrying a loaded warning.

She turns to her husband. 'Oh god.' Her hands press against her mouth and she makes a sort of gasping sound. She turns back to James. 'We liked you. Loved you, even. When she called me at the weekend I asked her what she'd done to cause you to stray.' Her eyes are wild, darting from person to person. 'What kind of mother asks that or even thinks it.' And she is gone, huge gulping, shoulder-shuddering sobs. James's eyes are carefully on the floor. His mother and Ben sit as far from him as they can. The Gerards cling to each other, both lost in their own grief.

'I wouldn't,' James says. 'I would never have hurt her.'

'Well you did hurt her, didn't you?' Zoe's dad says. 'I don't think you're capable of murder, though.'

'Thank you Phil...'

Mr Gerard holds a hand up to silence him. 'But you hurt her, that much is obvious, and you did it without a second thought, from what I can tell. Not once but twice you betrayed her and your vows. The truth, James, is that if she hadn't been leaving you, hadn't had to head home again, we might not be here and you...' He pauses. 'You'll have to live with that.'

James seems to sink into himself, crumpling back into the sofa. Seb sees his face flush bright red. He doesn't feel sorry for him. James is only concerned with himself. That much is obvious to anyone with eyes.

Phillip Gerard turns to Seb. 'She'll pull through this. She's strong.' Seb doesn't think this is likely, but knows better than to respond. 'You find out who did it, okay?'

'I intend to.'

CHAPTER THIRTY-NINE

STEVIE

The afternoon has turned into early evening. I've finished my marking, at least, and have spent most of the afternoon cleaning my flat with one eye on my phone. When it rings, I jump out of my skin. Ben. My heart hammers and I swear I can feel the blood rushing around my body.

'Ben, hi,' I say, forcing my voice to remain low and concerned.

'How was work?' he asks and I realise I haven't told him I'd come home. What reason could I give? He'd seen me so knew I wasn't sick.

'Fine, not that that matters right now. How is your sister-in-law?'

'No one really knows.'

'God,' I say, with memories of Zoe and I laughing side by side as we worked on our cores. Drinking coffee in the gym's shit cafe with her and realising, months in, that I liked her. Really liked her. We've been 'friends' for over a year now and those Thursday mornings have set me up well. 'I hope she pulls through,' I tell Ben, the emotion thick to my own ear.

'Me too; she's a good person.'

'I bet.'

'The police are here.'

'Bit off-key in these circumstances isn't it?' I say, my heart picking up speed again, hammering away in my chest as images of my hands held in front of me in cuffs assault my mind. Wouldn't that be hilarious, if I'd escaped the cloying prison my mum set me only to end up in a real one. No, I push that thought away. I've done nothing wrong. Well, I've done nothing illegal, anyway.

'Someone tampered with her brakes, Stevie,' Ben says, his voice low with shock.

'Oh my god,' I manage, the words falling into each other. 'How awful.'

'Yes,' he says. 'I need to be here, to support Mum and Dad, if not my pillock of a brother.'

'Yeah, I understand that,' I tell him. Adding, 'You're a good brother, I hope James knows that.'

'Ha. I'm a good son, more like. If it was just him I'd have been tempted to leave him to it,' he says, hot anger giving the words some bite. 'None of us would be here, would we, if it wasn't for him. Zoe wouldn't be lying in intensive care.'

'It's a horrible situation, Ben, and being in hospitals is always grim,' I say. Just before Mum stopped going out altogether, she had a fall that resulted in a broken hip and later surgery. I'd rushed to the hospital and she'd been panicked and incoherent. She'd accused us all of trying to poison her; she'd accused me, fear making her unpleasant, colourful language pelted at me like snooker balls in a sock. I still didn't leave. I'd spent the night in the awful waiting room, spread out over three plastic chairs. I'd regretted it when I woke up and every bone in my own body seemed to hurt. I'd woken up angry at her, meaning to go and tell her off.

But, then I'd been led in, seen her small, frightened, bewildered and wide-eyed, and I'd felt... sorry for her. This woman who'd sung to me, held me, taken me on walks and made me laugh so hard sometimes I could hardly breathe. I could see she was damaged, broken by her own mind. Once we got her home, she was initially visited by nurses, then carers. Then just me, and she hasn't left the house since.

Tomorrow, the cleaners will finish at her place. Tom suggested I pop over one evening. 'We could all get a takeaway,' he'd said. I told him I'd consider it. Not wanting to divulge the fact I didn't tend to eat food if my mother was near it.

Plus, I'm not sure I wanted to see them together. I consider Tom my uncle, my family. But first he was her brother.

'I wish I didn't have to be here, to be honest,' Ben says now. 'Which must sound dreadful.'

'I get it,' I tell him and I do.

As soon as I hang up, I call Michael's office, asking if he can squeeze me in for an emergency appointment. He says he can fit me in at 8:30, the end of his day.

–

As I leave my house, stepping out into the evening air, still warm but cool enough for a jacket, I feel real fear. The police are at the hospital. Zoe is in intensive care. Hannah Smith is dead. Sam Carmichael is dead. Somehow, without any desire to be, I am connected to everyone in that scenario. Worse, I'm now also connected to James's brother. We've been on a few dates. It won't take much digging, will it, for me to be uncovered.

All that innocent until proven guilty stuff is fine, but teachers are held to a higher scrutiny aren't they? Who wants to leave their child with a possible murderess?

Even thinking the word makes me feel the cold, hard stone of fear in my gut all over again.

I arrive just on time. Michael appears from his small room, which is too comfortable to be called an office exactly, and greets me in reception with a slight nod. 'Hello Stevie.'

'Thanks for fitting me in,' I say. My eyes flick to his receptionist's desk.

'Jean's gone home,' he says. 'Come on in.' His voice, as always, is even and calm.

I go in and sink onto the familiar couch, my hand immediately feeling along the ridged edge of the cushion for the loose thread I know is there. I see him watching and pull my hand away, forcing it into my lap, holding it still with its pair.

I came here to speak, to confess, to offload. To, I suppose, somehow share my worry with the hope that perhaps in sharing it may either lessen, unlikely, or perhaps a solution might be found.

'Was there something specific Stevie?'

I take a deep breath and avert my eyes so I am looking not at him but slightly over his shoulder, to the window which leads out onto the street, so familiar after more than a decade coming here.

'Do you remember me mentioning that girl, young woman I suppose, who died in the park?'

'I do, yes.'

'She was my ex's mistress.'

'Your ex?'

'James,' I say, giving him a moment to register.

'I see,' he says. 'Did you know this, when you found out about her death?'

'Yes,' I say, my voice clearer and stronger than I feel.

'Did you know her, Stevie?'

'I was...' I swallow and feel as if I am drinking phlegm. 'I was following her.'

'The woman who was murdered?'

'Yes.'

'Why were you following her Stevie?'

'I knew.'

'About?'

'Her and James, the affair.'

'I see.' There is silence then. Well, not quiet silence because my breath is hard, slightly laboured. 'Did you tell the police?'

'No.' A tear escapes and runs down my cheek. 'The night she died, I saw her going into his house.'

'You still watch him?'

'Yes.' I swipe at the tear.

'You told me you'd stopped,' Michael says, his voice even. There is no accusation in his words. No judgement. I realise there never really has been. I was the one who'd decided he couldn't help, couldn't understand. I was the one who felt like I just didn't need this stuff. Yet here I am, seeking refuge.

'I lied. I lie all the time.'

'Why?'

I shrug. 'I don't know.'

'Do you not find these sessions useful?'

'I don't know. I feel like when I've come at least I've tried.'

'Tried what?'

'To be honest, at least in some things.'

'But you protected this aspect of your life?'

'Protected?' I laugh. 'What do you mean?'

'By not telling me, you didn't need to interrogate it, therefore the behaviour is protected, by you.'

'Oh,' I say, feeling like he's punched me in the mouth.

'You've done remarkably well, Stevie. You didn't have the easiest start and yet you've made a good life for yourself.'

'Which I've put at risk.'

He ignores that but leaves a moment's silence before he speaks again. 'You saw her go into his house. Did you see her leave?'

'No. But I went out and got drunk.'

'Where did you go?'

'Into town, then to the Amersham Arms, right by the park. Right by where she was killed.'

'What did you do?'

'It's… it's hazy but I hooked up with a guy, Joel. I've seen him since. We, uh, went into the park and you know.'

'You slept with him?'

'Yes,' I say. 'Though I don't remember it and he left me at about one at home. He saw me go in.'

'Do you remember that?'

'Not really,' I say miserably.

'Are you blackout drinking often?'

'No,' I say quickly. 'But sometimes.'

'Spending?'

'I stole my mother's credit card details to pay off my debts.'

'Okay.'

'I'm sorry.'

'You don't need to apologise. I'm not judging you. I just want to help you see the situation clearly. Tell me where it's at now, if you can. You've been following James for how long, do you think?'

'Since he moved back here; about two and a half years.'

'How did it start?'

'I realised he'd moved in to that house. I told you that.'

'I remember.'

'I know you said it was just coincidence but I… I thought it was a sign.'

'Of what?'

'That we were meant to be together.'

'We've talked about magical thinking.'

I manage a half smile. 'I knew you'd say that.'

'I'm sorry Stevie, this is tough stuff.'

I burst into tears. He slides the box of tissues across to me and I take one, dabbing at my face, shoulders quivering but the sobs subsiding.

'It gets worse,' I tell him.

'Go on.'

'There was another woman, this stripper, he spent a few days with. I, uh, knew about her too.'

'Because you'd followed him?'

I nod. 'He checked into the club on Facebook. I went down there, saw him leave with her. Sam, her name was.'

'Okay.'

'She died.'

'When?'

'Just after he and Zoe got married, so two years. Same way as Hannah Smith.'

'Stevie,' he says and for the first time ever I hear real exasperation in his voice.

'I know. That's not everything. I started attending his wife's Pilates class. Then, we became friends.'

'Did she know who you were?'

'I gave her my real name. She must have mentioned me to James.' He waits, blinks. 'But no,' I add. 'I think he hardly remembers me to be honest.'

'Oh, Stevie.'

'She was in a car crash. It looks like it wasn't an accident and I was the last person to see her.'

He blinks again, taking in what I've said. 'Is she dead?'

'No, but she's in a coma. It doesn't look good, does it? James was a suspect, the primary suspect I think, in Hannah's death. And I went for a drink with his brother.'

'James's brother?'

'Yes.'

'They will find all of this out Stevie.'

'I didn't kill anyone,' I say, my voice high, my cheeks heating up. 'After Hannah, when I couldn't remember anything, I even thought maybe, maybe it could have been me. So I won't blame you, wouldn't think less of you if that's what you thought.'

'I don't think that.'

My shoulders slump, my whole body seeming to deflate. It mattered to me what Michael thought, what he thinks. I say, 'It doesn't look good though, does it?'

'No, you need to go and talk to the police.'

'I know,' I say. 'I also know that they might come here.'

'They might and anything I know that is linked to an active investigation like this...'

'Isn't protected, I know. I understood that when I walked in today and told you this.'

'So you know I'll have to talk to them if they come to me?'

'I do, and it's fine.'

'Tell them the truth.'

'That I'm a mad stalker?'

'That you had a hard time growing up and struggle sometimes with your mental health, but that you are working on it and are willing to cooperate.'

'Okay.'

'This is brave.'

'What is?'

'Coming to see me.'

'It's desperate.'

He smiles then. 'Sometimes desperation is a gift.'

I roll my eyes and he laughs, actually laughs.

'How do you feel about James now?'

'I know I'm not in love with him,' I say quickly. Realising it's true. 'What we had was never real.'

'No, but it represented something to you.'

'Normality,' I say. 'It's all I ever wanted.'

He shrugs. 'It's overrated. What you have is better; you have resilience.'

I sigh.

'Go to the police.'

CHAPTER FORTY

SEB

The mood back at the station is subdued. Seb is going over the notes that the scene of crime officers have sent over. What is clear to him is that the person who'd cut the brakes was no expert, but that hadn't stopped them almost causing Zoe's death.

Seb has called a briefing and his small team file in. He updates them all.

Ken asks, 'Will she make it? Zoe Cowley?'

'It's unlikely.'

Ken nods, solemn-faced.

Jackie is updating her superiors; Seb had spoken to her on the phone as he drove from the hospital to the station. Lucy is back at the hospital for now, just in case. Jackie said what Seb already knew and what he tells his team now: 'If Zoe doesn't make it, we're looking at three deaths, and three deaths makes our perpetrator a serial killer.' That rare beast that populates TV shows and films. 'We won't be saying that publicly of course,' Jackie had added.

'No, and Zoe's death is quite different to the other women, it's far less personal but really, what are the chances of three deaths where all victims are connected having two perpetrators.'

'Low, but not impossible,' she'd said, 'but reason enough to avoid panic inducing language.'

'I think that's right,' Ken says. 'The link is James Cowley but is he the culprit?'

Seb shakes his head. 'Yesterday I'd have said probably, now I'm not so sure, he had motive for Hannah and Sam but the motive was Zoe not finding out. Why harm her? But you are right, Ken, that he is the link.'

'Do you think they thought they'd get away with it, Zoe? That we wouldn't have been able to tell?' Harry asks, frowning at Seb.

Seb shrugs. 'Maybe. Or they didn't think that deeply about it, or maybe they just panicked. It's possible we are dealing with a truly disturbed mind and that that mind is unravelling. It could be someone suffering from psychosis or some sort of mania which would account for the carelessness.'

'True,' Ken says, 'though for now they've managed to evade detection over three crimes.'

'Yes,' Seb says. This case is making his brain hurt. 'Right now, we have Zoe's phone, and we're in?' He looks at Finn who nods. 'We are, yes, far easier than with Hannah's as James had the password.' The handset itself had been smashed in the crash but they'd managed to carefully remove the SIM, put it in a different handset and Finn was finally into her messages and call log lists. In so many ways, police work was easier now. Everyone left a digital trail and these small handheld computers contained so much information about an individual that it was almost like having a soul laid bare for all to see. Seb often found the level of detail jarring. He wasn't an avid social media user, and didn't have any devices at home like an Alexa or a Google Home. He'd used them too many times to gather information to be comfortable with one sitting on his kitchen side or his bedroom, or anywhere else for that matter.

'Going through all of Zoe Cowley's recent interactions is our immediate focus and Ken, you are right, I'm less certain about James now,' Seb says, 'but we're not at a stage where we can rule him out altogether.'

'I don't see why he'd have hurt Zoe.' Harry shrugs. 'Not when he'd so obviously be caught.'

'Maybe so, but like I said, we are ruling nothing out. Now let's get to it.'

–

'Guv.' Finn stands at the edge of Seb's desk.

'Yes, Finn?'

'I'm into Zoe's messages. Looks like a mate went and met her at the hotel on Sunday night.'

Seb gets up, following Finn back to his desk. He stands behind the younger man and reads the messages over his shoulder.

'Ken,' Seb says.

'Yes guv.'

'Bring up the notes from Lucy and Harry's interview with Ben Cowley, would you.'

Ken taps at his computer. 'Okay, got them.'

'He talks about going for a drink with someone near the end of that chat, a woman who had previously dated his brother?'

Ken scans the text in front of him. 'Yes, got that here.'

'The woman's name?'

'Stevie Gordon,' Ken tells him.

'The messages to Zoe are from a Stevie,' Seb says. 'Finn, can you trace her from her phone number.'

'Doing it now sir.'

'Why the hell would Zoe be in contact with her husband's ex?' Harry asks, frowning.

'I have no idea,' Seb says.

'Yes will do.'

'What do you think it means?' Finn asks Seb.

'I don't know, but it's an odd connection. Too odd to just be a coincidence. And also, generally exes are just that, aren't they, so why would Zoe turn to her, especially at a time like this?'

'Yeah, it's weird,' Finn agrees.

'Hmm.' He turns over various possible scenarios and dismisses them. 'Did Ben mention her being mates with his sister-in-law?'

'No.'

'I didn't think so, which leads me to think, perhaps he doesn't know.'

'Or they could be different Stevies?'

'It's an unusual name.'

'It is, yeah.'

'But you never know.'

'No.'

He stands. 'I'll go back to the hospital. Go see James. Finn, get me as much information as you can about her, okay?'

CHAPTER FORTY-ONE

SEB

They find James in the corridor staring absent-mindedly at a drinks machine. Seb's first thought is that he looks awful. A far cry from the dapper man Seb had met only a few days ago. He supposed, given the circumstances, James probably was a wreck.

'Mr Cowley,' Seb says and he turns to look at him. Seb throws Lucy a quick glance.

She says, 'Why don't you sit down with DI Locke. I'll get you a drink, eh.'

He nods. Forlorn, hands dangling by his sides.

'Coffee?' Lucy asks.

'Please.' He looks, thinks Seb, like a bewildered little boy.

James slumps onto one of the hard-backed chairs, running his hand through his hair. A gesture Seb has come to understand is like a nervous tic.

'Where is everyone else?' Seb asks.

'In the family room. I, um, well her mum, Ann… we had a few words. I said I'd step out.'

'It's a difficult time, emotions will be running high.'

'Yeah. Can see why they don't want to lay eyes on me though, can't you?'

Seb doesn't respond, because of course he can. If Tilly married an idiot like James, he'd be livid.

Lucy comes back, placing a mug of coffee in James's hand. 'I added milk and sugar, figured you might need it.'

'Yeah,' he says. 'Thanks.'

'Are your parents still here?' Seb asks him.

'No, nothing they could add by being here.'

'No,' Seb agrees. 'Your brother?'

'He drove them and said he'd come back.'

'How does he get on with Zoe's parents?'

'Yeah, they like him, always have. I think they'd probably have preferred him for a son-in-law to be honest.'

Seb ignores this comment. He'd actually started to feel a bit sorry for James himself, but finds the sympathy evaporates a bit with James's evident self-pity.

'You dated a woman called Stevie Gordon?'

James looks at him, wrinkling his nose. 'What?'

'Stevie Gordon, you dated her?'

'Like, a million years ago.'

'About four, we think?'

'Okay four. I knew her from school.'

'Were you together then?'

'Together?' He chuckles. 'I mean, I knew her when we were at school, we were seeing each other for a bit, like kids do. Then when I moved back here we hung out a few times.'

'Hung out?'

'You know.'

'I don't. Were you romantically involved?'

'Yeah, I guess.'

'You guess?'

'We hooked up.' He pauses, takes a sip of the coffee.

'Was it serious?'

236

He shrugs. 'Not for me. She was alright, easy-going, not too much hassle, but it probably went on for longer than it should have.'

'How so?'

'Um, I don't know. I, uh, got the feeling she was fairly into me.'

'You didn't reciprocate?'

'No. But like I said, she was easy-going.'

'So, what, you kept stringing her along?'

James sighs. 'She wasn't complaining.'

'Your brother Ben mentioned he'd seen her recently?'

'Oh yeah, that's right, I vaguely recall him saying they went for a drink. Fair play to him if he doesn't mind seconds.' He smirks when he says it and Seb feels a spike of annoyance. 'She was a proper good-looking lass,' he says as if that's the main point.

'You were cool with it?'

'What?'

'Your brother going for a drink with her?'

'Yeah, of course, I don't care either way.' Seb believes this.

'She knows your wife.'

James smiles now, shaking his head. 'I don't think so.'

'Did Zoe ever mention a friend from her Pilates class?'

His mouth falls into a comical O. 'Yeah she did. I even remember thinking it was funny she had that name, now you mention it.'

'But it didn't occur to you that it might be the same woman?'

'No, not really, why would it? That would just be weird.' He seems to realise where this conversation is going. He murmurs, 'What the fuck.'

'When you say she was more into you than you were her, how into you?'

'Well, I, uh, cheated on her. A couple of times actually. Didn't even hide it really, figured that would be the end of it, but she didn't bat an eyelid.'

'She was in love with you?'

'Yeah, I guess, looking back.'

'When did you break up?'

'I left to go travelling, seemed a natural cut-off point.'

'You've not seen her since?'

'No, not even thought about her.'

Seb sits back, folding his arms, and glances at Lucy, who leans forward.

Lucy says, 'What sort of a person was she?'

James puts the now empty cup down on the arm of the hard-backed chair. Seb notices a slight tremor in his hand. 'She was nice, sweet. A teacher, little ones I think.'

Lucy smiles. 'You'd need a lot of patience for that job, eh?'

'Ha, yeah, I guess so.'

'And you said you cheated on her?'

'Well, like I said, we weren't super serious or anything and we knew each other from when we were really young. We linked up again just as I was back from university; she was doing some sort of training year.'

'In the school?'

'Yeah, I think so, is that a thing?'

Lucy nods. 'I believe so. I think all teachers have to do it to qualify.'

'Right, so she was doing that.'

'So, she'd also just finished studying?'

'Yeah but she went to uni here, same place she grew up.'

'Oh? That's unusual.'

'I suppose it is. Might have been financial.'

'She lived with her parents?'

'No, there was some trouble back at school. She had a foster family maybe, I can't remember details. But now, or at least the last time I saw her, she had a flat that I think was maybe council or housing association or something.'

'Oh really?' Lucy asks and he nods. She swaps a look with Seb who comes back in.

'That's unusual, young woman out of university getting social housing.'

James shrugs. 'Got the impression she'd been there a while. Like I said, she was being fostered, so probably trouble at home growing up.'

'But you don't know what the reason was?'

'No.' He shakes his head.

Seb takes that in. Assesses it. This man had been 'dating' this woman for something close to a year, from the sounds of it a woman he'd had some involvement with whilst they were at school and whilst she was in care. She'd have been vulnerable, Seb imagines. Especially if she got social housing at a young age.

'Okay,' Seb says, standing up. Lucy follows suit.

'That's it?'

Seb raises an eyebrow in question.

'Well, what is it?' James asks, confidence creeping back in his voice. 'Do you think she's somehow involved in this? Maybe she's gone all Glenn Close or something?' That's accompanied by another one of his irritating smirks. The thin shreds of sympathy Seb still had slip away. He gives James a tight smile. 'Like I said, we'll be in touch.'

'Yeah alright, look forward to it,' James says, voice dripping with sarcasm.

Seb's phone buzzes. 'DI Locke.'

'Hi it's Marcus. I just wanted to let you know that we are fairly certain the car was tampered with at the hotel, rather than on her drive.'

'Huh.'

'Helpful?'

'Very.' Seb says, and it is, though it does make it a lot less likely that it was James who did the tampering. 'Thanks Marcus.'

CHAPTER FORTY-TWO

STEVIE

I wake up completely unrested. In fact, I think I'm more exhausted than I was when I finally turned the light out at three a.m. and decided I'd at least try and get some sleep. I did, but it came in thin, anxiety-laden slivers. Now I'm headed to work, jumpy from too much caffeine and weighed down by my overly heavy bag.

I wait for the bus. Perspiration jumping up across my entire body, the sweat worsened by the tiredness. By the time I get to school, I know I must be a complete mess. I put the bag down in my classroom and head to the loos. I manage to settle my humidity-frizzed hair with water and spray deodorant, aware still of a faintly stale tang beneath it.

But I finally feel like I can probably do the day. The classroom is ready. I can hear the children's happy hollers outside and, as usual, their raised, excited voices give me a spike of joy. I glance at my phone and see there is a message from Ben; I'll have to read it later. I slide the phone into my bag.

The door opens and the children file in, a long wriggly line of arms and legs. Each child drops their bag in a large basket by the door and each time a bag drops I feel it like a death knell, my headache aggravated by each thump.

'Okay children, let's take our seats.' My voice is steady, calm and welcoming, but my stomach feels like jelly.

Zoe is in hospital, in a coma. Someone put her there deliberately. I was the last person to see her, my number is on her phone, many messages swapped, and several phone calls. I desperately need to go in and talk to the police, had said to Michael I'd do so, but I haven't yet. The thought of it hangs over me.

'Miss, miss.' A small hand waves in the air.

'Yes, Jackson?' I say, my smile bright as everything inside of me smashes into a million pieces.

'Can I go to the loo?'

'Yes,' I say, holding down my irritation that he didn't do it prior to class starting. I feel bad as he stands and heads out, throwing me his wide gummy smile. But he hates the bathrooms when they are heaving and normally this wouldn't bug me in the slightest. It's not him, of course. It's not my class or my job bothering me.

I swallow, my throat feeling lumpy. 'Let's get our pencils out and start writing our morning thoughts,' I tell the children. I start this habit at the beginning of every year and we do this first thing each morning. To begin with, most of the children can't really write. Lots manage their name, some draw pictures. I assure them there is no right or wrong, it's just a place to record our thoughts. We are now heading towards Easter and most are fairly proficient writers. The head had frowned when I started doing this but three classes on she can't deny the benefit of it.

I'm good at my job. In fact, I love my job. The children are all quiet now, heads bent over their writing books, small faces scrunched up in concentration.

I have, I think, risked my career. For the first time, I think about what Michael said back when I'd been honest about James and my dalliances into his life.

'This obsession, Stevie,' he'd told me, 'isn't really about him. It's about you trying to fix yourself, and if you don't let it go, it will cause you problems.'

'When we were together,' I'd replied, speaking very slowly as though slowing down my words might make him understand, 'I *was* fixed.'

'Another person can't mend you.'

I'd sulked I suppose. And Michael had sat silently waiting for me to speak again. I spent the session in stony, angry silence. But when he raised it again I said, 'There may be some truth to what you're saying.' Though I didn't think that at all.

'You need to be careful, Stevie. Looking back at periods of your life through rose-tinted glasses will make living in the present almost impossible.'

'Yeah,' I'd agreed. 'I get it.'

'It's a sure way to lose the good things you've built, don't take them for granted.'

'Yeah, no, you're right and I won't.'

Now, as Jackson wanders back in with his gappy smile and a little wave, settling at his desk to update his thoughts, I finally understand what Michael meant. I have built a good life for myself despite my lack of gratitude for it and now it is in jeopardy.

CHAPTER FORTY-THREE

SEB

Ben frowns at Seb, looking from him to Lucy and back again. They are back at their offices. Today they were met by the receptionist, who was busily tapping away on her keyboard. It was much milder since the heatwave seems to have ended, and the area doesn't feel so much like a little oven. They are sat at the table in the middle of the room again. James isn't there and, according to Ben, was doing 'fuck all work wise right now'.

'How would Stevie know Zoe?' Ben asks. They have checked and confirmed that the phone number from Zoe's contact is indeed the same number that Ben has for her.

'They did a Pilates class together,' Seb says. His mind whips over the messages they'd all spent yesterday and this morning reading.

'Well, it's a small town, isn't it?'

'Still,' Seb says. It's a smallish town, he supposes, but ever growing as a borough with the university and expanding train line.

'Maybe she didn't realise Zoe's James was James.'

'She'd have recognised Zoe's surname though, wouldn't she?'

'Maybe she didn't know it.'

'It's possible,' Seb relents.

'That'll be it, then,' says Ben, and Seb wonders if he is just naturally optimistic or actually a bit silly.

'You reconnected with her recently?'

'Yeah, like I said, I bumped into her.'

'Where?'

'Oh, Fengates Road, near her school I think.'

'She's a teacher?' Seb asks, though of course they already know this.

'Yeah,' Ben smiles, 'seems to really love it too.'

'And you asked her out?'

'Yeah.'

'Did you always have romantic feelings for her?'

'I suppose I did. We were actually in the same year at school. I thought she was pretty even then, but she was my brother's girlfriend.' He shrugs.

'So out of bounds.'

'Well, exactly.'

'Were you jealous?'

'What?'

'Then, of your brother and Stevie?'

'Oh, I see. I mean, no not exactly jealous, but annoyed when they started seeing each other again.'

'Annoyed why?'

'Well, like I said to you the other day.' He nods at Lucy. 'James was pretty shitty to her first time round. I figured it'd be more of the same and I was right. She's nice, sweet.' He smiles. James had also described her as 'sweet'. A sweet harmless schoolteacher who was oddly still involved in many aspects of her ex's life. Her ex whose other romantic partners kept turning up dead.

Seb nods as if he understands exactly what Ben means, but he makes a mental note of the anger evident in Ben's tone and the rising red on his cheeks. Jealousy, Seb knows, can cause all kinds of problems. Jealousy can sometimes motivate murder. 'Must have been tough to witness, especially if you liked her.'

'Yeah, it was but' – another shrug – 'that's how James is with women.'

'He was the same with Zoe?'

'Yeah.'

'You liked her too?'

'Not in that way.' Ben frowns.

Seb brings the conversation back to topic: 'What's Stevie like?'

Ben smiles and it immediately takes his face back to its usual softer state. 'Like I said she's sweet. Like honestly, you should hear her talking about her class.'

'Has she mentioned James?'

'Not really, I mean obviously it's come up a few times, but it's old news. Or I thought it was.' He pauses, running a hand through his hair, a gesture that reminds Seb of James. They look very alike but are quite different characters, he thinks. Though he's now wondering if Ben's nice guy act is hiding simmering anger. 'You think she befriended Zoe what, to get info on him?' he asks now, not silly at all then.

'We don't know,' Seb says. 'It's possible she didn't realise at first and then felt awkward mentioning it.' Seb feels like this is unlikely. Especially given that she's now 'seeing' James's brother, who she just happened to cross paths with. 'You definitely bumped into her by accident?'

'Yeah,' Ben says, then sighs. 'Okay, no, not actually. I, uh… knew she worked at that school.'

'Right.'

'I saw her a couple of weeks ago, walking by the river, and remembered how much I liked her, you know. Figured, well, exactly as I said, her and James – old news. Maybe now I get my chance.'

'*You* engineered seeing *her*?' Bang goes Seb's Stevie theory, and back to Ben behaving oddly.

'Yeah, I did. Please don't tell her.'

Seb makes a non-committal sound and says, 'We'd appreciate it if, for now, you didn't mention this to her.'

'Oh right, okay.'

'We'll speak to her, of course.'

'Yeah alright. I mean, she's not a suspect or anything is she?'

Seb stands. 'Thanks for your time, we'll be in touch.'

–

Seb stands in the hallway of the station, talking on the phone. 'I'm sorry, Val,' he says, having broken the news he won't be home for dinner as planned.

'It's no bother Seb, really.'

'I know, but I wanted to go over Tilly's choices form with her.'

'She's finished it,' Val says.

'What, when?'

'Last night. Faye and I talked her through it again. Well actually Faye did; I hate admin, Sebastian, as you know. I made cookies, some of which you would have found in your school bag today.'

That makes him smile. She always refers to his work rucksack this way. And every time he opens it to fish out his laptop or notebooks, he sees some insanely delicious snack in Tupperware. Generally with enough supplied for everyone.

'Got it thanks, and from the team too.'

'You all need your energy.'

'Yeah, we're close but it's going to be a long few days, I think.'

'Well don't add needless worrying about us to the list. The form has been done and uploaded.'

'Great, thank you,' he says feeling a stab of guilt he assumes most working parents must get at times.

He heads into the main office and finds his small team around the table in the middle of the room. He suppresses a smile when he sees that at least three of them have a cookie in hand.

Lucy looks up and says, 'These are awesome,' while littering crumbs everywhere.

'Maybe a bit of kitchen roll would help there Lucy?'

'Yeah, sorry.' She grins. 'I'll grab some.' She heads into the kitchen and back, with the cookie, smaller now but still in hand, and sheets of kitchen roll for everyone.

Seb waits for her to settle then says, 'Right, Finn, Harry – what did you get on Stevie Gordon?'

Harry says, 'She was, as you suggested, a ward of the state, from the age of thirteen onwards. Her mother, Madeleine Gordon, suffered from bouts of psychosis which resulted in her poisoning Stevie on several occasions.'

'Ah,' Seb says. 'She was fostered?'

'Occasionally but mainly not; you know how it is for kids that age.'

Seb nods. He knows only too well. Despite the breach with his adopted parents, for many years he'd been grateful to them. They had adopted him when he was just three months old. They'd paid for him to have a good education and he'd always had a warm bed and food to eat. He knew, from his own experience on the Force, that this sadly wasn't the case for many of the children who ended up pumped through the system with a terrifying amount of change and bumps along the way.

'The mother?'

'She avoided prison. She was deemed mentally unfit. She spent five years in an institution and was released when Stevie was eighteen,' Harry tells him.

'Did they move back in together?'

'No, the mum was put in sheltered housing where she remains. Stevie was given the flat. She has since studied, become a primary school teacher and bought the flat. Though she has had a CCJ applied to her financial records.'

'Does she have a record for anything?'

'No, clean. On paper, at least, Stevie is nothing but an unlikely success story.'

'Right,' Seb says.

'What did Ben tell you?' Lucy asks.

'He engineered bumping into her.'

'Blimey.'

'Yeah, I know, I'd figured it was her who'd engineered it, in light of her knowing Zoe.'

'What did he make of that?' Lucy says.

'He was a bit taken aback but it's a small town.'

'That's true. Could they be in it together?'

Seb sighs. 'They could.'

'But you don't think so?'

'I don't know,' he says honestly, baffled every time a new piece of information shows up in this case; everything seems to feed into everything else. All roads had led to James, but now all roads lead to this woman, Stevie Gordon, too.

'Guv, look at this.' Finn is waving Seb over. Finn's screen has a photo of Stevie Gordon alongside an enlarged image of the couple leaving the pub the night Hannah went missing. 'Could that be her?' Finn asks, squinting.

'I think it could, yes,' Seb says. 'Any luck on identifying either man yet?'

'Not yet.'

'Okay, well maybe we can start by asking her ourselves,' Seb says. He's interrupted by his phone ringing. He takes the call, listens to the grave tone on the other end and feels his heart sink. Expected, but still. 'Thank you.' He hangs up, turns to face his team.

'Zoe Cowley has died we're looking for a triple murderer.'

CHAPTER FORTY-FOUR

STEVIE

I pick up a tearful message from Ben on my break and I walk numbly into the head's office, telling her I need to go, a bereavement, a friend. Which isn't a lie, not exactly.

'Of course, Stevie,' she says, all sympathy, because historically I'm not a skiver. I'm a dedicated member of staff. 'Take as long as you need, yeah?'

At home, I open my fridge; a bottle of Chardonnay stares back at me. I look at it for so long that the fridge starts beeping, a reminder to close the door, which I do. Leaving the wine where it is. I wish I had the strength to just grab it and tip it down the sink. I don't, but I also don't pour a glass. I sit out on the balcony, my eyes drawn as always to James's house like a beacon. Michael was right all along, of course. I'm not in love with him. I'm obsessed, or I had been obsessed, and that's a different thing. He'd been a welcome distraction, and to start with he'd been absolutely lovely. Charming and very attentive. If I look back at the whole thing rationally, though, that really only lasted until I went to his after school and let him take me to bed. I'd been easy-peasy, which, looking back, I guessed was my appeal. A story probably older than time. It was always I who pursued him, my persistence that made it last longer than it should have, then and more recently.

When he took me home and I met his family, I really was sold. They were all just so nice. Ben, younger than James by a year, but awkward. His mum cooked that day, he and her dad laughing between themselves as they laid the table. I went over there a couple of times for lunches on Sundays, a break from the foster family who made it clear it was temporary. It was that that I wanted more than anything else. More than him, even. It is lonely being in a family of two. Especially when one of them is my mother. Especially then, when I didn't even have her.

I have Tom now and that's good. I have my classes, a new one each year, and I adore them all for the most part. I've had my dates lately with Ben and I'd been surprised when we went out, how much I'd enjoyed his company. That will be over, of course, once he finds out I'm unhinged.

My phone rings; it's a withheld number.

'Hello.'

'Stevie Gordon?'

'Speaking.'

A man, deep voice, serious tone. 'This is DI Locke.'

'DI?' I say, knowing it's the police. Of course it is.

'Detective Inspector.'

'Right.'

'We'd like to speak to you in person if possible.'

'Can I ask what it's regarding?'

'Zoe Cowley.'

'Oh?'

'You're friends?'

'Um, yes. We do a class together at the gym.'

'And you know her husband, James?'

'I knew him.'

'And James's brother Ben?'

I squeeze my eyes shut. 'I do. He, uh, left a message about Zoe. He said she hasn't made it?'

'We'd like you to come and see us in person, we can discuss everything then.'

I don't ask why. They've laid out what they have, really. They know all the details I'd kept carefully hidden from each party. This means that probably Ben knows too. God.

'When?'

'As soon as possible.' I don't say anything, my heart hammering in my chest. 'This is very important,' he adds. 'If you don't come to us, we could come and find you at work perhaps?'

'No.' I say the word fast. 'I'm at home anyway. I'll come now.'

He gives me the postcode of the police station. I write it down and hang up.

–

I dress with care in a too smart, uncomfortable dress. I take it off, opt for dark trousers and a blouse with sandals. Smart but quiet. Hard to know what is the correct outfit for being questioned about murder.

I walk to the station, keeping my eyes peeled for any signs of being followed, the flashes of red I'd seen a familiarity niggling away at the back of my mind. I called Tom but he hasn't picked up. I left a voicemail, not with any detail, just asking him to call. He can be like this from time to time. He disappears; I never really know where to.

I walk slowly, but even so I'm starting to sweat. A combination of lack of sleep, the weather and a blinding internal panic because my life, this little life I have built and which I had lost gratitude for, or perhaps I'd never managed to be quite grateful enough for, is in peril.

Self-pity can consume you; to compare is to despair. These are things I have heard in group therapy over the years and from Michael on repeat.

Yet I always felt I was an exception to that rule. If you had a mad woman for a mother, you'd feel sorry for yourself too. If only I had her life, or hers or hers, I'd be fine.

If only I had *him*.

The man I'd been thinking about and wishing for wasn't even worth it, it seems.

The police station is a low-built, bland, grey building with the police emblem, which has seen better days, on a sign out the front. I must have passed it a thousand times but it's set back away from the pavement and I'd not noticed it before. I check my phone, still nothing from Tom.

I take a deep breath and walk up the steps.

CHAPTER FORTY-FIVE

SEB

Stevie Gordon is small, in stature and in her physical presence. She is scrunched into herself on the hard-backed, nailed-to-the-floor chair of the interrogation room. She looks, Seb thinks, like a frightened child. His mind flicks back to the notes on her childhood: blighted by her mother's mental instability, pushed from pillar to post. She'd made it through the care system and into education. He admired her grit even on paper and he feels a swell of sympathy for her now. But could this woman be the murderer because even success stories can snap.

'Hello, Ms Gordon. I'm Detective Inspector Locke and this is my colleague Detective Sergeant Quinn.'

'Stevie.'

'Stevie then. We'll be recording this interview and I'm going to pause briefly now to start that okay?'

She nods. He talks for the recording and reads Stevie her rights, which leads to her asking, 'Am I a suspect?'

'This is an official interview,' he tells her, 'and we just want to make sure everything is on record.'

She frowns at him 'Right.'

'You are entitled to legal counsel if you'd like.'

She shakes her head. 'Let's get this done.'

'You know why we've called you in?'

'You said it's about Zoe Cowley.'

'That's right, and Hannah Smith and Sam Carmichael. Do you know these women?'

'I know Zoe.'

'But not Hannah or Sam?'

A pause.

'Stevie?'

'I knew who they were.'

'In terms of?'

'Their relationship to James. I knew he'd slept with Sam and that he and Hannah were having an affair.'

'How?'

'I saw them together.'

'You know James Cowley?' Seb asks, already, of course, knowing the answer.

'Yes.'

'How do you know him?'

'We were a couple.'

A couple is quite different to the version that James has presented but in keeping with what Ben has told them. It definitely meant more to her than James, Seb thinks. He glances at Lucy, who is taking notes, back to Stevie, whose eyes are darting round the room.

'He says he hasn't seen you for years,' Seb says.

'That's true. I mean, we've not spoken.'

'He had no idea that you were friends with his wife.'

'No.' She looks down at her hands, which are clasped together on the table in front of her.

'But you knew who she was?'

She opens her mouth, closes it.

'You knew that Zoe was married to your ex-boyfriend?'

'I did, yes.'

'Is that why you attended that class?'

She nods, her face a picture of misery, red spots high in her cheeks.

'Did Zoe know that you dated her husband?'

'No.' Stevie shakes her head, eyes still downcast.

'Why didn't you tell her?'

Stevie looks up. Her lower lip trembles slightly and her eyes are damp. 'I don't know. I should have, once we became friends, I can see that, and how it must look.'

'How does it look?'

She shrugs. 'A bit… off-key. Creepy even.' Seb neither denies nor confirms it; instead he lets the silence surround them and she starts talking again. 'I liked her you see; I didn't set out to be her friend.'

'What did you set out to do?'

'I… I don't know really. I just wanted to know about her.'

'Why?'

'I'm not exactly sure.' She gives him a smile but it's fleeting and sad. 'I was in love with him, detective. Or thought I was. That relationship meant an awful lot to me. He was my first love at a time when the rest of my life fell to pieces, then when we reconnected and it seemed like… it was meant to be.'

'Meant to be?'

'I understand it doesn't make sense.'

'Try and explain it.'

'He moved into a house, the house he lives in now. From my flat, the balcony, I could see it, see him. It stirred it all up again.'

'You were stalking his partners?'

'I… didn't mean to.' She looks from Seb to Lucy and back again, wide-eyed. 'But I suppose I was, yes.'

'With what intent?'

She shrugs. 'I really don't know.'

And Seb finds, odd though her answer is, he believes she is telling the truth.

'I followed James one day. I saw him in town.' Her eyes go back to the wall. It's a space where there probably ought to be a window but there aren't any in here. No views to the outside world. It is an awful little concrete box designed to make people feel uncomfortable. 'I watched his house. I set up a fake Facebook account and followed him there. He often updates his locations. The night he went to the strip club, I went, saw him leave with Sam, saw where she lived.'

'Why did you follow him?'

'I can't say clearly,' she says, chewing her lower lip.

'And you saw him with Hannah?'

She looks back at Seb directly. 'I followed him a few times then when he started seeing Hannah, more often I followed her.' Her voice is small when she says this.

'Why?'

'It became a sort of fixation I suppose.'

'Were you hoping to get back together with him?'

'I don't know exactly,' she says, a crack in her voice.

Seb says, leaning forward, 'You saw it as a sign?'

Her eyes are skittering around again. Lucy has stopped writing. She and Seb are now sitting, staring calmly at this woman who is becoming flustered.

'You thought it was meant to be, him back in your life.'

'Yes, well, no... I...'

'So you saw him with Hannah the first time, when?' Seb changes tack.

'Um. God, I don't know maybe five months ago.'

'Where?'

'In Thamespark, near her office.'

'You know where she worked?'

'I found out. That day, actually.'

'What were they doing?'

'Eating lunch.'

'You suspected a relationship?'

'They… they went to the hill, by the pyramids.' A rock formation at the top of fairly secluded woodland. Not far from where Hannah's body had been found, in fact.

'You followed?'

'Yes,' she says, face pale, head hung low again. Her hands are now twisting in and out of each other. She sees his eyes flick to them and pulls them off the table, putting them in her lap.

'Then what?'

'They were… intimate.'

'You watched that too?'

'I left when it started.'

'Right.'

'I realise how this all sounds.'

'It sounds like you stalked James Cowley. Then you stalked his mistresses. Sounds like you were jealous of them and his wife and that you are obsessed with him. Those women are now dead. You were the last person at least one of them saw.'

'I get how it must look.'

'How does it look Stevie?'

'Like I killed them.' Her eyes snap up and meet his.

'Did you?'

'No.'

'Ever think about it?'

'I thought about them being out of the picture, yes. As I said, I thought I was deeply in love with James.'

'You don't think that now?'

'No, it was obsession, a distraction from real life.'

'So you thought you'd date his brother?'

'Ben asked me out, I didn't go looking.' This much, at least is true: Ben has told them as much.

'Where were you the night of April 5th?' The night Hannah Smith was killed.

'I went for a drink.'

'Who with?'

'On my own.'

'Do you do that a lot?'

'No. Occasionally. When I'm stressed maybe.'

'Why were you stressed?'

'My flatmate told me she was leaving.'

'Was she there that night?'

'No.'

'So you went out on your own?'

'Yes.'

'Anyone see you?'

'Um, a man I met.'

'Oh?'

Her face flushes. He pulls out the picture of the couple, one of whom he thinks is her, and the dark-haired guy whose face is obscured.

'Is this him?'

'I, yes, I think so.'

'That's you?'

'Yes,' she says her voice barely a whisper now.

'Hannah passed by there just hours later.'

'I know. Do you think I don't know that?'

'The man's name?'

'Joel. I can give you his details.'

Lucy slides a pad across. Stevie fumbles with her phone, dropping it twice while she looks for his number. She writes it down in a jagged scrawl. 'There.' She slides it back and Lucy nods.

'This weekend, you went to see Zoe at her hotel?'

'I did, yes.'

'Why?'

'She called in some distress.'

'Because of her husband?'

'Yes, the affair and…' Stevie pauses, licks her lips and takes a hitched breath in, which judders like an engine being slow to start. 'He was being questioned wasn't he, by you.'

'He was a suspect in Sam Carmichael and Hannah Smith's murders, yes.'

'Is he still?'

'I'm afraid I can't discuss that with you.'

'Right.'

More silence.

'Even at this stage in this situation,' Seb says 'you didn't tell her that you knew her husband, and knew before she did that he was having an affair.'

'No.' One of the shiny tears slips down her cheek. The rest of her face remains still and she seems not to notice. 'I'm a terrible friend, I get that.'

'You did consider her a friend, then?'

'Yes,' she says. 'I liked her.'

'You also didn't tell Ben you knew her.'

'No, I didn't.' She looks up and swipes at the tear. 'Can you keep me here?'

'Do you want to leave?'

'Yes.'

'You are free to, if that's what you want.'

'It is,' she says, standing and hitching her bag on her shoulder. Her face now is steely, pale still, but little red spots have appeared at the top of her cheeks.

'We will be in touch though, so do stay local.'

'Right.'

–

'Joel Clarke,' Finn says triumphantly.

'Great,' Seb says. 'Harry, call him and ask if me and Lucy can talk to him.'

'When?'

'Now.' He nods at Lucy. Harry gets on the phone. By the time they are at the car, Harry has texted them an address with *next door to his work*.

They arrive at the same time as him, definitely the man from the footage.

'Joel?'

'Yeah, detective?' he says, voice wary.

'I'm DI Locke. This is Detective Sergeant Quinn.' Lucy holds a hand up.

'Okay.'

'Thanks for seeing us and so quickly.'

'Your, uh, colleague made it sound urgent.'

'It is, yes.'

'Right.'

'You were with a young woman last Monday.'

'Stevie?'

'Right.'

'Yeah. I mean, she'd had a few, we both had, but nothing untoward...' His hands are raised now, his face fearful.

Seb shakes his head. 'We're not getting at that.'

'Oh okay, phew.' He laughs; it's a nervous sound.

'You saw her again?'

'We met for a drink. I've texted since, but she hasn't responded.' He shrugs. 'I assume she's not interested.'

'You read about the murder?'

'Yeah, in the park, just after we left, it must have been. Oh, hey, I didn't see anything – I'd have called in if I had.'

'Yeah, okay. So you left about one, she said?'

'Yeah that's right. We shared a cab. I walked her to her door.'

'How was she?'

'I mean, pissed but fine. I, uh, thought we'd had a nice time.'

'Which cab firm did you use?'

'Um, Road Runners. Hang on.' He fishes out his phone and shows them the saved number. Seb writes it down.

'Where did you go, in the cab?'

'Oh, home.'

'Live alone?'

'Um, well, with my parents at the minute.'

'Can they confirm what time you got in?'

'Yeah, I woke my dad up, we had a few words.'

'At about?'

'One twenty-six. I know exactly as he kept repeating it. Not too clever on a Monday, I guess.' His phone lights up, he frowns at it. 'It's work, I probably need to go back.' He looks up. 'Sorry.'

'That's okay, thanks for seeing us. Can we have your dad's details too?'

'Oh yeah, course.' Joel takes the pen and pad off Lucy and scrawls an address and a phone number. 'Is that okay?'

'Yes,' Seb says. 'We'll be in touch if we need anything else.'

'OK, great thanks.' Joel springs up and leaves.

Seb is already on the phone asking Harry to check with the cab driver and his dad. As he hangs up, Lucy says, 'What do you think?'

'I think he's telling the truth.'

'Which means that Stevie Gordon probably was home when Hannah was killed.'

'Most likely, though there might have been time.'

'Maybe,' Lucy says, sounding unconvinced. 'Could she have overpowered Hannah though?'

'With the element of surprise, it's possible.'

'Possible,' Lucy says.

'Yeah, I agree; it's possible but maybe not likely. What we can be fairly sure of is that she was the last person to see Zoe alive.'

CHAPTER FORTY-SIX

STEVIE

When I leave the station, I'm not entirely sure where I'm going but it's as if my legs are doing the thinking for me. For at least the past week, I've had that feeling of being followed on and off. I wonder if it's some kind of psychological comeuppance for my own stalking behaviours. I wonder, as I often do, if there is a god of any kind. If so, is this payback? Maybe paranoia runs in my family. I call Tom again and again but the calls go straight to voicemail.

I walk alongside the river, the now slightly chilled night air making goosebumps stand up on my arms. I pull my thin jacket close around me as if it can keep out all the badness, all the horror and the sorrow at Zoe. My first real fiend since... forever, probably. Angela had been close but we were companions by necessity, not real pals. When I was with Zoe I'd laugh, proper silly belly laughs. Tears sting my eyes; I blink them away. I am at my mother's. For a second, I stand outside looking at the door. Even this part of the house has been cleaned, the grey concrete step cleared of all debris, and I notice that either side of it are two potted plants flowering pink.

I open the door, step in and am amazed by the sheer space everywhere.

'Hello?' I call and my mum appears from the kitchen. My first thought is that she looks well, relaxed even.

'Stevie,' she says, genuine warmth in her voice. 'What a lovely surprise.'

'I uh, thought I'd pop in, see how the cleaners did.'

'Marvellously, I'd say.'

'I would too.'

'I was making tea; do you want one?'

'I'll get mine and finish yours. You go sit.'

'Yeah okay.'

I boil the kettle, not risking milk in mine as, at this point, it has already been opened. I check the dates on food; everything seems to be within a safe range.

I add sugar to hers and take both cups through.

'Wow,' I say, taking in the living room.

'I know,' she says, reaching for her cigarettes. 'I didn't realise quite how out of hand it had got.'

A silence. I can hear the clock ticking on the mantelpiece. My eyes go to it now. She's had that clock for years. All of the stuff from our old house was packed away into storage when she was sent to hospital, when I helped her move in here, unpacking boxes, the familiarity of the items had felled me.

'Does it feel better?'

'What?' she says, lighting a cigarette, the click and whoosh of the flame as familiar to me as the smell of her perfume.

'The house,' I say slowly. She stares at me blankly for a moment and blinks glassy-eyed while she puffs on her fag. They have her on all kinds of medication which can make her sluggish and disconnected.

'Oh, yes, I see. I guess it does. I didn't like it for the first few days, to be honest.' She goes blank again.

'Mum, are you alright?' I ask, feeling slight concern at her spacing out.

'What? Sorry, yes. Goodness. I might have had a bit of a meltdown, about the house. Tom was a bit concerned, booked me a psychiatric appointment, and they've upped some of my tablets.'

'Are they making you feel a bit funny?'

She gives me a faint smile. 'Yes, I suppose they are.'

'It will take time to adjust.'

'Yes, that's right. Until then, I'm a bit washed out, you know.'

'Yeah,' I say.

'Is it Thursday?' she asks, face screwed up.

'No, Tuesday.'

'You're not normally here then?'

'No. I'm not.'

She puts the cigarette out and her head starts drooping forward.

'Mum, maybe you should go to bed?' It's not even lunchtime, but she looks like she's about to drop.

She pushes herself up from the chair. 'I think you might be right. Sorry, Stevie.'

'It's fine, come on.'

I help her into her bedroom and help her undress, amazed as always at the fact that, despite the smoking, erratic eating and endless rounds of medication, she looks like she's in perfect shape. I tuck her in, pulling the covers up so they are tucked under her chin. Her eyes are already closed.

'Sweet dreams, Mum.'

I go to leave the room, my hand stretching to turn out the light, when my eyes catch on something hanging on the back of her bedroom door. Another glimpse of my childhood. A coat I haven't seen for years but one I remember now. My hand reaches for the material rather than the light, touches the soft wool I'd felt as a little girl. It has remained the same as since I'd last seen it, which must have been infant school. I used to love holding her hand when she wore this; I would rub the material between my thumb and forefinger. This beautiful, bright red wool coat. I pause. Frown.

This past week, everywhere I've turned, that flash of colour from the corner of my eye. The tang of cigarettes and floral perfume. Familiar but so out of context.

I whip round to look at her now, half expecting to find her sat up, eyes wide open, grinning like a ghoul.

She is asleep, snoring softly. I turn out the light, leave the room, close the door behind me with a trembling hand and head out into the hallway.

I pull open the small shoe closet by the front door and start going through her shoes. Most dusty and unworn. But there is a pair of white trainers that are not covered in dust and when I turn them over, I see grass and mud. When I press my fingers to it, I find they are still damp. I clamp a hand to my mouth and kneel next to the shoes. Heart hammering, a scream threatening to escape.

My agoraphobic mother, once a danger to herself and to me, has been outside. She has, I think, been following me. Now three women I had reason to resent are dead.

What does it mean? What do I do?

—

I leave, looking over my shoulder and around me now, but there is no sign of her.

I am a suspect.

That much is true, of course I am; it makes sense. If I was the detective, I'd have me on the list too. But it's not true.

What if my mum killed them? I try that thought out, letting it unfurl in my mind, approaching it slowly.

She tried to kill me, after all. But she thought she was helping me. She fully believed in a medical conspiracy. She got it into her mind that I needed to be cleaned out, that having my stomach pumped regularly would purge me of poison. We were always on a strict diet of non-processed foods and filtered water. She was also a fan of fasts which could last for dangerously long periods of time. But it hadn't been intentional, had it?

She loved me in her own way, or so I thought. Perhaps if she did commit these murders, that too was an expression of her love for me? Sick and awful but maybe, like the poisonings and starvations, she thought it was for my own benefit. I loved James. I told her about him once, a long time after we broke up, and she'd been sympathetic. I asked her if she'd ever been in love and she'd said, 'Yes Stevie, I loved your father very much.'

I swear in that moment I felt a loss I hadn't even acknowledged I was carrying.

'What was he like, Mum?' I'd asked.

'Oh,' she said, 'he really was wonderful, Stevie.'

'I wish I'd known him.'

'Well.'

He had disappeared one day, shortly after she'd told him she was pregnant. She'd said he had been fine, happy even to hear of my existence. But he'd stopped answering her calls, then she had gone to his flat; the landlord said the rent had been paid but he'd packed and gone without notice. They hadn't been together long, though. My

269

mother always maintained they were very much in love. But she didn't know his friends, nor his family. He was a travelling salesman and although she knew the name of the company he worked for, she'd never met his colleagues. Tom had tried to locate him several times over the years but so far hadn't had any luck. He did find out that my dad didn't return to work but that was about it.

My phone rings; it's Ben. I think about not picking it up but I'll have to face the music eventually.

'Ben, hi.'

'You knew Zoe?'

'I did, yes.'

'Why didn't you say?'

'Because I'm an idiot.'

Footsteps are coming up fast behind me. I lunge to the right, turning as I do so to look behind me, and almost crash into a jogger who yells, 'Mind out!' As if it's somehow my fault that we came close to collision. I shriek.

'Stevie, are you OK?'

'Sorry, yeah, a jogger hurtling past.'

'Everyone's an athlete since lockdown.'

'Ha, yeah,' I say. I had periods where I exercised a lot but it always seemed to fizzle out. Pilates, though, has kept me strong, and my link ups with Zoe had kept me mentally more stable.

'Did you know who she was?' Ben asks now.

'Yes,' I say, crossing the main road out of the park. I'm beyond lies now, there's no point. Almost home, where I can shut the door.

'Did she know about you and James?'

'No,' I say, and that's true because Zoe would have raised it. 'She mentioned me to him, I suspect. We met every week, after all.'

'Stevie, can you see how weird that is?'

'Yeah,' I say, 'I can, not least as the police seem to think I killed her.'

A silence at the other end of the phone.

'I didn't, by the way,' I add, wishing I didn't have to but understanding why I do.

'I believe you,' he says and I feel a flood of relief. 'James messed you up badly, didn't he?'

I try for a laugh but it doesn't quite come out and ends up sounding like a slightly strangled cough. I'm at the bottom of my block of flats. I press the phone between my ear and shoulder, and rummage around in my bag for my keys.

'I had problems before I met him,' I say.

'I remember.'

'I think I fixated on him as some kind of barometer for normal.'

'Are you still fixated on him?'

'No. Not at all,' I say, realising it's true and even with the awfulness of everything it's a freedom of sorts. A clearing of the mind.

'I guess he's a suspect too.'

'I don't think they are convinced he hurt Zoe.'

'No,' I say, not adding it might be my mum, unbalanced, unhinged, with good intentions and deadly actions.

'Her parents don't want to see James.'

'Understandable,' I murmur.

'It is, yeah. Entirely his own doing.'

More silence. All I can hear is my slightly ragged breath as I climb several flights of stairs to my flat.

'I am sorry Ben, for my behaviour, which hasn't been good.'

'No,' he agrees and I think he doesn't know the half of it. 'My mum did some odd things when my dad, you know...' I remember what he'd said about his father's affairs: how it had impacted them all in different ways.

'Oh?'

'Yeah.' He sighs. 'So, I get it.'

'Thank you,' I say. His understanding is more than I deserve. 'I liked Zoe and I had a good time with you.' I put my key in the door, frowning as I discover the chub is unlocked. I'm sure I locked it? I always do? Though, I left in a state after too little sleep. I get in, scanning each room, almost expecting someone to jump out from behind a door.

'I did, too,' Ben says. 'Better than good.'

'Oh,' I say, tears springing to my eyes. 'Thanks, and I'll get it if you never want to see me again.'

'I do – want to see you. If you want to see me?'

'I do, actually,' I say. He's nice and despite my fairly despicable behaviour he's still willing to take a chance. He's the better brother, I realise. Kind, sweet, forgiving. If I said something James considered stupid, he wouldn't hesitate in rolling his eyes, poking fun, or generally being unpleasant.

'I'm glad.'

I hang up the call feeling surprisingly better for having spoken to him, then I remember where I've just come from.

CHAPTER FORTY-SEVEN

SEB

'Is it possible?' Jackie Ferris asks Seb, her trademark glare firmly on him. He sees Finn flinch out of the corner of his eye and manages not to grin. Jackie is shitty with everyone she comes into contact with. It's just the way she is and it's not personal. Once you realise that, she becomes a lot easier to take. 'That Stevie Gordon killed them?' Seb asks.

'Yes.'

'She had motive. I mean, not that they'd done anything wrong to her per se but' – Seb shrugs – 'jealousy is a powerful emotion.'

Jackie chews her lip, watching him through narrowed eyes. 'But?'

'I believed her.'

Jackie makes a dismissive sound.

'Also, Hannah Smith was tall, young and athletic. Stevie is small.'

'Element of surprise?'

'Yeah, that's feasible.'

'But?'

'The guy Joel, his alibi checks out and he dropped her home at one.'

'She could have gone back out.'

Seb shrugs again. 'She'd have been pushed for time with the posing; whoever did this stayed a while, lingered over the body.'

'James's brother still on the list?'

'Oh yes.'

'Motivation?'

'Same as Stevie's, I mean, slightly different: he's jealous of what his brother gets away with, as he sees it. He's also had feelings for Stevie going way back.'

'Could they be working together?'

'I guess.'

'James?'

'I wouldn't have been at all surprised if he'd killed Hannah. Maybe not Sam, though possible.'

'Not Zoe?'

'No, he was at his parents' while Zoe's car was at the hotel.'

'CCTV?'

'Unfortunately the cameras are not working in the hotel car park.'

'Shit.'

'Yeah, I know. Sorry.'

'What's next?'

'Finn and Harry are going to do some digging around about Stevie and Ben. Lucy and I are going to talk to Ben again but probably their mum and dad first, see if we can get any more information about him there.'

'Okay.'

–

The Cowleys live in a nice detached house, not far from the park or from James and Zoe's place. When Janine

Cowley answers the door and sees them, she greets them with a sigh. 'Not done harassing us, detective?'

'We've not found the person who killed your daughter-in-law yet.' The words are out and said sharply before Seb can stop himself. 'We do appreciate your cooperation,' he adds, softening his tone.

She scowls but steps aside and lets them in. They follow her through to a large kitchen with an impressive lantern. Light streams into the room, making it look even bigger. Nice place, must have cost some proper cash. Ian Cowley looks up from the table where he is sitting, a paper spread out in front of him, a steaming mug of coffee to one side.

'Sit.' Janine waves at the table. 'Drinks?' Her tone lets them know she'd rather not and Seb declines. It's information they are after, not refreshments, though he'd be lying to himself not to acknowledge the coffee smelt tempting.

Lucy and Seb sit. Janine sits next to her husband, who looks relaxed. She looks wound so tight she might burst.

'This must be difficult,' Seb says, trying to pull back from his initial annoyance, and feeling a wave of sympathy for this woman whose son is a suspect in a triple murder case. In fact, he thinks, currently both her sons are suspects; he doesn't tell her this, of course.

'It's been an awful week,' she says. 'Zoe's parents have gone mad at James. They shouted at the hospital, it was terrible.'

'Preposterous that they think so badly of James though. They've known him for years, for heaven's sake,' Ian says.

'He did cheat on their daughter,' Janine reminds him.

'Pfft,' Ian says. 'Hardly in the same league as murder, is it?'

Seb's eyes flick to Janine; her mouth is pursed and thin. How much, he wonders, did it cost her to ignore an affair with her best friend, which Ben told them about. He himself knows that that kind of betrayal comes with its own pain. One difficult to explain to someone who's not been there.

'James is staying with you?' he asks them both.

'Yeah, poor bugger,' Ian says. 'Couldn't leave him there moping about all on his tod. Ben's seeing over the business for now.'

'Close, are they?'

'Sorry?' Janine blinks. Her fierceness when she opened the door seems to have subsided into a kind of dazed bewilderment.

'Your sons?' Seb clarifies.

'Oh, I see. Yes, they see a lot of each other. Business partners as well as brothers.'

'Ha.' Ian lets out a loud bellow and Janine glares at him.

'You don't think so?' Seb asks, eyes on Ian though he can see Janine desperately trying to get his attention.

'They're brothers aren't they? I've always encouraged a robust competition.'

'Between your own children?'

'Yes, quite right too. It's a dog–eat–dog world, detective, you've got to stand up and be counted.'

'So they argue?'

'I mean, not so much these days but when they were younger, yes. Little blighters got suspended for a week from secondary school for fighting.' Ian shakes his head but his smile lets everyone know that he doesn't really disapprove.

'What were they fighting about?'

Ian shrugs. 'Some girl.'

'Fiona Dean,' Janine says, voice quiet. 'She was Ben's first girlfriend. He adored her.'

'Oh?' Seb prompts.

'James asked her out, several times.'

'Likes to try his luck that one, always been a go-getter,' Ian says, grinning. Seb doesn't even acknowledge the comment or the general sickness of this awful man.

'What did Fiona say?'

'She said no, and she told Ben.'

'He confronted James?'

'Yes, that's why they were fighting. James broke Ben's nose. It was dreadful.'

'Boys' stuff, Jan, you're not meant to understand it.' Ian offers Seb an eyeroll that Seb ignores. He hates men like him and can see exactly how James ended up how he did, and Ben too.

They hear the door opening. 'Mum, Dad?'

James's face appears in the kitchen. Seb's phone buzzes in his pocket.

'Oh,' James says, scowling at Lucy and Seb.

'Alright son?' Ian asks as if everything is fine and there aren't two police officers at the kitchen table.

Seb stands. 'We'll be going then.'

'Good.' From Ian.

'We'll probably see you soon though.'

CHAPTER FORTY-EIGHT

STEVIE

Tom had finally sent a text saying he was working away, was I okay?

I hadn't really thought about how to respond to that yet. I want the feel of another adult around. I want to talk to someone about Mum. I sit by my open back door. It's still warm; the heat presses into my skin like an unwanted stifling blanket but a thin drizzle has started to fall. There will be a rainbow somewhere, I think. I remember when I was small and my mum told me the tale I'm sure all children get about the leprechaun, a tiny man hiding with a pot of gold who could grant wishes. I remember searching for it. I had an idea for a wish then that Mum and I ought to get a pet, though she was dead against it. I wanted company, I suppose, like many an only child before and after me. My mother disliked animals, didn't like the mess and thought they were prone to turning. I remembered thinking if I found the cutest puppy I could and came home with it, she wouldn't be able to say no.

Tears spring up in my eyes at the memory now. My well-meaning, confused and at times utterly terrifying mother. I remember going to visit her in hospital, after I'd been placed with my first foster family and she'd been locked away 'for her own good'. She'd attempted suicide at the first opportunity and I'd gone in to see her. She looked tiny. That was my first thought, that captivity had somehow diminished her and, worse still, it was my fault.

'Stevie,' she'd said, 'I thought you were dead.'

'W... what?' I'd asked her. Only just fourteen, thrown from our sick but familiar household into a whole new world of strangers and stocked pantries, three meals a day and clean bedding. It should have been better but it never is, is it, for the kids who get taken away. Or maybe it is for some. I never knew where I stood in the miserable pecking order of other foster children and other kids in the homes. My mother had tried to kill me, sure, but she'd done it because she loved me.

Crazy, of course, but her intention was to save and not harm me.

'Are you still cleansing Stevie, is that why you're okay?'

I'd looked desperately at the nurse who came over, patted Mum's hand and said, 'What a lovely daughter you have, Madeleine.' As I was reminded so blatantly of why I couldn't live with her.

'Oh yes. She's wonderful.' And she'd meant it and that hurt more than if she hated me. If she'd loathed me, actively disliked me, she'd have been so much easier to leave.

I call Tom. His phone rings until it hits voicemail.

'Tom,' I say, my voice shaking. I pause. Lick my lips and try again. 'There's been some trouble, the police, they... well I might be in some bother and I was wondering if you'd noticed anything different about Mum? Sorry, look, I'm rambling and I know you said you're working but call me. Please.' I hang up, hating the desperate tone of my voice but not knowing what else to do, where else to go. Because that detective isn't stupid and if my mum has anything to do with this, which I'm starting to think she must do, then he'll find his way there soon enough.

CHAPTER FORTY-NINE

SEB

'Guv.' Finn is looking up from his computer and calling Seb over. 'There is some footage from Park Hill.' The hotel Zoe had stayed at.

'Of the car park?'

'No but, have a look,' Finn says, red tinging his ears. He is a nice kid, Seb thinks, then immediately tries to reframe that in his mind. He's hardly an old man but this, he thinks, is what Tilly is on about. He seems older than he is. 'An old dude vibe,' is how she unflatteringly puts it.

'Let's see then.'

They all stand behind Finn and he hits play. Night-time, the car park is mostly out of view but there is a walkway between two doors, one of which leads to the reception area and one to a restaurant closed at that time. Not badly lit. Seb's eyes flick to the time. One a.m. Zoe's car is out of the shot, which he knows and still finds annoying. A man walks around the side of it, large build, darkish hair, white, Seb thinks, though can't be one hundred per cent certain. Carries himself confidently, not in a rush but not dawdling either. Seems to be minding his own business. Then he's gone.

'Is that it?' Seb asks.

'No, I'll come back to him, but keep watching.' Almost a whole minute passes. A woman appears in the frame, distinctive, thin, in a bright red coat. Her face is visible and she pauses to light a cigarette. She stands at the edge of the car park just in view of the little walkway. She doesn't seem to be doing anything, but she chain-smokes three cigarettes. The door leading to the hotel swings open. The woman disappears from view. A figure stumble-walks out of the hotel door; a familiar figure, Seb thinks, squinting at the screen.

'That's Stevie Gordon,' Lucy murmurs.

'It is,' Finn says. 'Watch this to the end, then I'll show you all the blown-up images.'

Stevie pauses, pulling a thin cardigan from her bag and putting it on. She looks around her, eyes darting. She's drunk, by the slight sway as she puts her arms into the cardigan. But she's naturally hyper-vigilant.

'She's looking for someone,' Seb says.

'Yes, or more likely senses someone there. Wait, watch.'

Stevie eventually walks away and less than ten seconds later the woman in the red coat follows along behind her.

'Shit,' Lucy says.

'And,' Finn says, pulling up two images side by side. The man from the video the night Hannah Smith went missing, not Joel but the mystery man, and the man in the car park. 'What do you think?'

'Same build,' Seb murmurs. 'Can you enlarge it?'

'Yes.' Finn makes the image more focused and they can see the man's face.

CHAPTER FIFTY

STEVIE

'Are you in, Mum?' I call as I step into her house. The windows are shut. The smell of wet rain and heat wafts in with me, mingling with all of the new, clean fresh smells since the place was scrubbed.

'Where else would I be?' she says, stepping out from the kitchen with a smile. 'How lovely to see you.'

'You too,' I manage, leaning down and giving her a kiss on the cheek. Her skin feels papery thin but soft as ever and she smells exactly the same as she always has. Her make-up is immaculate, her hair set. Her clothes ironed. She looks wonderful, and age-proof; if she didn't smoke, I don't think she'd have a line on her face.

'How are you?' she says.

'I'm not great actually, Mum.'

Her face falls. 'Oh dear.' She shakes her head as if she can rattle the bad things around and make them go away. I hate doing this, hate causing her any distress. When I was at my angriest, bruised after years in the care system, raging at the unfairness of it all, at having to be stuck with her and no one else, I stayed away from her. A few times I'd given her sharp words, flung out things intended to sting and they did; I saw them land every time and it never made me feel better. It made me feel like I was kicking a harmless puppy dog. It's how I feel now, how I felt when the doctor asked me if Mummy often fed me homemade drinks that tasted funny. Like I was betraying her.

'Do you remember a few days ago, we spoke about the woman in the park?'

She stares at me wide eyed and blinks. She looks like a doll when she does that.

'Do you, Mum?'

'Um, yes, the girl with the red hair.' Was that reported? Could she have known that? Yes, of course she would. Hannah's death was reported obscenely early in a bid for information. There were pictures of her on the TV.

'That's right, Mum, Hannah Smith, and there was another woman, Sam Carmichael.'

'Yes. Poor Hannah and you Stevie, walking back there across the park so late.' She shakes her head, makes a tutting sound.

'Did you see me, Mum?'

'See you what?'

'In the park, late?' I think of my tangled hair, small leaves woven into my long messy plait. The dampness on my dress, hardening by morning. Red streaks washing away down the plughole and my arms scratched and raw. Joel and I getting into a cab giggling and hyper.

'Um, I don't think so?' she says, framing it almost as a question. 'If I did, I'd want to keep you safe though, wouldn't I?'

'Yes, Mum. I know that.'

'I've always been trying to do that, you know.'

'I do know, Mum,' I say, my heart breaking in a hundred different ways. The usual questions buzz round in my mind. Why is she like this? Has she always been this way? Was it my fault?

Prior to me, she didn't have a criminal record, although she had stayed in an institution as a teenager. For depression, according to the notes. After that, she'd worked for almost a decade as a receptionist. Then she'd had me and slowly, perhaps over years, she'd turned into this.

'Maybe you were in the park too?' I say to her now.

She nods. 'Maybe, yes.' She's been out.

'And you saw the girl, with the red hair?'

'Mmm.' She leans forward, reaching for her cigarettes, her hand fluttering as she goes to get them. She is like a small nervous bird. She is delicate and breakable and… dangerous? She was to me, certainly.

'Mum, the girl, woman, you saw her?'

'The one with the fancy white car?' she says and my heart sinks. Zoe drives a white Tesla.

'Oh Mum.' I ask her, 'What have you done?'

CHAPTER FIFTY-ONE

STEVIE

Is murdering an adult in cold blood worse than poisoning your own child because you are having a psychotic
episode? Or is it not cold blood if it's more of the same?
It's the only reason I can think of for her to have done
this. Why else would she? She'd been drifting off as I left.
I waited for her to fall asleep, after laying her out on the
sofa, covering her with a mohair blanket Tom had bought.
All my life, I suppose, I've felt more like her parent than
her child. A tiring way to live. Michael has always said
my desire to caretake is understandable and not unusual
in a child who is parentified. I get it and it is, but it's
not healthy and it skews my view of people and where I
belong.

I close the door quietly behind me and wonder what
the hell I do next?

I decide to walk home hoping it will clear my head.

My phone rings when I'm almost there.

'Tom, hi.'

'Stevie my dear, I'm so sorry. You've been trying to get
me for days.'

'I have.'

'I was working, but I am free now.'

'Now as in right now?'

'Yes.'

'Um.' I pull the phone away and check the time. I'm due to see Michael in an hour. 'Where are you?' I ask as I get to the bottom of my block of flats. Then I stop and say, 'Oh.'

'Surprise,' he says, hanging up and heading over. He takes me into a big bear hug and I feel, if not like all is right in the world, at least like maybe I'm not in it alone.

'Thank you,' I manage, my voice barely a whisper.

'You, my dear niece, do not need to thank me, ever. Come on, I brought snacks.'

–

'Tom, did you bake these?' I ask him and he grins, which, as always lights up his entire face.

'I did, yes.'

'I never had you down as a baker.'

He chuckles, putting a cup of steaming tea next to me. 'They are best dunked,' he tells me, dipping his and making a show of enjoying it. I do the same.

They are exceptionally good. Far sweeter than anything I've eaten for a long time. They make my first sip of tea taste slightly bitter, in contrast.

'Obviously Stevie, a man of my physique looks unlikely to be the sort of fella who likes a sweet treat.'

'Oh,' I say, my face flushing. Tom is not a small man in any respect; he's not quite fat but definitely edging that way. He throws his head back and roars with laughter. I find I'm laughing too. At least in part with relief because I haven't offended him.

'I know I'm on the chubby side dear and I am fine with it. Life is too short to worry about these things.' He shunts the cookie box to me. 'Go on, have another.' With a grin.

'Okay,' I say, taking a bite and chewing.

'Did you go and see your mother?'

'Yes,' I say, swallowing the last of the cookie, washing it down with tea. Bumping right back down to earth.

'Ah, from your tone of voice, I'm guessing it didn't go well?'

'She's been going out,' I say.

He raises an eyebrow, all jolliness wiped from his face now. 'Has she?'

'Yes,' I say. 'She… knew something about James's wife.'

'Zoe?'

'Yes,' I say, nodding.

'What did she know, dear?'

'The car she drives.'

'I see, and you've never mentioned it?'

'No, I've never even told her I know Zoe, or about James really. Plus, I kept thinking someone was following me.'

'Following you?'

I nod. Feeling like just by speaking, just by confiding in someone, I am starting to relax. I hadn't realised how tired I was, how exhausting this whole thing has been.

'Tom, the police think I killed Hannah and Sam and Zoe but I think… I think it might have been Mum.'

CHAPTER FIFTY-TWO

SEB

'Zoom in on her face,' Seb says, squinting at the screen.

'Okay.' Finn does. 'Do you recognise her sir?'

'Maybe. Ken have you got the file on Stevie Gordon?'

'The file?'

'From social work.'

'Yes, right, here you go.'

Seb holds his hand out and Ken passes it to him and they all gather round. Seb rifles through, finds the picture he's after and holds it up to the screen. 'Can anyone else see that?'

'Yeah, it's the same woman?' Lucy suggests, tentatively.

'I'd say so. Older, darker hair, she might be bottle-dyeing it.'

'Yes,' Lucy says, 'I think you're right.'

'Who is it?' Harry asks.

'Stevie's mum, Madeleine Gordon, who has a history of psychosis and, according to her notes, is agoraphobic and doesn't leave the house.'

'Oh,' says Harry. 'Interesting.'

'Very,' says Seb.

'The man, let's see if we can get any hits on him.'

'On it,' Finn says hands flying across the keyboard now.

'It could be him,' Seb says. They are all staring at a picture on Harry's computer of Tom Gordon, Madeleine Gordon's older brother. It's a mugshot, over twenty years old now. He'd come up as a possible match. He was in the system because, it turned out, he had a criminal record.

'How long did he serve?'

'Just under a decade,' Harry says.

'That's a long stretch,' Lucy says.

Finn tells her, 'It was a heinous crime; he attacked the woman in broad daylight, dragged her off of a woodland path leaving her child in a buggy, then he left her for dead.'

'Christ,' Lucy murmurs.

'I'm into the sealed files pertaining to his underage offending.'

Seb moves over to Finn, reading over his shoulder. 'Shit.'

'Well?' Lucy says.

'Juvenile record for attacking his sister, aged seven at the time.'

'Madeleine?'

'Yes.'

'Finn, do we have an address for him yet?'

'Their parents' place was never sold, he inherited it.'

'Where is it?'

'Not far from here, out into woodland behind the park. It would be very isolated.'

'Okay, Finn, head there. Lucy go with him.'

'What about you?'

'I'll update Jackie, Ken can you contact Stevie and Madeleine, get them both brought in ASAP.'

'Yes, no problem.'

Twenty minutes later, Seb is walking out of the station when his phone rings. 'DI Locke.'

'Um, hi. They forwarded my call to you from the police station?' It's a question, but not. Seb gets in his car, starting the engine and switching his phone to hands free. They wouldn't have forwarded it if it wasn't important. Stevie Gordon is not responding to calls, so he's heading to her place now.

'Okay?' he says.

'I'm, uh, Stevie's therapist. Stevie Gordon.'

'Oh, yes.' He'd been on the list of people they needed to talk to but as far as Seb knew no one had contacted him yet. 'How can I help?' Seb asks, pulling out of the car park.

'Stevie was due to see me and, well, I know, or hope, she would have spoken to you by now.'

'She has spoken to me.'

'Well, it's just she hasn't turned up.'

'Is that unusual?' Seb weaves in and out of traffic. Not rush hour yet, but it would be soon.

'Yes. She'd call. And in light of everything…'

'Yes, look, I'm on my way to hers now.'

'Oh good, great. Can you let me know she's okay?'

'Will do.'

Seb sees a traffic jam ahead. Stevie isn't where she's meant to be. She is, in fact, the link in these murders, not James. His phone rings again.

'Yeah.'

'It's us, sir,' says Finn.

'From the house of horrors,' adds Lucy.

'What's there?'

'Photos, all along one wall, mainly Madeleine, Stevie. He's been following her for years and amassed quite a collection.'

'You're kidding?' Seb feels his stomach somersault.

'Wish we were,' Lucy says. 'That's not the worst of it.'

'Really?'

'No, there's…' A pause; he thinks she can hear her swallowing. 'Trophies, we think. Items belonging to the victims. There's a hubcap from a Tesla.'

'Zoe's car?'

'Yes, it was in the report that one was missing, never recovered.'

'Anything of Hannah's?'

'The pinkie ring, and Sam's Argos necklace.' Another pause. 'There's a lot of other things.'

'Jesus,' Seb says.

'It looks like it was a family house once and someone is definitely living here. Tom, I guess, but it's a mess. Harry got into the deeds, everything was left to Tom. Madeleine was deemed mentally unfit.'

'Stevie's therapist calls, she was due there and hasn't showed.'

'That's not good.'

'No,' Seb says. 'Right, I'm going to blue light it over to her. Get scene of crime officers in there okay?'

CHAPTER FIFTY-THREE

STEVIE

I must have fallen asleep again. I open my eyes and Tom's face is mere inches away from mine.

'Ah, there you are.' He's holding something that he dangles in front of my face. He's wearing gloves. The thin latex kind you get in doctor surgeries. It's a hair clip in his hand, I recognise it.

'That's Zoe's?' It is distinctive, made with real opals. I'd admired it and she'd grinned saying it had cost a ridiculous amount for something to keep her fringe in line, but James had insisted, on their first anniversary when she'd eyed it up in a shop in Spain.

'It is Zoe's. Or was.'

'Why do you have it?' I ask Tom, my head heavy, the answer there but just out of reach.

'I took her hubcap actually, which wasn't quite the personal touch I like, but I was fiddling about under the bonnet – better than nothing, I thought. When I went in to the hotel bar, saw she'd left this, even better. I didn't get to spend any time with her, mind. Can hardly count her but' – he shrugs – 'she died eventually and I know that will have to be enough.'

'Why?' My words are thick and sluggish.

'I've never quite known why I do the things I do, though I do know I am not like you. Or most people for that matter.' He adjusts his bulk, settling back on my soft, IKEA rug. 'How are you feeling?' he asks, tilting his head to one side.

'You… what was in the cookies?'

'Oh, no, nothing.'

I blink, heavy heavy eyes.

'They were, as you rightly said, delicious. No, I put an enormous amount of barbiturates in the tea.' He smiles. He is mad, I think. Not in the way my mother is. His intentions are grim, really awfully grim. 'I've been trying, Stevie, to get rid of you for years.'

'What?'

'Oh yes. She hid the pregnancy. When I found out, I have to say, I was extremely upset.' He sighs. 'She is mine, sweet little Madeleine. The only person I've ever truly cared for.'

'What did you do to her?'

He looks at me, blinks. 'Nothing she didn't want really. Until she met your dad. Until you.'

'You weren't around when I was small?'

'I was in prison, would you believe. Had a terrible stress reaction after finding out about you, and with having to get rid of your silly father.'

'Rid?' I say, my voice nothing but a thin gasp.

He smiles. He has small teeth and they are all very round.

'Yes. Didn't want to; no interest in men, so not a satisfying thing for me at all. But had to be done. Did leave me with an itch though, which is how I ended up in prison. Some girl in the park, pushing a pram. Reminded me of Madeleine, made me imagine her being a mother with some man's brat. Made me cross all over again. But I'd never hurt her. Anyway. I digress. So, you were born. I supported your mother as I always have. She likes to let me take care of things and, although I was incarcerated, I advised her on the phone, about potions and toxins and…' He laughs. 'She bought everything I said. She was so scared of not taking care of you it almost led to your death. Which would have been perfect but' – that sigh again – 'not meant to be.'

'Why Hannah?'

A shrug. 'I followed you, saw you following her, saw what was bothering you. Madeleine was getting jittery, had been on and off since sam. She can sense when something's up. We're very in tune, sweet but not ideal. I had to up her meds. She was prodding round, asking about you and I. As if I'd betray her like that. I said to her, a few years ago now, what do you want Maddie? What can I do for you?

'"I want her to be happy," she said, and I knew how you hated those women, how you wanted that silly man. I got rid of Sam as a favour. Then I remembered how much I liked it.'

'And now?'

'Now you really must go. You're my patsy, I think. I'm not going back to prison, not ever. Your death will look like a sad suicide. Then I'll be here as ever, a shoulder for Maddie to cry on.'

There is a sound from outside, a siren moaning. It makes him pause. He stands, heading to the window. His broad back is the last thing I see as my eyelids become far too heavy and everything goes black.

CHAPTER FIFTY-FOUR

SEB

'I'd like to see my sister, please.'

'She's unable to be here,' Seb repeats, for what feels like the millionth time.

Tom Gordon sighs, looking out at the thin sliver of window which only shows a hallway. He's been here for hours. Had his rights read to him. They've hurriedly found him a lawyer who is sitting alongside Tom now. Stevie is at the hospital unconscious. Madeleine is there too. Pale-faced, holding her daughter's hand and murmuring to herself. Harry is keeping an eye on them both.

Lucy and Seb are in this stifling room with a monster. The lawyer has mostly told Tom to say no comment and it's been a frustrating conversation so far.

'She says she doesn't want to see you,' Seb says and Tom's face snaps around.

He frowns. 'Now why would she say that?'

'Perhaps because you killed the love of her life.'

He snorts.

'Tried to kill her daughter.'

'Well, actually, I'm glad young Stevie is okay, I didn't want her dead, but figured she'd make me look innocent.'

'No comment is fine.' His lawyer says. Tom waves a hand at him offering the man an eye roll.

'You poisoned her.'

He looks away again. The lawyer relaxes slightly.

'That was the house you grew up in?' Seb says.

Tom turns back to him, eyebrows raised in surprise. 'It is, yes.'

'A happy household?'

'Not overly. My father was a religious idiot and my mother a simpering wreck.'

'And your sister?'

His face softens. 'Maddie was adorable. The only good thing about the place. I had to look after her, though, after Dad left.'

'How did you look after her?'

'Fed her, clothed her.'

'Abused her?'

'You wouldn't understand,' Tom says.

'Then make me,' Seb presses.

Tom leans forward, 'Madeleine needed me. She wanted me even if she couldn't say it.'

'She was a child, you were a grown man, her brother. Sixteen when you were first arrested for assaulting her.'

'It wasn't assault. Our stupid mother overreacting as normal.'

'Because Madeleine was in pain. You hurt her, your own sister.'

He grins. 'The heart wants what the heart wants.'

'She wanted Nigel Slade.' Stevie's father, whose tie was found in Tom's macabre box of trophies.

'No, she didn't.' Anger flashes.

'She did. She loved him, enough to have his child, and he loved her.'

'Nonsense.'

'He did and you couldn't bear it, couldn't stand that she didn't want you.'

'She didn't know what she wanted or needed. She never did. I had to show her.'

'You destroyed her.'

He looks away again. 'I want to see her.'

'Give us what we want and we'll consider it.'

'Really?'

'I will when you tell me what you did.'

Silence except for the clock ticking and a faint whirring from an ineffectual fan.

'You're going to prison anyway; we have more than enough evidence.'

'Yes,' Tom says, smiling, 'all my bits and bobs, though you can't possibly know who they all belong to.'

Seb feels anger rise.

'Tell you what: I'll give you names and dates if you call her.'

'Can I have a word with my client please?' the lawyer leans forward.

'No need,' Tom tells him.

'I strongly advise…'

'I said no need,' Tom repeats.

'You're happy to make this deal?'

'I am and don't worry it's on tape am I right?' he says to Seb.

'Yes.'

'Fine then.' Tom smiles at his lawyer who scowls.

Seb picks up the phone, dials Harry and puts the phone on speaker. 'Harry are you with Madeleine Gordon?'

'I'm nearby.'

'Put her on.'

The sound of footsteps then. 'Hello?'

Tom leans forward. Seb cuts the call. The big man frowns.

'Talk first,' says Seb.

Once he starts, Tom gets into a flow: he gives names, dates, and details neither Seb or Lucy will ever forget. All in all, he has killed five women. Sam, Hannah, Zoe and two women in between. He also murdered Nigel Slade and there was the woman he attacked in the park, who had lived but who would be forever damaged, and then there was Madeline, who he had spent a lifetime manipulating even when he was locked up. The ripple effects spreading out to infect Stevie's childhood. No wonder Madeleine dissociated, so much trauma never resolved.

'Why did you leave the bodies the way you did?' Seb asks almost not wanting the answer.

'Hmm?' Tom looks far away, dreamy almost, a small smile plays on his lips.

'Hannah was holding flowers; Sam had a blanket pulled up to her neck.' Seb reminds him.

'Oh I see.' He shrugs. 'I enjoy spending time with them, afterwards. When they are like that they remind me of her when she was small and helpless and I used to have Maddie do the same, there's photos, I suspect you'll find them soon enough.' He scowls. 'And you'll steal them no doubt.'

The entire conversation gave Seb a chilling insight into psychopathy that he'll never forget.

The afternoon drags on as his voice keeps going, soft and low. He is, Seb thinks, a stone–cold psychopath, a paedophile and a misogynist of the worst variety.

The only comfort he can take way from the whole thing is that he will never get out of prison; he will never hurt another person again.

When Tom is finished, he smiles. 'Now, Maddie.'

Seb stands, ends the interview and walks out with Lucy. They can hear Tom's furious ranting from outside the room. Lucy bursts into tears and Seb puts an arm round her, pulling her close.

'We got him,' he says, though he is aware that this capture came far too late for some.

CHAPTER FIFTY-FIVE

STEVIE

Time is funny in a hospital. It's almost always unbearably warm in here and no matter how many times I ask the nurses to open the windows they always seem to end up closed again. Today, though, I manage to get out of bed by myself and push it ajar. It had taken me nearly forty-eight hours to stop feeling as if I couldn't open my eyes. Almost as soon as I was able to sit up, eat and talk, the detective came. I spoke to him, told him what I could about Tom, and he in turn gave me details of a case that spans more than the three murders linked to James. I listened to him, tears making my eyes sting, as he told me about my mother's history. She's barely left my side. I often find myself drifting off with my hand in hers and coming to to find her sprawled across my bed. She must be exhausted. Not just from this but from a lifetime of being misled, mistreated and mistrusted. It strikes me as a real injustice that it was her who was diagnosed with various things when it was always Tom who was sick.

'Mum,' I say now, putting a hand on her shoulder.

She snaps fully awake, eyes wide and looks at me startled. 'Stevie?'

I smile. 'You fell asleep.'

'I'm sorry,' she says.

'You don't need to be,' I say and it's true. 'The detective was here. Tom will never get out again. Not this time.'

She nods. The next step for us will be forging our way forward. I have no idea how that will look and I'm sure it will be full of bumps in the road, difficult things to navigate. What I am certain of is that we will manage, together.

'Why don't you go home, Mum, get some rest.'

'I don't want to leave you.'

'You're not,' I say, yawning.

'I don't really want to go back to the house,' she says, her voice barely a whisper. I have found out that despite being away a lot, Tom visited my mother a lot, often at odd hours in the night. Her prescribed meds were strong, but he'd been spiking her on top of it. Rohypnol mainly, and doing god knows what to her.

'Give me my bag,' I say. She does and I ferret around, find my keys. 'Here, go to mine.'

'Are you sure?'

I nod. 'I was thinking maybe when I get out of this place you might stay for a bit?'

'Oh, I'd love that,' she says. Face lighting up like a child at Christmas.

'Me too.' And I would, I think. 'Ask the detectives to pack some bits for you and take them over there.'

'Are you sure?'

'Yes,' I say.

'I'm so sorry Stevie, for everything.'

I grab her hand. 'It wasn't your fault,' I say. 'We'll be okay now, Mum.' I think it's going to take a while, especially for her to come to terms with everything, and for me; living with her even temporarily will be a challenge, but we'll find a way. Tom has stolen so much already. I won't let him snatch our future away as well.

'Okay love,' she says, leaning over and pressing her lips to my forehead. 'Sweet dreams.'

'Thanks, Mum,' I mumble, yawning again.

–

'You've got a visitor,' the nurse tells me.

I frown. 'The detective?'

'Not this time. A young man. Ben?'

'Oh,' I say, and scooch myself up on the bed. 'How do I look?' She smiles kindly. I sigh. 'Okay don't answer that.'

'Shall I send him in?'

'Yes, do.'

When he opens the door, he's hidden behind an enormous bunch of flowers, which makes me laugh. He moves them aside, grinning. 'Hey,' he says.

'Hey yourself.'

I've not seen him since Tom attempted to kill me and I study his face. He looks tired, I think. 'How are you?' I ask.

'I was about to ask you that.'

I grin, holding out my arm with its IV tubes. 'I've been better.'

'Yes, god.'

'I know.'

'It's on the front page of all the papers.'

'Yeah, I've seen,' I say. Leaving it at that. 'How are you all doing, Ben?'

'Well, James has taken himself off.'

'Off?'

'Yup, upped sticks and gone travelling.' He shakes his head. 'Leaving me with all the work.'

'That's crap.'

'Actually, it's not so bad. I think I might try and buy him out anyway.'

'Oh?'

'He's my brother but...' He shrugs.

I nod; I get it. 'Your parents?'

He sighs. 'Dad's defending James, Mum's pretending everything's fine. How's your Mum?'

'Fragile,' I say. 'But stronger than she thinks.'

'Yes, she really is.'

She's given the police a lot of information. Including that Tom had befriended Hannah and Zoe. Just an older man prone to chatting. Mum suspected he was up to something. She'd been reducing her pills the last few days and trying her hardest to find out what was going on. As it stood, her evidence would go a long way in the court case. 'She's at my place.'

'Really?'

'Yes,' I say. 'I don't think she should be on her own right now.'

'Probably not. Will you be okay with her there?'

'I guess we'll find out.' I move and the room swims a bit. I'm on a kind of detox.

'Maybe when you're home, we could have dinner.'

'Maybe,' I say.

'Not definitely?'

I pause. 'Maybe, just not yet.'

'Okay,' he says. 'I understand.'

'Which is why I'm not saying no.'

CHAPTER FIFTY-SIX

SEB

Tilly is singing loudly in the kitchen. Seb and Faye can hear her in the living room. 'She's got headphones on,' Seb says.

'Yeah, figured,' Faye says. 'What the hell is she listening to?'

'Pop of some kind.' Seb sighs. But actually he loves hearing her; he's been in a brilliant mood all week. Tom Gordon is behind bars. He was a serial killer and a stone-cold psychopath. He would never get out of prison, which was something, Seb supposed.

Stevie was in hospital recovering. Stevie's mother Madeleine had seen Tom following her. She had sadly suffered so many years of abuse by him that he was able to convince her things weren't what they seemed. But ultimately Madeleine loved her daughter and now everything was out in the open, Seb hoped she'd find some peace in life.

Tilly comes in, sliding her headphones off. 'Going out.'
'Where to?'
'Over to Donna's; she's having people round.'
'Oh yeah. Are you okay getting there?'
'Yeah, meeting Kai at the bus stop.'

'Great, that's cool,' Seb says, hoping his voice sounds like he means it.

'You okay?' Faye asks him as Tilly leaves, slamming the door so hard the house shakes.

'Yeah,' he says. 'Tired.'

'Me too.' She grins. 'Bed?'

'Um, yes.'

They head upstairs.

—

The woman standing across the street is shaking so hard it feels like her bones might crumble. She watches the light go out downstairs, sees the familiar silhouette of him and the woman he is with. Tall, she thinks. A light goes on upstairs; she assumes it is the bedroom. Just seconds ago, she'd seen the girl leave the house. She'd felt… she didn't know what exactly but, she'd felt… something which was unusual for her. She doesn't know why she's come, what it was she wanted or expected, if anything. She'd been back in Thamespark now for just under a week and it seemed to her that everywhere she turned there was some ghostly memory she'd rather forget. She should move on again and she will, as soon as she can.

Charlie Locke turns on her heel and walks away.

A LETTER FROM NJ MACKAY

I've really enjoyed getting back into Sebastian Locke's world and hope readers enjoy the second instalment. I knew I wanted to explore stalking from a slightly different perspective and Stevie was the perfect character to do this. Her obsession with her ex is unhealthy, but in a world where we're all so connected and often have front row seats to other people's lives, I think what she does is just an exaggerated version of how many of us spend our time online. It's easier than ever to create an alternate fantasy world and I guess you can start to buy into your own fiction – as Stevie does with terrible consequences.

In this novel, we see Seb and Faye's relationship develop and deepen and she also offers some psychological insights into Seb's case. I'm a fan of the TV show, *Criminal Minds* and have alluded to it in the text; I'm fascinated by criminal profiling (I think many writers are armchair psychologists of a sort) and have added a bit of that into this book, though I am aware profiling isn't a big thing in the UK nor an exact science.

Thank you for picking up *The Sweetheart Killer*, I hope it kept you turning the pages. The next case for Seb will be very personal and I hope you'll join him (and me) again for it.

ACKNOWLEDGMENTS

Thank you so much to my fantastic editor, Keshini Naidoo at Hera Books. Also, a huge thank you to the wider team at Canelo and Hera, Jennie, Thanhmai, Claudine and Kate. Thank you to Phil Williams for copy editing so thoroughly and Vicki Vrint for proof reading. I'm delighted to have another fabulous cover, thank you to The Brewster Project.

Thank you to Hattie Grünewald for making the deal and helping me bring Seb to readers. Thanks to the Criminal Minds group for the chat that never ends, and to my husband, the teen and the little loon who are everything.